Clan Lord

Highland Heroes Series: Book 5

Theo Mann

The Invisible Publishing Company

Highland Heroes Series

Contents

Chapter 1

Zero turned a small copper box over and over between her fingers. It looked so small and insignificant, but that was an illusion.

"Are you ready, Zoe?"

Zero looked up at Liam Barnett. "What did you call me?"

"That's your name, isn't it? Zoe Dutton. Right?"

"How did you know?"

He smiled kindly at her. That might be the first genuine smile she'd ever seen from him—not that she had seen many. She barely knew him.

"I know all your real names," he replied. "I've always known, but there's a limit to what information I could give to the others."

"So all this...." She looked around the featureless, empty room. It had no windows, no furniture, no nothing.

Magical projections filled the space on all sides. The map of Kald, the Boundless, and Icemeet—the genealogy of Duncan Buchanan and Lady Rhona Armstrong—they floated in space all around the room. They gave off eerie colored flashes as they hovered before Zoe's eyes.

They laid out such a detailed picture of everything going on in Scotland three hundred years ago, but they also left so many questions unanswered. All four of Zoe's closest friends had vanished into the past, never to be seen or heard from again and it all started with this small, insignificant little box.

How long ago had Liam showed up at the Last Division's headquarters at Ironforge in Detroit? He took his sister Lily to Scotland followed by Snowflake, the Last Division's commanding officer.

Now Dead Betty and Echo Boxwood were back there, and unlike the times when he took Lily and Snowflake, Liam couldn't tell Zoe what Betty and Echo were doing.

They went to Scotland to rescue Lady Rhona Armstrong from an evil wizard who wanted to kill her. The Last Division's mission was to help Duncan Buchanan ascend the Seat of Armstrong and marry Lady Rhona, but how far had Zoe's four friends gone toward accomplishing any of that? They might be dead already for all she knew.

Now it was her turn.

"Don't worry," Liam told her. "The time portal is harmless. It won't hurt you."

"I'm ready." She squared her shoulders and handed him the box. "I want to go."

He raised his eyebrows. "You want to go? That's a first."

"I'm an orphan. I stayed with the Last Division for so long because they're the only family I've ever had. I have no one left. Everyone I care about is on the other side of that portal. I couldn't go back to Ironforge without them. I have nowhere else in the world to go."

He set the box on the floor in the center of the room. "The portal will take us as near as possible to Duncan's location.

"Do we need to do anything?" she asked. "Should we arm ourselves or anything?"

"I don't think that will be necessary. Just hold onto me so you don't get lost in the portal."

He held out his hand and she took it. This was it—the moment of truth. She didn't know what she would find on the other side of the portal, but it had to be better than staying here alone. She entered this room with Betty and Echo. She couldn't leave it all by herself.

Liam pressed some of the strange symbols on the box and it clicked. The portal started as a strange feeling in the pit of her stomach. She felt motion sick and then the whole room started to whirl and churn.

She tightened her grip on Laim's hand as an unstoppable undertow dragged her feet off the floor. The portal spun faster and faster. She felt herself flying apart at the seams and her body disintegrating.

All at once, a sudden flash exploded in front of her face and her feet touched down on something solid. A second later, a blast of bitter, icy wind struck Zoe full force. It cut straight through her clothes and whipped her face with a million ice crystals.

"Hold onto me!" Liam yelled. "Don't get lost!"

"Where are we?" she hollered back. "You said...."

"I know!" he yelled. "Duncan must be around here somewhere."

Zoe looked right and left. The snow pelted her so fiercely that she couldn't see any-thing. An iron-grey sky blocked out all sunshine, but it had to be daytime even if the snowstorm cast the whole world in perpetual twilight.

"We have to find some shelter!" Liam bellowed. "We should dig into a snowbank and build a cave."

Zoe didn't answer. She felt very strange. What was wrong with her?

She might have explained the feeling away as an aftereffect of coming through the time portal, but it wasn't that. She was never more certain of anything.

"Zoe!" Liam roared. "Come on! We'll freeze out here!"

She barely heard him. She stared off into the white-out. She couldn't even explain to herself what she was staring at.

"Zoe!" Liam thundered. "Answer me!"

"There." She barely spoke above a whisper.

"What?" he yelled.

"Over there.... He's over there."

"What are you talking about?" She slipped her hand out of his and he went ballistic. "Zoe! Hold onto me! If you get lost out here...."

"He's over there. He's on that mountaintop."

"Who?"

"Duncan. He's here."

Liam spun around, but Zoe wasn't looking at him anymore. An irresistible power drew her forward. She couldn't see anything but a curtain of white. Snow and wind lashed her face and body, but everything felt a million miles away.

That otherworldly power attracted her with some mysterious magnetism she couldn't explain. She started walking through the storm until a shadowy cone appeared out of the murk. It started as a jagged silhouette barely visible in the driving storm.

"Zoe!" Liam roared. "Zoe, come back! You'll die out here!"

The wind swallowed his words and still she walked on. She didn't feel the cold. She lost awareness of everything but the dark figure on the mountaintop. It rose out of the black outline and separated from the peak.

Liam hurried after her still shouting in her ear. "Duncan isn't here! No one could survive out here!"

She halted at the base of the hill and looked up. The peak towered over giant mountains surrounded by more equally high mountains. She and Liam were in the middle of a vast remote mountain range thousands of miles long and hundreds of miles wide.

So much snow surrounded the peak that she still couldn't see anything but shadows, but she knew one thing. Whatever she sensed was up there. She couldn't force herself to look away.

The mountain shuddered and a long, slithering shape dislocated from the rock. It snaked around and over itself and then loomed huge and black and deadly over the surrounding countryside.

It straightened up and her eyes popped out of her head as an absolutely gargantuan dragon raised himself from his perch. He gripped the rock with razor talons and unfurled massive wings that covered the whole sky.

He uncoiled a long scaly tail that whipped and swished through the frosty air. He arched his serpentine neck and his pointed arrow-shaped head bobbed before her while he examined her with slitted, smoldering eyes. His intense gaze bored into her very being seeing everything that she was and everything she was thinking.

She stared up at the dragon in shock. Hearing from Liam that the Royal House of Clan Creighton were dragon shifters didn't prepare her for the reality of coming face to face with one of them.

He was so much bigger and more menacing than she ever imagined, but he didn't frighten her. He attracted her like nothing she had ever encountered in her life.

Her eyes took in the impossible depth of black in his scales, his sinuous muscle, and his hypnotic stare. His skin swallowed all light until he became one with the shadows and darkness of his mountain hideout.

She took a step nearer, but Liam grabbed her arm and pulled her back. "You can't go up there! It's too dangerous."

"Duncan isn't dangerous." She couldn't explain why she thought that. He looked plenty dangerous.

"You don't know what he might do. He might attack you."

She laughed. "Duncan won't attack me. He's waiting for me."

"How do you know?"

She looked up the hill. The dragon watched them with small, narrowed, deadly eyes. She didn't know how she knew that he was waiting for her, but she did know. Whatever drew her to him attracted him to her with the same mysterious pull.

She twisted out of Liam's grip and started climbing to the pinnacle. She couldn't stay out here. She needed to be near him. That feeling of falling and drowning got stronger the closer she got.

Zoe.

Did that deep, rumbling voice come from the dragon? It sounded like it came from inside her mind or maybe from the mountain itself. It sounded so low that it vibrated the bones in the center of her chest.

You know who I am?

I ken all about ye. I ken yer friends—Lily, Echo, Betty, and Jaimee—the woman ye call Snowflake.

Are they here? Are they safe?

They arenae here on this mountain, but they're in this country. They are safe now.

"Don't go up there, Zoe!" Liam yelled from below. "He could kill you!"

She couldn't stop staring at the giant creature before her. Duncan sounded Scottish even when he wasn't speaking out loud. She understood now that he was speaking inside her mind. He must have established some psychic connection with her.

She scaled the last rocks and stretched out her hand to touch his skin. His strange body fascinated her. She wanted to experience every surreal detail of him. He arched his head sideways to watch her come to his side.

"No, Zoe!" Liam hollered. "Come down before it's too late!"

He shuddered when her hand came to rest on his shoulder. His scales radiated heat and his muscles rippled just below the surface. His skin felt like armor, but it breathed with life and strength and some other hidden power she didn't understand.

He let out a low rumble at her touch and that one Liam definitely heard. He sprang back to get away from Duncan and then Liam leapt in to yank her away.

She tried to fight him, but when she stumbled to catch her balance, Liam did something with his other hand. He aimed his palm at the dragon and a flash burst from Liam's hand.

It hit Duncan and he imploded into a man. His neck and tail shrank and his wings disappeared. He collapsed to a fraction of his size and his scales vanished to reveal plain skin.

He shifted into a tall young man with black hair and flinty black eyes. He hadn't shaved in a while and the beginnings of a beard covered the lower half of his face.

He wore no shirt, socks, or shoes. A leather belt held his kilt around his waist and a length of tartan hung crossways across his chest. Other than that, he was totally naked, but he didn't seem to notice the cold.

He stood on the mountaintop studying Zoe even more closely. His eyes gave her a whirling feeling of floating or maybe of swimming in the air. She only registered at a distance that she was in the middle of a snowstorm. She felt herself falling into Duncan's eyes with no way to stop herself or even any desire to stop herself.

"Zoe!" Liam shrieked, but his voice vanished into the storm.

She heard him yelling about how Duncan was dangerous, but she didn't see anything dangerous about Duncan or the dragon. Was this man the same creature as the dragon? They had to be, but somehow that connection didn't quite form in her mind.

Whoever this man was, he wasn't dangerous—not to her. She belonged here somehow. She had never belonged anywhere more than right here next to him.

Chapter 2

Duncan turned away from Liam to face Zoe. She looked even more captivating like this, now that he was looking at her with human eyes.

Her straight, dark brown hair just touched her shoulders and her large, soft eyes warmed him through and through. She wasn't as tall as Jaimee. Zoe's lithe figure and lean features made her look small and vulnerable to him.

She lacked Lily's curves and Betty's striking blonde curls. Anyone looking at Zoe would probably think she looked plain and forgettable, but he couldn't remember ever meeting a more captivating woman.

He lifted her hand and pressed it between both of his. "It's grand to finally meet ye, lassie."

She gasped. "You can talk?"

He laughed. Her presence made him unbelievably happy. Now he knew why his brother Colton acted like such a schoolboy when Jaimee first came to Icemeet.

"Of course I can talk, lass. I'm only a man like any other."

"I mean.... I didn't mean...."

"Come. Sit ye down. We've much to discuss."

"We do?"

He laughed again. Everything about her delighted him.

He pulled her up to the hilltop where he'd just been sitting. He guided her to a flat stone and tugged her hand to encourage her to sit down.

Liam hustled up to the peak and started yelling into Zoe's ear. "We have to find a place to spend the night! We can't stay out here! The wind is getting stronger! We'll freeze out here."

Duncan did his best to ignore Liam. Duncan could still remember Liam's behavior when he came to Icemeet with Jaimee. Liam didn't make any friends then and Duncan was even less inclined to indulge this idiot now.

Liam also seemed to be going out of his way to avoid addressing Duncan. Liam pretended not to remember Duncan and his brother Reid trying to kill Liam before their battle against the Creightons. Maybe Liam didn't remember that incident at all, but Duncan doubted that.

Fortunately, Zoe didn't seem to hear Liam or even to notice his presence. She sank down on the stone and gazed up into Duncan's eyes. He couldn't tear his eyes off her. He felt himself falling deep, deep, deep into those bottomless soft pools of delicious brown. She seemed to be looking so far into him that he didn't even see her anymore. He swam in some endless awareness of her innermost being mingling with his innermost being.

What was she doing to him? How could such a simple girl exert such power over him?

Liam waved his hand in front of Zoe's eyes. "Zoe! Answer me! What is wrong with you? You're really starting to worry me."

She finally looked away from Duncan, but she only glanced at Liam for an instant. "I can hear you just fine. You don't have to yell. I'm fine."

"You won't be fine if you stay out here." Liam turned to Duncan and started talking without even bothering to introduce himself or to greet Duncan. "You have to come back to Kald with me, Duncan. The Creightons and the Buchanans have been warring and we all need you to unseat Laird Balfour. You're the only leader that both sides can agree on."

Duncan said nothing. He concentrated only on Zoe. Nothing else mattered.

Duncan knew all about the most recent battle between the Creightons and the Buchanans. No one had to tell him about his brothers nearly getting killed or about Dead Betty using her magic to drive the Laird out of Tyrekirk or about the Buchanans retreating back to Icemeet with Grant Ritchie and Lily Barnett.

No one had to tell Duncan about Echo Boxwood and Elliot Ritchie coming out of the forest to aid the rebels or about them fleeing back there when the Laird retook Kald. Duncan knew a lot more about that battle than Liam did. Duncan had seen the whole thing from his mountaintop hideaway.

"We know from the records from our own time that you become Laird in your grandfather's place!" Liam went on. "You have to marry Lady Rhona Armstrong and...."

Duncan tuned him out and didn't listen to anything else. Duncan had heard all about Lady Rhona Armstrong from Jaimee and he trusted her a lot more than he trusted Liam.

Duncan pressed Zoe's hand again. "Come over here, lass. We cannae let ye get cold out here."

"Zoe!" Liam roared into the wind. "Duncan—listen to me!"

Duncan exploded out of himself so suddenly that he knocked Liam off the pinnacle. Duncan made sure to shift in a way that he didn't put Zoe in danger, but he didn't give a hoot about Liam.

Duncan burst out of his skin and shifted back into a dragon. This pathetic wizard might have some magical power, but his transforming spell couldn't hold Duncan.

He unfurled his tail and wings and whipped around to glare down at Liam's puny body. Liam somersaulted backward off the peak, tumbled through the snow, and fell flat in a snowbank on the level ground where he and Zoe first appeared.

Duncan eyed him just long enough to make sure Liam landed unhurt. Then Duncan turned back to Zoe. He rumbled deep in his chest and all her thoughts became clear to him beyond words. He didn't have to speak out loud.

Come lie down over here, lass. I'll keep ye warm.

She rose from her seat in a dream and advanced to the spot he indicated. He didn't have to do anything more than think it. It transmitted into her mind by thought alone.

She sat down on the cold, unforgiving stone and then stretched out on her back. He didn't have to tell her to take that position. She did it automatically—almost as if his every desire unfolded and came true before his eyes even as he thought it.

She gazed up into his eyes. Her face shone with an inner light that twisted his heart. Was this what it felt like to finally find his destined mate? Could this be real?

He slithered his giant body over the rock to surround her. He coiled his tail and body into a tight ring with his own scales closing her in on all sides. He spread one wing over her to form a roof that blocked the snow.

Last of all, he put his head under his wing so he could peer down at her in the darkness of his own coils. His glowing eyes gave just enough light for him to see her and for her to see him, but he didn't even really need to see her anymore. Her being shone straight into his heart. She saw everything that he was and might be in the pure, angelic depths of her eyes. Did she feel the same way about him? Did she feel him seeing all her perfection through her clear, open eyes?

He became distantly aware of Liam shouting and pounding Duncan's scales. Liam raced back and forth punching Duncan's armored spine and trying to reach Zoe. Liam kept demanding that Duncan listen to him and for Zoe to come out and talk to him.

Duncan didn't move. He didn't want to break Zoe's gaze, but some part of his mind realized he had to get rid of Liam. Liam would only interfere with Duncan's plans as long as the three of them remained on this mountaintop.

Chapter 3

Zoe woke up deliciously warm. She opened her eyes and looked up, but Duncan's eyes no longer glowed above her. She had fallen asleep staring into them, but they weren't there now.

She didn't have to worry, though. Her whole body and mind vibrated with this inexplicable connection between the two of them. She felt him near her and this intense heat radiating into her from all sides told her that he was still there, surrounding her in warmth.

His presence surrounded her, too. It crushed her in its intensity, but she couldn't get enough of it. It excited her, fascinated her, and obliterated her whole self all at the same time.

She stretched her arms above her head feeling every inch of her body full of his radiant aura. Her hand touched his scales and a shiver went through her. "Are you awake?"

"I am awake." His voice sounded so deep that it shook the mountain underneath her.

She sat up straining her eyes to see something in the darkness. "You can talk!"

"Of course I can talk. Ye heard me yesterday."

"Yesterday! Have I been asleep all that time?"

"Aye. Ye've slept long and deeply. Ye must have been tired."

"Was I?" She thought about it. "I don't remember being tired."

His scales rustled in the darkness and then his two gleaming eyes burst out of the dark. He opened them and pierced her with his all-powerful glare.

She gasped, but she couldn't tell if she gasped in surprise or ecstasy that she was looking at him.

"Ye cannae ken how wonderful it is to have ye on this mountain with me, lass," he boomed. "I've been alone too long."

"Why have you been alone? Don't you have a family back in Icemeet?"

"I came here to hide from the Laird. He's been trying to kill me ever since he found out who I am."

"I know, but...." Her hand flew to her head. "I guess I don't know as much about the situation as I should. My information all comes from Liam and the others thought he might be keeping information from us."

"He kept information from us all," Duncan growled. "That's why I decided to get rid of him."

"You what?" she blurted out. "You.... did you kill him?"

"Of course not. I wouldnae do that although I wanted to. He's a snake and a traitor and a liar. I dinnae think much of him."

Duncan's tone completely changed when he spoke about Liam that way. Now Zoe understood why Liam thought Duncan was dangerous. Duncan *would* be dangerous to anyone he considered a snake and a traitor and a liar, but she couldn't think of Duncan that way. She had never felt safer in her life, not even at Ironforge.

"I ken what ye want to ask, lassie," he rumbled. "I didnae kill Liam. I sent him back to Icemeet."

"How did you do that?"

"I cast a spell on him. He fancies himself a wizard, but he doesnae ken I'm a wizard more powerful than himself. He shifted me into a man yesterday so he thought he had me in his power. Now he kens differently."

"Why did you send him to Icemeet of all places? Why didn't you send him back to the modern era where he came from?"

"He cast a mate-bonding spell on me sister Edeena."

"He what?"

"The Highland tigers of Clan Buchanan mate for life. Once we mate-bond with one person, nothing can break the bond until one mate dies. He didnae ken that and he expected the spell to wear off in a few hours, but the bond remained."

"Then he didn't do it on purpose."

"He didnae, but he still forced her to mate with him for life against her will and then he abandoned her to a life of despair and decay. I sent him back there to make things right with her. Colton and Reid will see he does his duty."

"What if he gets caught in the war?" she asked.

"He's already caught in the war and he'll find out the news once he gets there. Colton and Reid winnae leave him in any doubt on their position."

"What *is* their position?"

"Ye dinnae want to talk about that, do ye, lassie?" His eyes bobbed back and forth in the dark. They exerted an even more hypnotically attractive spell on her mind and heart. "Ye didnae come all this way to talk about the war."

She didn't understand what he meant, but that didn't seem to matter much. "You didn't talk yesterday.... I mean, you didn't talk as a dragon."

"I didnae want to reveal all me secrets to that rat."

She grinned. He was talking about Liam.

"Ye find it funny, lassie. Do I amuse you?"

"I like you." She caressed her hand down his scales and another tremor of electric thrill coursed through her. "I don't understand why. You're a dragon and I'm a person."

"I am a person, too, lass."

"I know, but you're a different kind of person, aren't you? It's strange. This connection between us seems even stronger when you're a dragon."

"Didnae ye like me as a man? I'm disappointed, lassie."

She laughed out loud. "I didn't mean that. Don't tease me."

He chuckled deep in his chest. His whole body rumbled with the sound. Her happiness flooded him through their connection. He never had to wonder what she was thinking or what she really meant.

He hummed a deep, resounding purr that filled her mind with contentment and serenity. "Yer family name is Dutton, am I right, lassie?"

"Yeah. It's weird how you know everything about me without being told."

"Aye. I ken all about ye. I ken about yer time in the war and yer years with the Last Division."

"You could have heard about that from Jaimee and the others. The Last Division is hardly a secret anymore."

"Jaimee couldnae tell me about the foster home where ye grew up. She couldnae tell me about the older boys who tormented ye there or the teachers at yer school who told ye that ye were soft in the head. Jaimee couldnae tell me about the teacher who told ye that ye wouldnae ever become anything worthwhile."

She looked away and gazed off into the dark. She would have been unsettled by a total stranger knowing such intimate and carefully guarded secrets from her past.

He said them so casually, but it didn't bother her at all that he knew everything about her. It seemed natural.

"Now ye tell me, lassie," he went on. "Tell me all about meself that ye can see when ye look into me eyes. I cannae be the only one of us that sees and kens all."

She looked up without meaning to, and when she gazed into his shining eyes, she saw it all. "Your father Neill Buchanan abandoned you when you were a baby. Your grandfather Laird Balfour kidnapped your mother and left you alone. Colton and Reid raised you.... basically—them and your Clansmen."

He growled low and menacing, but she sensed instinctively that he wasn't angry at her. The memories hurt him to recall, but he didn't mind her mentioning them any more than she minded him mentioning hers.

"Then you found out you were a Creighton. That hurt a lot, didn't it? Colton, Reid, and Jaimee tried to stand up for you. A few of your Clansmen stood up for you, too, but some abandoned you. They said terrible things and the things they didn't say hurt even worse."

She winced at the pain she felt so exquisitely through their unbroken connection. She felt the sting of those insults, the glares, the disgusted grimaces when he passed in the corridor.

She twisted over on her side. The emotions coming from him hurt so much that she inched over to his side and kissed his scales. She would give anything to take that hurt away, but she couldn't. It was all in the past.

"I'm sorry," she croaked. "I'm sorry that happened to you....and then you ran away. You couldn't stand it anymore and then...."

She frowned. The next part of the memory became a confused jumble of wild images. She saw Echo and Betty in the forest with Reid and Elliot. She felt the terror and explosive insanity of Duncan's magic flying out of control and then the confrontation when Elliot shifted into a dragon.

She couldn't speak. So many memories and impressions flooded into her mind that she couldn't process them all.

"I am sorry, lassie," he murmured. "I shouldnae have shown you that."

"Why not? You know everything about me. You said you wanted me to know everything about you. How can I if you don't show me?"

"I'm.... sorry. I havenae ever had this with anyone before."

"I feel the same way." She barely breathed the words, but they seemed to echo through her whole life. Something massive was happening to her beyond her control. She didn't know what to do with it.

He murmured under his breath again and started to move around. "Ye must get up, lassie. Climb onto me back. We're leaving this mountain."

"We are? Why? Where are we going?"

"Liam's visit has got me thinking. I must consult with someone."

"What did Liam say? What does he know that we don't?"

"He doesnae ken ought, and even if he did, I wouldnae trust a word he says. I winnae ever trust that man as far as I can throw him."

She giggled. "You could probably throw him pretty far."

"Not far enough. Come along, lass. I'm going to consult with a man I ken for certain that I can trust."

"Who is it?"

"Elliot Ritchie. He's me brother."

She got to her feet and touched his scales. She didn't question the prospect of riding on this giant dragon's back. She never experienced a connection like this with anyone, either.

She didn't understand everything he said and did, but she didn't need to. She knew enough to know she would be safe with him.

She traced her hand down his scales and he trembled at her touch. Did she have the same effect on him that he had on her? She seemed to.

"Ye winnae be able to mount up until I uncoil, lassie," he told her. "I winnae be able to protect ye from the snow so ye must climb up quickly and then lie down on me scales. I'll keep ye warm on the way there."

"Okay. I'm ready."

Chapter 4

D uncan uncoiled himself much more quickly than he coiled himself around her. He stood up and rose to an incredible height. He extended his neck and tail to hundreds of feet in either direction.

As soon as he removed his wings and body, the blizzard struck Zoe with all its brutal power. It brought tears to her eyes and her nose and fingers instantly started going numb.

He pumped his wings and then crouched down to bring his enormous body closer to the ground. She stepped onto his bent knee, swung her leg over his shoulders, and burrowed between his wings.

His heat spread through her. She hardly remembered what he told her to do, so she stretched out on his warm scales for protection from the weather.

Another rumble sent tremors through her as he sighed with satisfaction. He flexed his wings harder and stood up straight.

She couldn't raise her head to look around without ice crystals stinging her in the face. She shut her eyes and rested her cheek against him. He felt incredibly strong and comforting. She settled in a cradle of safety so satisfying that she didn't want to leave it.

He launched off the ground, and for a second, the tempest raged so hard that she thought it might strip her off her back. The wind built to a punishing scour of razor shards and then he burst through some invisible barrier.

The wind whistled past her head and stripped her hair back, but the cold died in a blink. She cracked her eyes open to find him plunging down the mountains at supersonic speed.

He skimmed dense forests and rocketed over vast lakes buried in black, impenetrable mountains. He covered thousands of miles in a matter of seconds.

The wind became warm enough for her to sit up. She held on for dear life, but for some reason, she never feared that she would fall off.

Exhilarating pleasure made her burst out laughing in sheer delight. He clipped tree-tops, vaulted more mountains, and streaked down the other sight in the pure enjoyment of flight.

The rippling sinuous motion of his body rocked her in blissful rapture. She'd never experienced anything like this. How could she have lived her whole life under a cloud of depression, death, and isolation?

Even the years she spent at Ironforge—the happiest years of her life—stretched behind her in a wasteland of loneliness, desperation, and constant vigilance against unseen threats.

How could rapture and euphoria exist in the same world as all those dark shades? Why did she have to travel three hundred years into the past to find this happiness?

She didn't, but she didn't know that before. She had to come here to meet Duncan so he could show her.

He came to another trackless forest and coasted over the treetops. He lowered his head and scanned the ground looking for something.

She didn't see anything out of the ordinary, but he must have. He flicked his wings forward, braked, and dropped into a clearing miles from any sign of human civilization.

He twisted his head around and nudged her with his nose. "Climb down, lassie. This is where we stop."

She slipped off his neck and her feet landed next to his shoulder. "What are we doing here? There's nothing here."

"We're going to visit Elliot, but I cannae get near his fort like this." He shifted and collapsed again, but he didn't change into a man. He kept getting smaller and smaller until he transformed into a large cat.

She blinked down at him for a second. Liam had told her that the Buchanans could shift into Highland tigers. Duncan was much bigger than a regular cat and his yellow eyes mesmerized her with a strange striped pattern. Dark lines radiated outward from the pupil and exerted an even more hypnotic effect on her mind.

He flicked his tail and trotted off into the forest. He looked back at her and tripped a few more steps to wait for her.

She followed him and they started walking through the woods. For some reason, she didn't find anything unusual about this, either. Everything Duncan did seemed natural.

"What did you mean when you said Elliot had a fort?" she asked.

The rebels from Kald live in a fortified encampment in these woods. Elliot is their leader.

She looked down at him. "Why aren't you talking to me anymore?"

These tiger forms dinnae have the vocal cords to make speech. I cannae talk to ye any other way than this, but it's as good as the other, lassie. I can still talk to ye this way.

"Do all the Creighton dragons talk like you do?" she asked.

I'm the only one I ken of.... but I've only Elliot to go on. I havenae spoken to any of the others.... or I should say I havenae spoken to any of them including Elliot. He's the only Creighton dragon I've ever kenned.

She spun around and blinked down at him again. She still found it nearly impossible to keep in mind simultaneously that she was talking to a cat and that she was also talking to a man....and a dragon.

"So...you didn't talk to Elliot?"

I didnae speak to him when he was in dragon form...or when he was in human form or when I was in dragon form. I havenae spoken to him at all.... Och, no! I have, but we were both men that time.

"I don't understand."

It's complicated, lassie. I've only spoken to him a handful of times and we were both men then. That's all I can tell ye.

"How do you know he can't speak when he's a dragon, then? How do you know they can't all do it?"

They cannae. I ken.

She let it go at that. "If you haven't spoken to him very much, how do you know you can trust him? Oh, right. You said he's your brother." She shook her head trying to clear her thoughts, but it didn't work out too well. "You're right. It is complicated."

I can trust Elliot. He's on our side. I ken that, and after the last battle, he's as much in danger from the Laird as I am. He winnae steer us wrong and he can give us any news.... any news I dinnae already have.

"How do you know so much about what's going on in the war?"

I see. I see more than the Laird realizes.

His sharp eyes surveyed the woods and a shiver went up her spine. He could see, all right. He could see more than just what was in front of him. Was there anything in the world he couldn't see?

"Why is Elliot in danger from the Laird?" she asked.

He's the Laird's grandson. Grant is the Laird's heir although the Laird has tried to kill him several times, too.

"Why would he try to kill his own heir?"

To stop any of the three of us from taking the throne from him. He's especially worried about me as I'm both Buchanan and Creighton. He kens both Clans would follow me and both Clans want to put me in his place. He wants to kill me more than anyone, but he doesnae need Elliot for ought. Grant has some value to the Laird, but Elliot's naught but a threat.

"Wow. That's messed up."

Duncan cocked his head to study her and a bubbling sensation of mirth communicated to her mind through the airwaves. How strange it felt to hear and feel him laughing with no sound or any outward sign of laughter. He was just a cat and cats didn't laugh.... kind of like they didn't talk.

She shook her head again. She couldn't understand all this, but she didn't have to. She was with him and this all-consuming sense of rightness couldn't be wrong.

"How close are we to the fort?"

Not far now, lassie. Dinnae ye bother yerself about it.

She smiled to herself. His voice sounded so musical and pleasant in her mind. She loved having him inside her head where they heard and understood everything whether they were speaking or not.

He trotted a little way off to the side and came back. As soon as he reached her, he shifted back into a man again. He did it so fast that he startled her and she took a step back.

He inclined his head to one side again. "Did I frighten ye, lassie? It's only me."

She let out her breath in a shaky sigh. "I'm just not used to it." She scanned him from the top of his head down to his bare feet and back up to his face. "How do you do that and still keep your kilt on?"

He burst out laughing, and this time, she heard him loud and clear. His whole face lit up and crinkled in boyish wrinkles. "Dinnae ye joke about that, lassie!"

"I'm serious. You had your kilt on when you shifted on the mountain. Then you turned into a dragon and now you're a man again. How do you do it? How does your kilt reappear each time you shift?"

"I dinnae ken how it works, lassie! Dinnae ask me."

"So....do all your people do it that way?"

"Of course, lass!" He laughed even harder. "Listen to ye—asking such questions! How would it be if we shifted and ended up naked each time?" He giggled like that was the funniest thing he'd ever heard.

"Is it like that for the other Creighton dragons? I suppose you didn't get a chance to ask Elliot that when you talked to him last."

He chuckled and turned away to start walking again. "I didnae need to ask him, lassie. I saw him shift both times, and aye, he had his kilt on." He laughed and shook his head at her audacity.

She thought it over. "It's a legitimate question. I can't believe no one has asked it before now."

"Neither can I, lassie, now that ye mention it. It does seem odd."

"About as odd as changing into a cat," she remarked, "or a dragon."

He stopped and turned to face her. His eyes twinkled with fun and mischief and his cheeks flushed with pleasure. "Aye. Only ye could ask that."

She scowled at him. "Are you making fun of me?"

"Och, no, lassie! I'm laughing because ye make me happy. I cannae tell ye how happy I am that ye're here."

"Why are you so happy about it? I'm nobody."

He only beamed at her more delightedly. "Ye're somebody, lassie. Ye're most certainly somebody."

"So why are you so happy that I'm here?"

He stopped and studied her again. "Arenae ye happy to be here with me? I thought ye were."

"Yes, I am. I just don't understand it."

He got serious, but only slightly. "I dinnae understand it, either, lassie, and that's the truth. It's a great muckle mystery."

"What does 'muckle' mean?"

He laughed again. He really looked like a different person when he laughed. He didn't look like a dragon at all. "It means grand—large."

"Oh. Yeah. It is—a great muckle mystery."

He laughed until tears came to his eyes. He kept shaking his head and chuckling.

She followed him a little further and thought of another question. His human form didn't have the same mind-numbing effect as his dragon form. She could think more clearly when he was like this. "How do you know so much about Elliot's fort?"

"I've kept an eye on the place since Elliot got here—the last time, I mean."

"What do you mean—since the last time? Were there two times?"

"Aye. Echo and Elliot came and took control of the place. Elliot rallied the rebels to help in the war....and then they had to flee back here. That's the second time."

"So.... Echo and Elliot.... are they together?"

"Aye. They're together the same as Lily is married to Grant and Jaimee is married to me brother Colton and Betty is with me brother Reid. They're all paired off, like."

"Oh." She stared straight ahead of her. "I see."

"It's all right, lassie," he told her. "None of them has ever been happier."

She nodded. "They must be if they're all married."

He didn't answer and she sensed, with that other knowing she first experienced on the mountaintop, that he wasn't able to read her mind now. Why not? What changed?

She didn't want him to read her mind. She didn't want him to know how disturbed she was that all her old friends had found love and gotten married in ancient Scotland. It didn't seem fair. Why should they all be deliriously happy while she got left behind?

He woke her from her dark thoughts by speaking in a low murmur. "Och, there's the fort now. I'm sure they'll be happy to see ye here, lassie."

Chapter 5

Duncan's heart leapt at the sight of the rebel fort tucked amongst the trees. This would be the first time he'd been around people since he left Icemeet.

He didn't count the few days he spent with his brother Reid, Elliot Ritchie, Echo Boxwood, and Dead Betty. Duncan had been out of his mind then. He was a danger to himself and everyone around him.

Leaving them and going to the mountaintop to be by himself had been a relief. He couldn't even bring himself to leave his hideout to help in the battle that ended in such a disaster. He didn't trust himself not to make the situation worse than it already was.

Now it would be different. He felt it in his gut. Elliot was his brother—the brother he never knew he had. Duncan couldn't wait to spend time with him and Grant.

He took a step forward when a piercing shriek made him look up. He recoiled as six brilliant dragons descended through the canopy and extended their talons to pounce on him and Zoe.

Duncan sprang in front of Zoe, guarded her with his body, and backed her into the trees where the dragons couldn't reach her. The dragons pumped their wings and strutted forward to surround the pair.

Duncan's heart burst out of his chest. The dragons flashed blinding green and blue in the sunshine. None of them was as big as he was in his dragon form. He could shift right now and flatten them, but if he did that, the sentries at the fort would see him. If he ever got into the fort, they would know he was a Creighton. That wouldn't go down well.

Zoe shrank into the trees and huddled behind him for cover. The dragons bobbed their heads and eyed him with menacing glares. Their necks slithered back and forth as they wound up to unleash their fire.

He widened both his arms to protect Zoe. If it came to saving her life, he would shift and take the consequences. He didn't need this fort or the people in it. He didn't need them or Elliot as much as he needed Zoe.

He couldn't explain why, but she was the lynchpin in this whole thing. He couldn't think of any other person alive who could entice him to leave his mountaintop. He wouldn't do it for Colton and Reid. He wouldn't do it to defeat the Laird. Nothing in this whole wretched country meant enough for that, but she did.

Now he had finally left his sanctuary and come back into the real world with her. The Laird knew exactly where he was and sent these dragons to attack the pair.

One of the blue dragons sidestepped to the right to flank him. Duncan's eyes darted from one dragon to the next. Which of them would attack first? He could defeat them easily with his magic, but he didn't want to give himself away to the fort.

One of the green ones on his left squawked. Duncan realized a split second too late that the creature made that sound to distract him. The instant Duncan turned his head, the other five dragons all unloaded at the same time.

Their heads darted forward on their necks and five matched streams of fire spurted toward Duncan. Zoe froze behind his back and Duncan reacted without thinking.

He shot out his hand and all five jets struck his palm. He deflected them back at the dragons and the flames.... went right through them. The fire didn't touch them.

They snuffed out their fire and Duncan stared at them thinking fast. What could cause that to happen?

"Oh, my god!" Zoe breathed in his ear. "What's happening? Why didn't they......?"

"These dragons...They arenae real."

"What do you mean?" she gasped. "They look real enough to me."

"They arenae. They're apparitions cooked up by the Laird." Duncan straightened up and his shoulders relaxed. All the tension drained out of him. He knew what he had to do now. "Watch."

He faced the dragons. They hissed and shrieked at him, and as he suspected, that sound didn't rouse the sentries at the fort. No one at the fort could hear them.

One of the dragons lunged for Duncan and snapped its jaws on empty air. The dragons rustled their wings and flicked their tails to threaten him.

He took a step away from Zoe, extended his hand, and blasted a devastating magical pulse toward the dragons. He didn't even have to aim at any particular one. He swept them away with hardly any effort and they vanished.

Zoe crept up behind him and pressed herself against his back. He felt her trembling with fear and her breath came in small gasps. "What.... what was that about?"

"It's the Laird. He's trying everything he can to stop me from returning to Kald. We can expect more of this.... but dinnae bother yerself about it, lassie. I'll protect ye and those dragons werenae even real. They were naught but the Laird's magic."

He massaged her shoulders and rubbed his hands down her arms, but she wouldn't stop quivering. Her eyes skipped around the empty forest, but the dragons didn't return.

He couldn't stop touching her. Guarding her and comforting her flooded him with a feeling of immense power and confidence unlike anything he had ever known. He reveled in using his magic and all his other powers if it meant protecting her.

He loved the feeling of her clinging to him for protection. He couldn't get enough of that feeling of her trembling body glued to his back while she cowered behind him from the dragons' fire. He wouldn't even have cared if they were real dragons. He would gladly take real dragon fire right on his bare, unguarded skin for her sake.

He couldn't stop smiling at her. He never felt this happy in his life. He took hold of both her hands. "Come along, lassie."

He turned to his left and led her off into the woods. "Where are you going?" she asked. "You said the fort was that way."

"I'm taking ye somewhere else and I'll go on to the fort alone."

"Why? You said *we* were going to the fort." She stopped on a dime. "Did I do something wrong?"

"Of course no, lassie. Ye did everything right."

"Why aren't you taking me to the fort with you, then? Is there some reason you don't want me to see Echo and Elliot? Are you trying to hide me from them?

He sighed, and when he faced her and saw her distress written in her eyes, his heart ached. He longed to take her in his arms and kiss her right now. She was his fated mate. He sensed that.

He'd seen it happen a dozen times. Two people met for the first time and they just knew, but this girl was no Buchanan. These women from the future didn't operate that way. Duncan knew enough from his acquaintance with Jaimee to understand that.

These women took time. Even the idea of mating with one man for life took time for them to get used to. They had to grow into the idea.

He couldn't kiss Zoe now, much as he wanted to. That would only upset and confuse her more than she already was. "I'm not hiding ye from Echo and Elliot, lassie. I'm hiding ye from the Laird. If he sent these spell dragons to attack me, he might attack the fort with me inside it. He already wants to kill both me and Elliot. He'd be more likely to destroy the fort to kill both of us in one stroke."

"But.... then Echo will die, too."

"Aye, and I cannae put ye in danger by taking ye there. I'll go alone and cast a spell over the fort to protect it from the Laird's magic, but he's much stronger than I am. I dinnae ken if I'll be able to stop him if he tries it. If it works and it seems safe, I'll come back for ye."

Her eyes softened with emotion. "You promise?"

"I promise." He touched her arms again, but he had to stop before he let his emotions run away with him.

He guided her the rest of the way through the forest until they came to a cave cut into a giant stand of rock. He escorted her inside and pointed to some cartons, boxes, and crates stacked in the corner. "Ye'll find food and water in there....and this one has weapons."

"Weapons!" she exclaimed.

"Aye. The Creightons, the Buchanans, and all the Laird's forces are searching for me, so ye arm yerself and stay out of sight at all costs. I'll be back as soon as I can."

He walked away fast and left her alone in the cave—not because he wanted to. He never wanted to be out of her presence again as long as he lived.

He had to think of her safety, though. He had to put as much distance between himself and Zoe as possible before the Laird came after him again. Duncan was a liability to her and the Laird wasn't after her. She'd only been in the country for a few hours. The Laird probably didn't even know she existed.

Duncan set off for the fort at a fast clip. He kept a lookout on all sides, but no more ghost dragons came around to attack him again. Of course not. The Laird wouldn't pull the same trick twice.

Duncan used his magic to scan the forest and even the mountains in the distance, but of course he couldn't detect the Laird. Duncan had been using his magic to try to locate the Laird for weeks, but it never worked. The Laird could mask his presence too well.

Chapter 6

D uncan didn't try to walk quietly. In fact, he made as much noise as he could to let the sentries know he was coming and it worked.

They spotted him fifty yards from the wall and they turned their weapons on him. The archers drew their bows and yelled out, "Stop where ye are, laddie, or we'll shoot!"

Duncan raised his arms above his head and inched the rest of the way into the clear space around the fort. "I'm Duncan Buchanan, younger brother of Colton Buchanan, Chief of Clan Buchanan! I'm here to see Elliot Ritchie, yer leader! Tell him I'm here!"

"Turn yer back and get down on the ground!" one huge man bellowed. "Keep yer hands in the air!"

Duncan sighed. None of these men realized that Duncan could destroy the fort himself if he wanted to.

He turned his back and used his magical sight to watch what they were doing. They scurried around behind the wall whispering to each other.

"He's wearing Buchanan tartan!"

"Did ye see his eyes? He's one of those tigers!"

"We'll tie him up so he cannae attack us."

"Ye can tie him up all ye want. The moment he shifts, no rope will be able to hold him."

Word flew through the fort that a Buchanan was standing outside trying to get in. More armed men assembled from all over. Where was Elliot? Why weren't any of the sentries sending word that Duncan wanted to see him?

The heavy log gate scraped back and at least two dozen men came out. They pointed their sabers and arrows at Duncan and surrounded him. "Dinnae ye move, laddie," the big guy growled.

He grabbed Duncan's arms, yanked them down, and tied Duncan's wrists behind his back. "That isnae necessary, man," Duncan replied. "Ye can see I'm unarmed."

"Quiet!" the guy snapped. "We arenae any of us stupid enough to fall for that. Get down on yer face."

"Bind him up tight, Athol!" someone else called. "Tie him tight enough that he cannae shift into a cat."

Duncan sighed again. This was getting ridiculous. "Did ye tell Elliot I'm here? He'll tell ye I'm not yer enemy. I'm his...."

"Get down, ye bastard!" Athol grabbed Duncan's bound arm and shoved him face down on the ground. Athol jammed his knee into the back of Duncan's neck and tried to tie him up with more rope around his body.

The situation quickly disintegrated into a farce. Athol couldn't get the rope around Duncan while he pinned Duncan down on the ground. Athol couldn't decide whether to remove his knee or give up trying to bind Duncan tightly enough to stop him from shifting—as if any rope could stop him if he wanted to.

Athol finally cursed and started to straighten up. "Watch him, Athol!" someone yelled, but Duncan didn't move. He had no desire for this to erupt into a battle, but the tension kept building until it seemed inevitable.

"Did ye tell Elliot yet that I'm here?" he mumbled into the dirt.

"Keep yer mouth shut!" Athol kicked Duncan in the ribs.

Duncan winced in pain, but he still kept control of himself. Killing or injuring these men was the last thing he wanted to do. He needed them as his allies and that meant keeping them on good terms with Elliot.

A few feet shuffled around and inched closer to Duncan and Athol. Duncan twisted his head around to keep the rebels in sight.

"Watch him, Athol!" someone called. "He's making his move!"

Duncan turned back the other way trying to see who had spoken when a different man on his left dropped his saber. The weapon hit the ground and the blade made a boinging sound as it bent and sprang back to land a few feet away.

Four men spun toward the sound and then someone standing at Duncan's head gave a guttural yell. Duncan wrenched his head back just in time to see another rebel lunge in and thrust his saber straight at Duncan.

Duncan reacted on sheer instinct and pitched sideways. The saber stabbed into the dirt right where he'd been lying and Athol went flying.

The man crashed on the ground next to Duncan and the whole party erupted exactly the way Duncan feared. More armed men charged him and two raised their sabers to hack him to pieces.

The roars of attacking men surrounded Duncan in noise. He couldn't think and the ropes cut into his wrists. He had to get out of this.

He shifted without thinking. He did it automatically by force of long habit. He had always used his tiger form to cope with dangerous situations and he fell back on that now when he saw his life in danger.

He shifted in the blink of an eye and the ropes slipped off his wrists. He shot off the ground in the blur of battle, but enough of his rational mind remained for him to realize he couldn't kill these men. He needed them alive.

He sprang for Athol and sailed out of his attackers' range. Duncan struck Athol and just stopped himself from ripping the man's throat out.

Duncan's claws sank into Athol's tartan and all the rebels charged the man trying to stab and slash and kill Duncan. They would have killed Athol to get to Duncan. Duncan couldn't let that happen.

He retracted his claws and ricocheted off. He vaulted from man to man trying to stay out of reach of their blades.

Every move he made sent them further into a frenzy. They kept rushing here and there trying everything in their power to keep up with his speed. He landed on another man's arm, caught hold, and ripped down the man's shirt sleeve.

The guy shrieked, raised his saber, and tried to slice into his own arm to cut Duncan off. This couldn't go on. The rebels closed in tighter. Duncan couldn't let them trap him here.

He spotted one young man standing over by the edge of the trees. Duncan could bounce off him and escape into the trees. Duncan sprang for the young man, missed, and landed in the soft soil at the base of the trees.

He veered toward the woods, but a dozen rebels swarmed his position to cut him off. He whipped around to defend himself when, without warning, something huge and glowing golden-black erupted out of the ground right in front of him.

Duncan crouched low, flattened his ears to his head, and hissed up at the thing as a massive dragon ruptured out of nowhere. It appeared in a split second and grew to an incredible size. It knocked the rebels back and the dragon planted its enormous bulk between them and Duncan.

Duncan flattened himself even lower and raised his hackles spitting and baring his fangs at the dragon, but the creature didn't turn around to face him. It squatted above him protecting Duncan between its feet.

Duncan's adrenaline-fueled brain switched back into gear. He knew this dragon. It was his brother Elliot and Elliot faced off against the rebels blocking them from reaching Duncan.

Elliot lowered his head and snarled a deep, threatening growl at his own men. He slashed his tail in a whip-cracking motion.

The rebels who had toppled over backward at Elliot's sudden appearance staggered even farther away. They defended themselves with their blades for a moment and then slouched even farther away. Half of them slunk back inside the fence where they belonged.

Elliot glared at those who remained, but no one moved in to threaten Duncan. They wouldn't dare to threaten Elliot.

He eyed them for a minute and then he shifted again. He dwindled to a fraction of his size and became a man, but he didn't turn his back on the sentries.

He faced them glaring and compressing his lips. "Didnae ye hear him, ye glaikit dobbers? Didnae ye hear him say he's here to see me on behalf of his brother who's Chief of Clan Buchanan? What do ye have to say for yerselves?"

Athol shrugged, but no one answered.

Elliot waved his hand at his men. "Go on with ye! Ye've all got work to do, I suppose. Go on and dinnae let me see yer faces again so long as he's inside our walls."

A few more obeyed him and slouched away. Athol and his comrades stayed where they were. They glanced back and forth between Elliot and the tiger still coiled to spring between his ankles.

Elliot stood there for a long, silent moment before he decided to turn around. He took his eyes off his men and looked down at Duncan. "It's all right, laddie. Ye'll have to excuse them. They dinnae ken a Buchanan from a hole in the ground." Elliot frowned down at the cat. "Are ye in trouble, lad? What brings ye over here of all places?"

Duncan checked to make sure that Athol and the others stayed where they were. So much adrenaline surged in his veins that he had to think hard before he could make up his mind to shift.

Even then, he straightened his legs and shook himself. He walked a few paces to one side trying to work the tension out of his muscles.

Elliot kept studying him and frowning. "What's amiss, lad? Are yer brothers safe in Icemeet? Tell me what brings ye."

His voice finally got through Duncan's anxiety and he shifted. He straightened up in front of Elliot and Elliot's frown turned upside down. He burst into a huge grin, laughed, and grabbed Duncan in a rough hug. "Laddie! Ye cannae ken how good it is to see ye alive and well. We were all worried sick about ye."

"Ye didnae have to do that." Duncan allowed Elliot to hug him and then push him back. Duncan didn't expect a reception like this.

"Well, lad?" Elliot insisted. "Is anything wrong at Icemeet?"

"Och, no! They're all grand."

"What brings ye, then? Ye were safe.... wherever ye were. I didnae think we'd see again with the Laird at large. What brings ye out of hiding?"

Duncan jerked his thumb over his shoulder. "I've found one of Echo's lassies—the fifth one—the last one. She's just come through the portal with Liam."

Elliot scanned the woods looking just as excited as before. "Where is she? Echo will be delighted."

"The Laird just attacked me a moment ago. He kens where I am now that I've left the mountains."

Elliot's face drained of all color. "The Laird....is here? We thought he was in Tyrekirk."

"He didnae come out himself. He sent magic to ambush me. I didnae like to bring Zoe here in case it wasnae safe."

Elliot's eyebrows flew up. "Zoe! Echo says her name is Zero."

"That's her nickname—just like the others. Her name's Zoe."

Elliot waved that away. "I suppose it doesnae make much difference. Come inside. Echo will be thrilled that ye're here."

He started to leave, but Duncan caught his arm. "Wait, Elliot. There's more."

"What more could there be? Ye're here. Ye dinnae ken how anxious we've all been to find ye."

Duncan snorted. "Ye arenae the only ones. There's teams of men searching for me. If they find me here, they'll kill us both and all yer men along with us."

Elliot laughed and squeezed Duncan's shoulder. His behavior startled Duncan. He wasn't expecting such a warm welcome.

"Those teams are coming from Grant and Colton, lad," Elliot told him. "We couldnae agree on who should take over Tyrekirk after we drove the Laird out. Grant and Colton agreed to send out two teams—one Creighton and one Buchanan—to bring ye in." Elliot frowned at him again. "Didnae ye ken about all this?"

Duncan covered his eyes and sighed. "The Laird may have hidden it from me. He must have kenned ye sent out men to find me and he masked their intentions from me. I thought they were coming from him."

"Aye. He would have done. He would have wanted ye to hide from them. Come inside, laddie. Ye cannae stand out here in the open. It isnae safe and we can talk there."

"Wait, Elliot," Duncan called again. "There's something I must do before we go in."

He raised his hand and sent up a shower of magical sparks into the air. They rained downward and formed a gleaming, iridescent dome over the fort.

Elliot stood back and watched. "It's amazing! To think ye were out of control just a few weeks ago...and now ye can do this."

"I can do a lot more." Duncan grimaced. "I'm sorry about all that business in the forest. I didnae mean to hurt ye."

"Ye didnae. Ye showed me me own true self and I'm grateful for that. I wouldnae have Echo now if ye hadnae. I'm grateful and I'm delighted that ye're back." He put his arm around Duncan's shoulders and pulled him toward the fort. "I have a wee brother! I always wanted one. Ye dinnae ken how welcome ye are, lad!"

Chapter 7

E lliot stepped through the log fence and strode into the fort. His men stood around with their weapons drawn as though they still needed to protect themselves from Duncan.

Elliot pretended not to see them. He dragged Duncan to a large roundhouse that occupied most of the back half of the fence. The rebels stared at Duncan when he and Elliot went inside.

Their eyes popped glancing from Duncan's tartan to his eyes. He must be the first Buchanan ever to set foot in this place.

Elliot led the way down a corridor to an office and entered a large apartment. "Echo!" he yelled. "Echo—look who's here!"

Elliot went from room to room and left Duncan in the main living area. It was a very nice apartment—much nicer than Neill Buchanan's apartment at Icemeet. This one had obviously benefited from a woman's touch.

Elliot finally returned, grabbed Duncan's arm, and towed him into another even larger living area that had been set up as a dining room. A large table occupied the center and a window in the ceiling flooded the room with sunshine.

"I dinnae ken where that lassie's got to," Elliot told him. "She's off somewhere doing something or other. I tell ye, laddie, she runs this place as much as I do. I wouldnae ken what to do without her and she practically organized the new moon assault herself. I only wish we'd got to Tyrekirk a few minutes sooner."

Duncan started to say something about the assault when a door slammed in the very back of the apartment. He heard voices back there and Elliot raced away calling out for Echo again.

They came back a minute later. "Look who it is!" Elliot exclaimed and stood back to watch the fireworks unfold.

Echo's jaw dropped when she saw Duncan. "Duncan! What are you doing here?"

"I've come for...." he began, but she cut him off by charging him. She hugged him and then held him at arm's length while she touched his hair and cheeks and devoured him with her eyes.

"You're all right!" she blurted out. "You're...I mean, you're sane."

He had to laugh. "Aye, lassie. I'm all right."

"He's got Zero with him," Elliot chimed in.

Echo gasped out loud and her eyes popped. "You do? Where is she?"

"She's in the forest. I had to make sure it was safe and all before I brought her in."

"You have to go get her!" Echo exclaimed. "You have to bring her here. I have to see her."

"Easy, lassie," Elliot told her. "She's only just arrived in this country. She will have been in yer time until only a few minutes ago."

"Not quite," Duncan countered. "She came up to the mountain to find me. She had Liam with her and...."

"Liam!" Echo snorted. "What is he doing here?"

"He isnae here any longer," Duncan replied. "I've sent him back to Icemeet to make things right with Edeena."

Echo laughed. "I would give anything to be a fly on the wall when he meets up with Colton and Reid again."

"Aye." Duncan chuckled. "That would be a sight to see."

Elliot stepped forward. "Ye must join us for a meal, laddie. This is a great day for us all. As soon as Grant and yer brothers find out we've found ye—or ye've found us—they'll get up another offensive to put ye on the throne. It's that simple."

"Not so fast," Duncan countered. "I cannae just waltz into Kald and take the throne. The Laird is back in Tyrekirk and he wants to kill me as much as ever—if not more."

"That's precisely why we must mount another assault as soon as possible. The last attack didnae work because we didnae have ye with us."

"I dinnae ken about all that," Duncan muttered. "I suppose there were a mite few other reasons it failed."

"Not a bit of it, lad," Elliot told him. "We took the castle...."

"At great loss, I might add."

"At any rate, we took it and we would have kept it if we'd had ye in place to put on the throne the way we planned."

"The Laird drove ye out," Duncan reminded him. "If I had been there, the Laird would have defeated me along with ye and I'd be dead now."

"Anyway," Echo added, "the last offensive only made it as far as Tyrekirk because your brothers had Grant in place. He worked behind the scenes from inside the castle. He's the only reason the Buchanans got across the Boundless to begin with. Now he's in exile at Icemeet. All the advantage we got from him is gone."

Elliot grimaced and shuffled his feet. "Ye may be right about that part, but the whole idea of finding Duncan is to rally both Clans. If ye lead us, we can succeed this time."

Duncan snorted. "That's a joke, lad. Ye saw what happened outside just now. Everyone has a reason to hate me, including yer own men. They winnae follow me anywhere and they will never allow me to take the Laird's place."

"Dinnae rob us of all hope," Elliot exclaimed. "The hope of finding ye is the only thing keeping us all going."

Duncan held up his hand. "Dinnae ye go announcing to the world that ye've found me and where I am. That's the last thing I need."

"What about your brothers?" Echo asked. "We can't keep this from them. They should at least know that you're alive and safe and back in your right mind. I wouldn't feel right about keeping it from them after everything they've done and suffered in this war."

"And how do ye plan to inform them of that, lassie?" Duncan asked. "How would ye tell them without anyone else finding out?"

Now it was her turn to squirm and shuffle her feet. "I didn't think of that."

"Liam will tell them. That's enough for the moment. I'd only be putting them in more danger if I mounted an assault that didnae have any chance of succeeding."

"I dinnae like it," Elliot countered. "We've pinned all our hopes on finding ye."

His expression twisted with much more anguish than he betrayed with his words. His distress wrung Duncan's heart and the temptation to reconsider almost overcame his better judgment.

"Just command us, Duncan," Echo insisted. "Just tell us what you want us to do. We all consider you our one true Laird. Whatever you tell us to do, we'll do it and I'd bet anything that Clan Buchanan feels the same way."

"I'm touched, lassie. I really am, but this is the only way. Give me a chance to see what's what, but now, I must go back and get Zoe."

"Who's Zoe?"

"Zero," Elliot explained.

"Oh." Echo blinked and then shrugged. "I guess all the skeletons are coming out of the closet. Jaimee's using her real name so I guess Zero will do the same thing."

"I must go find her. If it's safe, I'll bring her back with me, but if I don't...."

"I understand." Echo hugged him again. "Be safe. Do whatever you have to do to stay alive. We'll hold the fort for you until you need us. Just.... just tell us what you want us to do."

He beamed at her and then Elliot seized him. He crushed Duncan in a tight hug and squeezed the back of Duncan's neck.

Elliot pushed Duncan back and Elliot's features spasmed even more. "I cannae believe I'm losing ye again so soon."

"Ye arenae losing me. Ye never will."

Duncan couldn't stay here any longer. That irresistible pull drew him back to Zoe. He didn't like leaving her even for an instant. He'd been inside this fort for only a few minutes and it was already too long.

He walked out of the roundhouse. The same men stood guard and they flanked him on his way back to the gate, but he only had to glare at them to make them back off.

They left him at the gate and he broke into a run. He shifted and dove into the shadowy woods making for the cave.

He ran faster and faster as he got nearer. His nerves twanged with tension. Something was wrong. He knew what he would find long before he got there and he confirmed his worst fears when he ran into the cave. It was empty.

He sniffed all over the place and found Zoe's scent trail entering it along with his own. She went over to the food stories the way he told her to. She sat down on this rock and then paced around for a while, but that was it.

He went back outside going out of his mind with anxiety and confusion. Where was she?

He covered the ground for a hundred yards in all directions, but he couldn't find any trace of her. He halted in front of the cave and radiated out a powerful locator spell to pick up any sign of where she went or who took her, but she was nowhere. She had completely vanished.

Chapter 8

Zoe paced around the cave and then sat down on the same flat rock to wait. She kept staring into the trees where Duncan disappeared. She studied that spot with obsessive fascination.

She didn't understand this gut pull toward Duncan, but it felt right. She didn't even have to wonder if he was still at the fort. He was definitely over there in the same direction he went when he left her. This unspoken instinct told her where he was and kept tugging her heartstrings to get back to him.

She fidgeted, stood up, and walked around a little more. The time dragged. She should get something to eat. She hadn't eaten since she left her own time. She must have been on the mountain with Duncan at least overnight, but it only felt like a few minutes.

She sat back down, but she only ended up standing again almost immediately. She couldn't settle down and not because she wanted Duncan back so badly. He had business to attend to at the fort. He probably wouldn't come back for hours.

Something else unsettled her. What was it? She listened. She didn't hear anything, but something was definitely moving around out in the woods. She was certain of it.

She went over to the weapons stores and found a bunch of sabers and dirks. The sabers were all too big for her and she had never trained with them. She took two dirks instead.

She approached the cave mouth and held her breath to listen again. She didn't understand this foreboding sense of danger, but it bothered her so much that she couldn't ignore it.

Her bond with Duncan should have made her feel better. She didn't have to worry about him coming back for her. He would come back and this feeling didn't come from Duncan. It came from somewhere off to her right. Something was out there and it wasn't friendly.

She took one step out of the cave and scanned the trees for any sign of movement. Did something happen to Duncan?

She instinctively looked back toward the fort and her heart leapt when she saw him running toward her in his tiger form. He skimmed along the ground at breakneck speed. He charged for her covering the distance impossibly fast.

She automatically tightened her grip on her weapons, and at the same instant, a bunch of armed men surged out of the trees. They surrounded Duncan and one of them started firing spells at him.

The first volley struck the cat broadside and sent him somersaulting through piles of dry leaves. The other three men rushed him and positioned themselves to encircle him.

The wizard bombarded him with dozens of spells before Duncan had time to recover. He pitched into a heap at the base of a tree and the other three men pounced on him trying to catch hold of the cat.

The tiger erupted out of the leaves screeching to wake the dead. He flew at his attackers slashing his claws and teeth everywhere. One spry young man caught hold of the cat's fur and held on despite Duncan's ferocious efforts to break free.

Duncan whipped around in the young man's grasp, flayed at the man's arms and hands, and kicked out with his hind legs to swipe the younger man's chest.

The young man held Duncan at arm's length straining every muscle to restrain him and the others moved in. The wizard ran over to help them bind Duncan.

Zoe couldn't watch this. She couldn't let these bastards catch Duncan—not if she could do something to help him.

She sprang forward, dive-bombed the young man holding Duncan, and clocked the guy hard across the side of the head. She hit him hard enough to dislodge his hold on Duncan and the cat sprang clear.

The wizard and the other two rounded on Zoe and two much larger men brandished their sabers at her. She checked herself when she realized her mistake. She had two small daggers and they had a wizard and full-sized sabers. Each of the attackers fought with a saber in the right hand and a dirk in the left.

They advanced one menacing step at a time and she braced herself to fight for her life. She couldn't back down when Duncan's life was at stake.

The young man picked himself up, grabbed his weapons, and took his place with his comrades. Blood ran down his cheek from a wound in his scalp and he didn't look happy about it at all.

Zoe raised her blades to defend herself when, without warning, all the attackers' weapons sailed out of their hands. Their dirks and sabers flew sideways, they all looked down at their empty hands, and then they all spun around to come face to face with Duncan.

He faced them as a man and glared at them in undisguised fury. He sliced his forefinger at the biggest one and sent the guy wheeling sideways to slam into a tree.

The young man on the far end of the line launched at Duncan and shifted in midair. He transformed into a Highland tiger and flew shrieking straight for Duncan's face.

Duncan swiped his hand back to the left and the cat slammed into a different tree. The cat grunted in pain and crashed to the ground, unconscious.

Zoe stared in horror at the last two men. The last remaining attacker shifted, too, and another hair-raising screech tore through the woods as he closed on Duncan. Why were the Buchanans attacking Duncan? Weren't they his own Clansmen? They should be trying to help him.

Zoe didn't care anymore. She sprinted across the clearing, dropped her dirks, and dove for the cat. She had no idea what she would do once she got hold of it, but she couldn't let it harm Duncan.

At that moment, an ear-splitting bang exploded right next to her head. The impact ripped her feet off the ground and she fell flat on her back.

She barely had time to realize she was looking up at the treetops with the sky beyond before a man stepped over her and pointed a saber tip at her eye. "Dinnae move a whisker, lassie, or I'll kill ye right here."

She tightened her grip on her dirks to fight back.... except that she didn't have any dirks. She was totally unarmed and defenseless.

Chapter 9

The young wizard that captured Zoe stood back and aimed all ten of his fingers at her. Streams of golden light flowed from his fingers and wrapped around her. She couldn't move no matter how hard she struggled.

He surrounded her in these magical filaments and lifted her off the ground. He moved her over to a tree and used more magical lines to tie her to the tree.

She didn't try to struggle very much, though. She'd seen enough magic in the last twenty-four hours to understand that fighting back would be useless.

She surveyed the surroundings and saw right away that Duncan was gone. That didn't bother her as much as it should have. He vanished in the middle of fighting these High-landers, but his presence still gave her much more confidence than she expected. Was he still here? How could he be when she couldn't see him?

She understood why he didn't show himself. These Buchanans were trying to capture him and maybe kill him. She couldn't understand why, but she wouldn't show herself to them either if she'd been in Duncan's place.

The young wizard left her sitting there and went over to his friends. He helped them up and did something to the young guy who had smashed into the tree trunk. The wizard did something to his head and stopped the bleeding, but that didn't improve the guy's mood.

The young man strode over to Zoe and kicked her in the leg. "Do ye have any notion how long we've been hunting for Duncan, ye blasted witch? Now ye've lost him for us all over again."

"Leave her be, Fletcher!" the wizard ordered. "She's traveling with him. If we treat her well, she may help us find him again."

"Keep dreaming, asshole," Zoe snarled. "I'll never help you capture him."

"We arenae trying to capture him, ye daft nupty!" Fletcher spat. "He's our own cousin! Do ye think we're out here looking for him to harm him? Ye're off yer head!"

The wizard grabbed Fletcher from behind and dragged him away. He gave Fletcher a shove in the opposite direction. "I told ye to leave her be! Go get some wood and make a fire. We arenae going anywhere tonight."

Fletcher shot Zoe another hateful glare that she returned just as fiercely. She didn't care if these idiots were Duncan's cousins. She wouldn't help them catch him. How did she know they didn't come from the Laird?

Duncan's warning came back to her. Everyone was hunting him and too many people were trying to kill him. She didn't trust anyone.... except maybe Elliot Ritchie. Duncan trusted him, but none of these guys was Elliot.

These were all definitely Buchanans. She recognized their tartan, now that she no longer had the option to fight them. They all wore the same tartan as Duncan, but that didn't make them her friends—far from it.

The wizard went over and helped his other two Clansmen. Then he gave them jobs making camp, too. He must have told them to stay away from Zoe because none of them came near her.

The wizard came back and squatted down in front of her. He sighed and passed his hand across his eyes. "Ye've given us a heap of trouble, lassie."

"Good," she spat. "I hope you never find Duncan."

He put his hand down and furrowed his brow to study her, but he didn't glare or snarl. "Ye're one of Jaimee's friends. She's the woman ye call Snowflake."

"I know who Jaimee is, pal. I'm not stupid."

"Ye've come from the future, am I right? Ye and Betty."

She spun around before she thought to stop herself. "You know Betty?"

"She's mated to me cousin Reid—Duncan's brother. Did Duncan tell ye that?"

She looked away. She kicked herself for letting him get inside her defenses.

"I'm Connell, lassie—Connell Buchanan. Me cousin Colton is Chief of Clan Buchanan. He's Duncan's older brother. Did ye ken that, lassie?"

"I know," she mumbled under her breath.

"Colton sent us out to find Duncan—not to harm him, but to bring him in alive so we can all put him on the throne in the Laird's place. Do ye understand that, lassie? None of us means ye nor Duncan any harm. We only want to find him."

"It doesn't look like he wants you to find him," she returned. "You better keep me tied up with your magic because, the minute I get out of here, I'm gonna kill you and your cousins. What did you do with Duncan?"

Connell cocked his head and frowned at her even more deeply. "Dinnae ye ken where Duncan is?"

"How the hell should I know where he is? You were fighting him and then you captured me. What did you do with him? If you harmed him, I'll kill you all!"

"He vanished, lass. He up and vanished in the middle of the fight. Ye distracted us by attacking and then he was gone."

She gaped at him in disbelief. "He can't have!"

"He's a wizard, lassie—a much more powerful wizard than I am. If he'd have fought me, he could have defeated me and retaken ye. He could have killed us all, but he didnae. He let us capture ye. Why?"

She blinked at him trying to get some sound to come out of her mouth. Duncan.... did he abandon her? Why would he let these men capture her if he could save her so easily?

Did she misjudge Duncan? Did she fall under some insidious spell that he cast to befuddle her? What if she was completely wrong about him?

She shook that thought out of her head and rounded on Connell. "What did you do with him? Did you use magic to take him away?"

"We were trying to help him, lassie. Why did ye attack us? Why would ye stop us from saving him?"

"Saving him! You were trying to kill him! I saw you with my own eyes so don't waste your breath lying about it!"

Connel's shoulders slumped and he shuddered. "This is all a grand mix-up, lassie. I see that now."

"Where is Duncan?" she demanded. "He wouldn't just vanish without a trace."

"Well, he did." Connell stood up and turned away. "I cannae free ye, now that ye've threatened all our lives."

"What are you going to do with me, then? You can't just leave me lying here tied to a tree."

"No. I didnae mean to. I'll send ye to Icemeet."

"What?! No!" she exclaimed. "You can't do that!"

She really started struggling then, but he had bound her so tightly that she couldn't move her arms or legs. She only managed to hurt herself tugging against his magical restraints.

"Ye're the last person to see Duncan alive. Ye'll be safer at Icemeet and Betty and Jaimee can take charge of ye. Perhaps Colton and Reid can get some information out of ye about

Duncan's whereabouts." He got to his feet and turned away shaking his head. "I dinnae ken where to look for him now, lassie. If ye can help us, I'd be most grateful."

He wandered over to where Fletcher was busy building a fire. They talked for a while, but they didn't talk about Zoe or Duncan. They kept the conversation casual and discussed where they would go next and potential rebel movements in the area that they had to avoid.

She listened long enough to realize that the other two men were Fergus and Callum. They wandered over and Connell used his magic to heal their injuries. Fergus came back with a rabbit he had caught and the four of them started cooking something over the flames.

The roasting meat smelled incredible and Zoe's mouth watered. Now she felt really hungry and none of them acknowledged her presence or offered her anything to eat. She should have eaten at the cave when she had the chance.

Her heart sank and despair started to catch up with her. She could face this strange country when she had Duncan by her side. Now she was alone with these men.

She gulped down a lump in her throat and turned away. She didn't want to see them relaxing around the fire, eating their roasted rabbit, and enjoying each other's company while she remained tied up in the dark, alone and hungry.

She searched the surrounding woods for any sign of Duncan, but he wasn't there. She became more and more convinced that he had left her, now that circumstances turned against him. Why should he expose himself for her sake? She was nothing. She'd known him no more than a day.

She shouldn't have let herself start feeling anything for him so quickly. Did he bewitch her? She could have sworn he felt the same way about her, but what if that was all a ruse?

Darkness settled over the forest. She wouldn't be able to see Duncan out there even if he was there to see.

No, that was all wrong. These fears only reared their ugly heads because she was alone and couldn't see him, but her primal instinct told her that the bond between them was all too real. She didn't imagine it and it was no magic.

The connection transcended all rational thought. She saw that in his eyes and that inexplicable link tied her to him even when he went to the fort. She felt it now. It kept moving around in the woods out of sight, but it was still there. He was here. He didn't abandon her.

That certainty made her even more desperate to get away. She never felt this way about anyone. She had to find him somehow. She had to feel that unbreakable connection between them when she looked into his eyes. She would stop at nothing to feel that again.

She startled to high alert when someone touched her leg. "Lassie...."

She whipped around to find Connell bending over her. She tried to kick him away and failed.

"Easy, lass," he murmured. "I've only brought ye something to eat."

She swallowed hard and looked away. "Go away. Don't pretend to be nice to me."

"I would free ye entirely if I thought for an instant ye wouldnae run away."

"Why shouldn't I run away?" she fired back. "I have no reason to trust you."

Silence fell over the forest except for the flames crackling. She realized with a jolt that Fergus, Callum, and Fletcher were all staring at her and listening to the conversation.

Connell passed his hand in front of her chest and one of her arms came free. "Sit up and have something to eat, lassie. We've a long march back to Icemeet tomorrow and ye'll need yer strength. I dinnae dare to free ye more than that after the threats ye've made against us. We've all had far too much to do with Jaimee to risk ye attacking us."

Fergus laughed loudly. "Ye can say that again, laddie."

"And Betty," Fletcher grumbled. "She nearly killed me."

Zoe stared at them and then at Connell. He held out a piece of bark with a bunch of rabbit meat on it. It smelled mind-blowingly good and her mouth watered even more. She couldn't resist.

She squirmed her body into a better position and took the bark plate from him. She eyed Connell and then the others suspiciously, but once she started eating, she couldn't stop until she finished it all.

Connell smiled at her, took the plate, and handed her a wooden cup. "Here's some water, lassie."

She took it and drank it. She was too grateful to refuse.

He took the empty cup and set it aside, but he didn't leave. "I want to use magic to scan yer mind, lassie. Will ye let me do that?"

"Let you?" She snorted. "I didn't let you tie me up. Are you asking for my permission to keep me as your prisoner?"

"Ye must care for Duncan as much as we do, lassie. Ye tried to defend him and protect him from us."

"Ye witch!" Fletcher snapped over by the fire. "Me head's down the cludgie thanks to ye."

Connell chuckled like Fletcher just made a joke. Zoe didn't understand what either of them meant—not that she cared. "Come near me again and I'll crack it a second time," she growled at Fletcher. "Maybe I'll finish the job that Betty started."

"Enough," Connell cut in and waved his hand between them to get Zoe's attention. "Show me where ye've been with Duncan. It will only help us find him and take him to safety."

"You can't take him to safety. The Laird is trying to kill him. Finding him will only put him in danger. Don't you get that?"

Connell studied her with his head on one side. "Show me, lassie. I winnae do it without yer permission."

"Fine." She turned away. "Do what you want."

She didn't want to watch to see what he did to her. She half-feared what he would find even though she knew she couldn't tell him anything that would put Duncan in danger. Wherever he was, he wouldn't be any of the places he had been with Zoe. He wasn't that stupid.

A warm, watery sensation flooded her body and finally fizzed inside her head. The memories of the past day played through her mind and filled her with the same peace and happiness. She felt again the blessed relaxation and relief of curling up inside Duncan's warm coils and flying over the landscape on his back.

"My God!" Connell whispered.

She turned around to find him staring at her in stunned disbelief. "What? What's wrong?"

"What did ye see, laddie?" Fergus asked from the fireside.

Connell sprang to his feet and started pacing up and down next to Zoe. "This is.... this is astounding!"

"What's so astounding about it?" she asked. "You can see there's nothing wrong with him. He understands the danger he's in. He can protect himself a whole lot better than you can."

Connel's hand flew to his head. "I never realized.... My God! The power he must have!"

"What is it, lad?" Callum asked. "What did ye see?"

"He can shift into a cat and a dragon....and he has magic—incredible magic!"

"We've seen that," Fletcher added. "How do ye think he defeated us?"

"Ye dinnae understand. He might even be powerful enough to defeat the Laird."

The three men and Zoe all whipped around to stare at him. "Are you serious?" Zoe asked. "Duncan doesn't think so."

"But the Laird does." Connell squatted down in front of her, and this time, he murmured in a breathless rush. "Ye're bonded, lassie. Ye're mated to him for life."

"How can we be? I don't even know him."

"I dinnae ken how it happened. I've seen it a thousand times, but never like this. It happened instantly—the moment ye met."

She blinked at nothing. Was that it? Was that the amazing feeling of understanding everything about him so quickly? Was this the mate-bond linking them together for all time?

Not even that bothered her. It explained everything and made her happy. She wasn't crazy after all, and if it was a real mate-bond, it meant that Duncan must feel the same way she did. He wouldn't leave her. He wouldn't let anything happen to her.

That one thought gave her all the energy she needed to escape and get her revenge. She reacted instantly, shot out her one free hand, and grabbed Connell by the throat.

Fury and hope made her squeeze a lot harder than she ever thought possible. If she killed this guy, his magic would vanish and she would be free. Then she would kill the other three and run away to Duncan again.

She clamped her fingers around Connel's neck in a death grip. She crushed his windpipe. He tried to struggle and she yanked him down on the ground next to her. She could only use one hand and she couldn't get up, so she pinned him against her leg and gritted her teeth to choke the life out of him.

She hated him. She hated him for seeing into her private moments with Duncan. She hated Connell for understanding what was going on between her and Duncan better than she did herself. Connell deserved to die for that.

His face turned blue. He clawed at her fingers trying to free himself. Strangling him might have interfered with his ability to use his magic because he didn't use it on her. He grabbed her wrist and tried to pull her hand away, but that was it.

She vented her hate and vengeance on him and his eyes started to bug out of his head. The men at the fire kept talking to each other in normal tones of voice. They didn't see what was happening. In a few seconds, Connell would be dead with them none the wiser.

She bared her teeth in pure loathing. She focused on the colors spreading over his face. His struggles became more disordered and frantic. He was almost dead....

A crushing blow struck her across the side of the head. She felt herself falling over and tried to pull herself back from the darkness enveloping her. Another blow slammed her down and she blacked out entirely.

Chapter 10

Duncan slipped a little closer to the camp and listened to Connell and Callum talking.

"How is that even possible?" Callum was saying. "She isnae one of us. Her kind dinnae mate for life.

"How many times do I have to say I dinnae understand it?" Connell countered. "I only ken what I saw."

"Tell us again what ye saw," Fergus urged.

"Dinnae," Fletcher growled. "She tried to kill ye. Isnae that enough to ken about her?"

"She's cut from the same cloth as Jaimee and Betty," Fergus replied. "That's clear enough."

"That doesnae explain how she mate-bonded with Duncan the moment she laid eyes on him and he wasnae even a man at the time," Callum pointed out. "She mate-bonded with a dragon."

"He's still a Buchanan even if he is a dragon," Fergus countered. "He's Neill Buchanan's son. What more do ye need to ken?"

None of the others answered and Duncan slipped away. The conversation between Connell and Zoe and now this one between Connell and his Clansmen gave Duncan the thrill of his life. She felt the same way! She was mate-bonded with him and he was mate-bonded with her. No wonder he felt this way about her.

She had certainly been acting like his life's mate since she met him on the mountain. She didn't seem nearly as distressed by Connel's revelation as Duncan expected. He expected her to resist more and maybe try to deny it.

He snuck over to the tree where Connell had retied her. He had overlooked leaving one of her arms free and it almost cost him his life. He didn't make the same mistake a second time. He might even keep her bound and carry her back to Icemeet.

Duncan slipped in front of the tree. She didn't look up at him. She stared off into the dark woods with her head turned away from the four men at the fire. He shielded himself with an invisibility spell and she didn't see him standing right in front of her.

He gazed down at her and let this flood of exquisite emotion sweep over him. He couldn't define the way he felt about her. He felt pain and sadness and ecstasy and longing all mixed up together. He ached to touch her, but he couldn't do that without revealing himself.

He let the magical cloak drop and it flowed off him in a sheet of colored sparks. She jerked around fast and gasped. "Duncan!"

His heart flipped at how happy she was to see him. Only Connel's spells kept her on the ground and stopped her from coming to him. She might even come all the way into his arms.

"Keep still, lassie," he whispered. "Dinnae let them hear ye. They cannae see me nor hear me. Only ye can, but they can hear and see ye. Lie quietly."

"But...." She tried to sit up, but the men still didn't notice. "Where have you been? I was worried you might have left."

"I've been here the whole time, lass. I wouldnae ever leave ye." He squatted down in front of her and caressed her cheek. Touching her tore at his heart, but he couldn't let it go any further without giving himself away.

"Duncan...." she stammered. "Connell said...."

"I heard what he said, lassie. Dinnae concern yerself about ought. I'll be here and I'll be with ye no matter what they do."

"Do you trust those men? They say they're your cousins, but how do we know they don't really want to hurt you?"

"They dinnae want to hurt me, lassie, but I cannae say the same about ye."

"What do you mean? Why would they do anything to me?"

"I dinnae ken. Perhaps they wouldnae, but they winnae be near as careful about ye as they would about me.... but dinnae bother about that. I'll be here and I'll see ye're kept safe."

"But.... how long do I have to stay like this?"

"It serves me purpose to track them without showing meself for now, but I winnae ever leave ye alone. If they really mean to take ye back to Icemeet, this may be the best way for me to get back to me brothers."

"And if they don't?"

"Then they'll lead me to some other part of this war where I can do some good. It doesnae do any good to stay out here in these woods where I'm a danger to everyone I care about."

She gulped and her countenance twisted. "Duncan...."

"Hush yer wheesht, lassie," he whispered, and without thinking, he leaned in and kissed her. "I'm watching. I winnae let anything happen to ye. Ye have me solemn word of honor on that."

He pulled back. Her soft eyes feasted on his face and he recognized that look. He'd seen it on dozens of Buchanan faces when people looked deep into the eyes of their fated mates. She wasn't afraid. She only wanted him. She didn't want him to leave her alone.

He petted her cheeks, and when he pushed her hair back, he saw the pulverized bruise on the side of her head where Fletcher hit her to break her hold on Connell.

Duncan touched it and his magic erased the wound. He made her whole, but it was really his kiss that completed her and made her his.

She didn't mention it. Did it frighten her or did it just make her as happy as it made him? That kiss felt so natural, so destined. Nothing could ever be wrong about him kissing her except that he wouldn't be able to do more of it.

"Do ye think ye can stay here a little longer, lassie?" he breathed. "Ye can hate the lads all ye like. I winnae blame ye for that, but let them keep ye as a prisoner just a little longer. If they're right, we'll be back in Icemeet before long."

"I don't want to, but I'll do it for you."

"That's me own lass." He kissed her again and allowed his lips to linger there for a long moment before he pulled away. He didn't think he could break the hold of her eyes so easily. "I've never felt this for anyone before, lassie. There's no one before ye in me heart."

He took a step back and let the cloak fall over himself again. Her eyes remained riveted on him until the cloak came down and then she looked around everywhere trying to find him in the darkness. He was invisible again.

Her face went through several rapidly conflicting emotions. He longed to touch her again, to whisper some assurance in her ear, but he couldn't do that without revealing himself again. He already took a massive risk doing it the first time. He couldn't take that chance now.

He just had to stand back and devour her with his eyes. God, he loved her so much! How did he lose his heart so quickly? He would give anything for her, including his life. His whole life would be a small price to pay for one kiss.

He couldn't sacrifice *her* life for one kiss, though, especially not when Connell and Fergus stood up and came over to check on her.

Duncan moved out of their way and hid behind a tree where he could eavesdrop on them.

"We'll need to post a watch on her each night to make sure she doesnae try anything," Connell began.

"I'll take the first watch," Fergus offered. "Ye need yer rest, laddie."

Connell sighed and rubbed his temples. "Thank ye. I need it."

Fergus chuckled and slapped him on the back. "I'll wake Callum at midnight and then Fletcher can take over sometime after that."

"Do ye still mean to take her back to Icemeet?" Callum interjected from his place. "Colton winnae like ye coming back without Duncan."

"What would ye have me do—leave her to run free? She's a danger to us all."

"Ye dinnae want to face Jaimee," Fletcher interjected. "That's your concern. Ye dinnae fancy explaining to Jaimee that ye had this lassie and let her go."

"Ye dinnae dare to cross Jaimee yer own self." Connell threw himself down on the ground. "Ye'd take the same course in me place. Ye ken ye would for there's no other course to take."

None of the others answered. Jaimee would skin them alive if they let Zoe get away and returned to Icemeet without her.

Fergus sat down not far away, but he made sure to sit far enough away that Zoe wouldn't be able to threaten him even if she somehow got her arms free.

He eyed her with a sharp look and she looked away first. She squirmed under his gaze. He knew all about her. He knew perfectly well that she was planning to escape and kill them all. Jaimee's and Betty's reputation preceded the whole Last Division. Everyone knew what they were capable of.

Connell stretched out on the ground by the fire and folded his arms under his head. Callum shifted into a cat, curled into a furry ball, draped his bushy striped tail over his face, and shut his eyes.

Fletcher sat up for a long time staring into the flames and Fergus never slackened his vigilance for an instant. He took his watch very seriously.

Zoe looked back out at the forest and Duncan felt her searching for him. She had seen him and now she knew for certain that the bond between them was real. She wouldn't question anymore. He was here and he would keep watch over her much more carefully than Fergus would.

Chapter 11

Zoe woke up in the middle of the night to find Callum and Fletcher standing over her and whispering. She couldn't make out the words.

Two Highland tigers curled up by the dying embers of the fire. Connell must have shifted, too, and now both he and Fergus were sound asleep.

Callum said something and Fletcher nodded. Callum went over to the fire, shifted, and curled up next to his cousins.

Fletcher sat down in Fergus's old place, but he didn't look at Zoe. He picked up a stick from the ground and started whittling it with his dirk.

She relaxed back against the tree and looked out at the forest. Her heart turned another somersault when she sensed Duncan out there. She could feel him so much more clearly, now that she knew he felt the same way she did.

They were mated for life. He had only kissed her twice, but somehow, it already seemed like a done deal. She didn't understand how, but it was definitely real.

The palpable tension coming from Fletcher didn't soften as the minutes dragged on. She couldn't sleep with him looming over her, but if the men divided up the watch the way they said, it must be close to dawn anyway.

They would either release her or take her to Icemeet this way. Either way, she wouldn't have to spend too much longer in these woods. Duncan wouldn't let her down.

She stiffened when Fletcher stood up and went over to the fire. He put more wood on it and the flames crackled higher. None of the three cats stirred.

He came back toward her, but he didn't sit down. He squatted next to her and pointed his dirk at her. "Now it's just ye and me, lassie. Go on and scream out. Tell these lads that ye're a coward the way I ken ye are."

She stared at him seething with a combination of hate and confusion. What was he going to do—attack her right here and now when she was tied up? Who was he calling a coward?

The other Buchanans wouldn't let that happen even if Duncan wasn't here to stop it. She didn't know much about their Clan, but she understood enough. Connell sure wouldn't let Fletcher do anything to her.

She could call out, but his taunt about her being a coward made her too foaming mad. She wouldn't give him the satisfaction. She might have all four limbs restrained by magic, but she would still teach Fletcher a lesson he wouldn't forget.

He dragged his dirk down her body and the point set off more sparks from the magical filaments that bound her. The blade tip tried to penetrate the field, but it couldn't get through.

"This is the only thing keeping ye alive, lassie," he hissed. "Ye're not Jaimee, are ye? Ye cannae do ought but lie there and pray I let ye live."

He gritted his teeth trying to drive the dirk deeper into the field even though he already knew it was impossible. Connel's magic protected her. Fletcher couldn't cut through it or she would be dead already.

"That's neither here nor there, lassie. I can still kill ye this way." He brought his dirk back up and pointed the tip at her face. "What will ye do to stop me? Ye're weak and helpless. How did ye become one of their comrades, anyway, if ye're this weak?"

He brought the dirk point right against her cheek. The tip stabbed into her skin. It hurt, but not as much as his words. She hated him beyond reason for saying she didn't belong in the Last Division. How dare he?

She had to strike back somehow, but she didn't have a weapon or even the use of her arms and legs. She had to think of something, so she fell back on the only weapon left to her.

She wrenched her body sideways with all her strength and sank her teeth into his hand. She bit down on the fleshy muscle of his thumb and her teeth cut to the bone.

He let out a broken shriek somewhere between a bellow and a scream. He tried to pull away, but she held on. She wanted to punish him for everything he did and said to her.

She snarled through gritted teeth and yanked him down on top of her. His body struck the magical field surrounding her and a loud crack exploded all around her. The field evaporated in a split second and Fletcher's weight landed on top of her. She was free.

The noise of struggle roused the other three and Callum, Connell, and Fergus all shifted. They scrambled to grab their weapons and whirled around to find Zoe and Fletcher locked in a death struggle.

Zoe saw the three men coming for her and lightning flickered from Connel's fingertips. She couldn't let him retake her.

She summoned all her strength, unlocked her jaws from Fletcher's hand, and hurled him off. She curled her legs under him, planted her feet on his chest, and kicked him at Fergus and Callum.

Fletcher's body struck all three men. Fergus and Callum tried to catch him and Zoe took that chance to vault to her feet. A wicked fork of lightning splintered the tree bark right next to her head as she ducked behind the tree for cover.

She took off into the woods, but she was making too much noise. Radiant pulses of magic popped out of the camp and came perilously close to recapturing her. She had to get away and she had to find a way to hide from Connel's magic.

She ran blindly and she didn't dare to slow down to try to find a place to hide. Twigs ripped her hair and cheeks. She glanced back to see a giant ball of glowing blue light floating through the woods behind her. Connell was coming for her.

She spun around to run on and she collided with something solid. Powerful arms surrounded her and held her still. She screamed and tried to break away when a hand clamped over her mouth. "Quiet, lassie!" Duncan whispered. "Dinnae make a sound."

He pulled her behind a tree and held her there while her heart fluttered in a whirlwind. Her blood pounded in her ears so she couldn't hear if Connell and the others were still following her.

Duncan's dark eyes glistened in the darkness. His arms surrounded her in blissful protection. She didn't have to worry. His magic would keep her safe from Connell finding her again.

Now that she stopped running, her mind cleared enough to hear what the men were doing. They blundered into the woods yelling back and forth to each other.

"I swear she came this way!" Callum called.

"Did ye see her?" Fergus asked.

"How could I see her in this darkness? Of course I didnae see her! I heard her, though. She's here somewhere."

"We'll have to shift to find her," Callum returned. "We cannae wait until morning to search."

"That filthy, rotten cow!" Fletcher fumed. "She's mangled me hand."

"I told ye not to get near enough for her to reach ye," Connell countered. "She made threats that she'd kill us all and ye didnae listen. Ye should know better than to underestimate these lassies. Now ye've lost her for us."

"Me! I havenae lost ought." A thud echoed through the woods followed by Fletcher bellowing. "What did ye do that for?"

"Shut it, ye droog!" Connell hissed. "Ye've mucked up enough for one night. Now we've lost both her and Duncan into the bargain."

The four men marched closer to the tree where Duncan and Zoe hid. Zoe tried to warn Duncan, but he didn't release his hold on her mouth.

His voice came into her mind. *Keep ye still as still, lassie. I'm covering us with me magic. They cannae see us. Be silent and they winnae find us.*

Connell, Fergus, and Callum walked past the tree. They all faced the same direction and they searched the dark woods for any sign of Duncan and Zoe.

Zoe froze against the tree. Callum and Fergus looked straight at her more than once, but they didn't see her. Connell kept sending out pulses of magic, but they didn't touch Duncan and Zoe.

Connell finally straightened up and let his shoulders slump. "They arenae here. Duncan must have taken them somewhere."

"How in the name of Christ are we meant to find them, then?" Fletcher growled from behind the tree.

"Dinnae ye give me yer mouth when ye're the one that's got us into this fix," Connell fired back.

"Dinnae ye blame me for this!" Fletcher roared. "I didnae do ought to her."

"And that's why she attacked ye, is it?" Connell gave a sick laugh. "I winnae believe that if I live a thousand years. Ye were up to no good and I dinnae envy ye the welcome ye'll receive back home when Colton finds out."

"Ye winnae tell him ought when ye've naught to back yer claim," Fletcher muttered. "Ye're all talk, lad."

"Would ye like me to back me claim.... *lad*?" Connell hissed in a deadly undertone. "Would ye like me to use the power to find out why she attacked ye and bit yer hand nearly in half? I can do it if ye've a mind for me to."

Fletcher went deadly quiet and Connell sauntered the rest of the way to where his cousin stood. "I didnae spend the last seven weeks with Jaimee and Betty not to ken they dinnae attack anyone without a muckle great reason for it. One of these days, that lassie will come wandering back to Icemeet and she'll have plenty to say about what went on here tonight. Ye remember that before ye open yer mouth to me again.... *lad*."

Connell strode past him on his way back to camp. Fergus and Callum hustled to catch up with him. "We cannae go back to Icemeet empty-handed," Fergus pointed out. "Colton ordered us not to return without Duncan."

"We havenae any choice now," Connell muttered over his shoulder. "We must report all this to Colton either way. We can only hope to come back out afterwards and pick up the trail. Now come. It will be day soon."

Chapter 12

Duncan let his hand slide off Zoe's mouth and he felt her relax. Blood covered her mouth and ran down her chin to stain her shirt. "Are ye all right, lassie?"

She nodded staring up at him with huge eyes. "Are you?"

"Of course." He traced his thumb across her lips and chin. That blood made her look primal and wild like an animal fresh from hunting its prey, but it only made her more impossibly beautiful to him. "Ye're heart's racing like a bird, lass."

Her eyes darted down his mouth. Was she thinking as much about kissing him as he was thinking about kissing her?

He finished wiping the blood off her face, but he couldn't stop beaming at her. She was with him, in his arms. They held each other close in the darkness deep in the woods. No one could see or hear them.

"Are they gone?" she whispered. "They won't come back for us, will they?"

"They winnae come back. They'll go to Icemeet and we'll follow them under cover of invisibility. They winnae ken we're there until we're safe inside the walls."

"Are you sure we'll be safe at Icemeet? I mean—will *you* be safe there? Will you be safe anywhere?"

He burst into an even bigger smile. She cared about him! He could kiss her for that, but he didn't want to do it here.

He took her hand. "Come with me, lassie. I'll take ye somewhere we can spend the night."

"It isn't another cave, is it?"

He laughed and she spun around to look behind her toward the Buchanans' camp. "Ye dinnae need to jump at every sound, lassie. We're safe."

She took longer to relax and he stood aside waiting until she was ready to follow him. Even her hesitation enchanted him.

She was so beautiful in a simple, humble way. She didn't even realize how special and angelic she was. That was her charm. She thought she was nothing when she was really the most priceless treasure imaginable.

She finally followed him deeper into the woods, but not without pausing every now and then to listen and survey the surroundings.

He came to a thick stand of trees much older and broader than the rest of the forest. They grew side by side with barely enough space between the trunks for a person to walk.

He wound his way deeper into the grove until he came to a massive tree bigger than the others. He halted next to her and stretched his hand toward the bark.

"What are you doing?" she whispered.

He took hold of the bark and it reformed in his hand. He molded it with his fingers until it formed a door handle.

He pulled it open and a door opened in the side of the tree. He led her into a magnificent room flooded with soft candlelight. A fire crackled in the stone fireplace against one wall.

He shut the door behind her while she stared at the opulent furnishings and the carved oaken table loaded with food. A giant canopy bed laid with brocade quilts filled the other half of the room.

"What is this place?" she breathed.

"I wanted ye to have a nice place to spend the night. I didnae want ye sleeping on the cold, hard ground in the forest. It wouldnae be right."

"I don't mind. I'm used to it."

"I ken that, lassie, but I still wanted to give ye this." He pulled her over to the table and then turned away. "Ye'll be comfortable here and no one will find ye."

Her eyes widened when he returned back to the doorway. "Where are you going? Aren't you staying with me?" She gulped. "I want you to."

"I cannae, lassie. Me Clan mates for life. I dinnae want to stay with ye until I have a chance to introduce ye to me Clan Chief and that's Colton."

"But...you're going to Laird of the whole country. Don't you outrank him?"

He laughed and kissed her hand. "The old ways die hard, lassie, and I'm a stickler for tradition. I've been raised with it all me life and I couldnae besmirch yer reputation by doing this any other way."

He kissed her knuckles one more time and pulled away with an effort. "Ye'll be safe here, lassie. I'll come for ye in the morning."

She watched him open the door and slip away. He shut it and the golden light and warmth of that room vanished. It left him out in the cold by himself, but her beautiful heart overwhelmed him with emotion.

He would give anything to stay with her in that room, but he wanted to do things the right way. He didn't want anything to interfere with him mating with her the right way. He didn't want any of this craziness to mess this up.

Her heart and soul pulled him back to that room inside the tree. She was in there waiting for him. She would welcome him back with open arms—literally.

How easy it would be to fall into her arms and forget everything else, but he couldn't do that. She exerted a much more powerful influence on him.

It had been easy for him to retreat to his mountain and stay out of the war. He could watch everything from a distance. He consoled himself that staying out of the way helped everyone. He tricked himself into thinking that everyone would be safer with him far away from the conflict.

She changed all that when she arrived on his mountain. He couldn't ignore the war anymore. He couldn't let his Clan and his friends fight and die while he hid in safety.

He couldn't hide her, either. That was the worst part. She might be safe tonight, but she was part of this. One of these days, she would fight in this war, and when that happened, he would have to fight to protect her. She was his mate. He couldn't do anything else but protect her or at least fight on the same side.

Fighting on the same side meant defeating the Laird. The Laird was after him and Duncan had to preserve himself for her sake. Protecting his own life was as much his responsibility as protecting hers. He had a responsibility to her to keep her mate alive and well. What kind of mate would he be if he didn't?

He had to fight the Laird and he had to find a way to win. He had to find a way to stop the Laird from destroying Clan Buchanan and all the rest of Kald. Duncan suffered a pang of guilt that it took Zoe coming to him before he actually took responsibility for winning this war.

He set off through the woods toward Connel's camp. Duncan had to keep his cousins in sight. He didn't know when they would move out for Icemeet and Duncan had to be ready to follow them when they did. He hoped it wouldn't be too soon. Zoe needed sleep after the night she'd just endured.

Duncan stuffed down his fury at Fletcher, especially when he reached the camp and heard Connell berating Fletcher in the harshest possible tone.

"Arenae ye even going to heal me hand?" Fletcher grumbled. "What good is a wizard without that?"

"Ye sit and suffer with it, ye rotten bastard!" Connell countered. "I dinnae use me magic to heal traitors and cowards."

"How the devil am I supposed to fight like this?" Fletcher started wrapping a piece of cloth around his hand. "It's me right hand she's bitten. I cannae even hold a saber."

"Then ye'll die and rot in these woods where ye belong," Connell snarled and turned his back on his cousin.

Fergus and Callum looked back and forth between the two cousins without saying a word. They clearly didn't understand why Connell was so mad at Fletcher, but no one would dare to argue with Connell. They trusted him to know what he was talking about because he did.

He threatened to use his magic to find out what Fletcher did to provoke Zoe and Fletcher backed down. That told everyone loud and clear that Connell had guessed right about Fletcher being up to no good.

Connell stormed over to the coals and started kicking dirt over them. "It's nearly dawn. We may as well go now and get across the water. If we make good time, we can report to Colton and be back before nightfall."

Fergus and Callum both stood up to obey him. Fletcher moaned again and Duncan turned away. He better hurry back to the tree room and inform Zoe before she went to sleep. Maybe Duncan could cast a spell over her so she could sleep while he magically transported her to Icemeet.

He hated to disturb her when he just gave her that room to relax in, but he had no choice besides leaving her there and going on to Icemeet alone.

A high-pitched whistle set his nerves on end. He whipped around to see a rocket blast corkscrew through the woods and detonate in the air right above the fire.

The outward blast flattened all four men and, before any of them could recover, a cloud of black-clad figures swarmed out of the woods.

Duncan stared in amazement as they materialized in the firelight. The fire had flared to a towering column of flame even though nothing had hit it. The light shone outward almost as bright as day.

Duncan's blood ran cold when the ghostly apparitions formed in that circle of firelight. They hovered off the ground, but in that flash, he saw them clearly.

The shapes of men wavered under the dark outline of what looked like hooded cloaks, but that was just the magical halo that allowed them to move around at such impossible speeds.

Most of the men inside were young Highlanders. They all resembled each other.... almost as though they were all related. They pounced on the four Buchanans.... all except for one.

The last one wasn't young. In fact, he was beyond old with deep, etched wrinkles lining his ancient face. He stood back and watched the other wizards attack the four Buchanans in overwhelming numbers.

Two wizards crowded each of the Buchanans and separated them from each other. Fergus and Callum grabbed their weapons to defend themselves, but they couldn't harm the wizards no matter how they slashed and stabbed.

Connell unleashed a hellish barrage of spells and one of the dark wizards shattered into a million flying specks that vaporized into the night.

The other wizard flew at Connell and they traded dozens of spells. Connel's arms whirled spouting a steady stream of incantations and enchantments that rocketed from his fingertips.

He drove his enemy back, but Connell couldn't destroy him entirely. Fletcher grabbed his saber and it fell out of his mangled hand. The two wizards attacking him swooped in with a vengeance and ran him against a tree.

One of them shot out a hand and glistening magical power surrounded the wizard's fingers in a sheath of light. The wizard stabbed the mystical blade into Fletcher's stomach and he screamed in agony.

"Connell!" he screeched. "Connell, help me!"

That sound detonated in Duncan's mind. Connell couldn't help Fletcher. Fletcher might be a rotten scumbag, but he didn't deserve to die like this.

Duncan's feet left the ground and he flew into the clearing. Both wizards stood over Fletcher's slumped frame hitting him with magical weapons that Duncan didn't recognize. He had never seen anything like this and their dark, vaporous forms made it difficult for him to see through them.

He couldn't tell exactly what they were doing to Fletcher and he didn't care. He rushed them, and in the second before he reached them to intervene, the old man whooshed into his path.

Duncan froze as the truth struck him between the eyes. This whole attack.... Fletcher's death.... the whole scene was nothing but a trap to get Duncan into a face-to-face confrontation against Laird Balfour Creighton.

Duncan stared at the man realizing for the first time that this was his grandfather—his mother's father. This was the man who wanted to kill him. Duncan had managed to avoid the Laird.... until now.

Duncan had dealt with the Laird's magic more than once, but he'd never looked directly into the old man's eyes. Duncan had never had the misfortune of seeing just how much murderous hatred and deadly intent burned in those cold, cruel eyes.

An instant's clarity confirmed the conclusion that Duncan came to a moment before. He had to take this man down. Duncan had to destroy the Laird and take the Seat of Armstrong for himself. That was the only way to save the country from the insidious darkness the Laird spread far and wide.

Duncan summoned all his magic to unleash a killing stroke against the Laird, but he never got the chance even to raise his hands to fire a single spell. The Laird only blinked at him and a loud snap popped in Duncan's eardrums.

It came from inside his own head, ricocheted outward, and surrounded him in a magical orb. It enveloped him instantly and all his magic snuffed out. He couldn't summon it. He couldn't even think about it.

The Laird smirked at him and those burning dark eyes held Duncan in a stranglehold. He heard Fletcher screaming as the two hooded figures descended on him. Duncan heard Fergus and Callum yelling, but Duncan couldn't even turn his head to see what was happening to them.

Explosions kept going off behind Duncan's back. What was happening to Connell? Was he trying to free Duncan?

Duncan shifted into a dragon, but the orb only expanded to adjust to his new size. He shifted into a tiger and the same thing happened. The orb collapsed and expanded no matter what he did.

He shifted back into a man, but he still couldn't access his magic. The Laird grinned in sadistic triumph. His shoulders shook and his eyes gleamed with silent laughter as the orb started to sink.

The bottom edge drifted into the ground and the whole orb started to submerge underground. Duncan tried in vain to scramble up the orb's sides, but he only slipped down its smooth curves.

His feet sank into the dirt up to the ankles. The earth turned to spongy goo under him. He couldn't even pull his feet out. The rim connecting the orb to the ground expanded as its sides floated lower and lower.

Duncan wrenched around to scream to his cousins, but he couldn't even see Connell. The wizards had backed Fergus and Callum so far into the trees that Duncan couldn't see them at all.

The other two wizards bent over Fletcher and Duncan couldn't see him, either. Was he dead? Duncan couldn't see what they were doing to him and Duncan didn't want to see.

He fought to free himself, but he couldn't get away. He submerged up to his waist and he lost all sensation in his legs. No amount of struggle would free him now. He clawed at the soil, but that only got him even more stuck.

The Laird stood back and laughed at Duncan's pathetic efforts as he sank up to his armpits and then to his neck. The soil crept up to Duncan's jaw and started to rise over his cheeks.

He tilted his head as far back as it would go. He panicked and struggled until he thought he would break himself in half, but he could hardly move at all now. The orb's top edge shone directly above his eyes as he gasped for his last breath of air before he drowned.

His eyes darted everywhere and his frenzied mind switched back to Zoe in the tree room. She was sound asleep in the big luxurious bed. She had no idea what was happening to him.

He inhaled a massive breath of air, but when the dirt touched the corners of his mouth, terror made him scream out one last cry to the one person he most needed right now. "Zoe! Help me!"

The earth crumbled into his mouth and strangled off his last sounds. It muffled him and then it cut off his last dying breath before the earth swallowed him alive.

Chapter 13

Zoe drifted in a beautiful dream and listened to the birds twittering in the tree branches overhead. The sun played on green leaves above her head and soothed her heavy eyelids.

Her fingers brushed the soft grass underneath her and the small river nearby giggled gently over stepping stones down the bank from where she lay.

Her fishing line twanged, but she felt too lazy to sit up and check if she had a fish on her hook. Fluffy clouds rolled by in the sky above. She could just lie here forever and never get tired of all the pleasant sensations surrounding her.

She sighed in blissful contentment. She didn't want or need anything more than this. She must be in heaven.

All at once, a piercing scream shattered her dream. *Zoe! Help me!*

She jolted upright and looked around for whoever called her, but she wasn't on a grassy riverbank anymore. She wasn't lying in a magnificent bed with a fire crackling in a stone fireplace and food covered the hewn oak table.

Duncan. The tree room where Duncan left her had completely vanished. She was lying on the cold ground in the forest and it was the middle of the night. Duncan was in trouble.

She sprang to her feet and checked her surroundings one last time to make sure she knew where she was. She was in the same place where he took her to the tree room, but there was no tree room. How long had she been asleep? Was it still the same night when Fletcher attacked her or had a full twenty-four hours passed? Was she already too late?

She found her own tracks walking side by side with Duncan. This was the direction he had led her to get here. She took off running through the woods following their trial. She had to stop more than once to check her bearings.

She found the place where she and Duncan had hidden behind the tree. Finding her way back to Connel's campsite was much easier, now that she could follow six sets of tracks instead of just two. The four men didn't try to cover their tracks, either. They left a highway of markings for her to follow.

She pulled up short when she saw the camp. Fletcher lay dead and cold against a tree with at least five knife wounds in his chest and stomach. His dead eyes stared up at the canopy out of his ghastly colorless face.

She knelt down next to him and squeezed his arm just to make sure. She might have threatened to kill him, but she never would have wished this on him. Who did this to him?

She sprang to her feet and searched the area. She found dozens of tracks. Someone attacked the camp and they attacked five people—Connell, Callum, Fergus, Fletcher, and Duncan. He was here. He fought these people—or he tried to.

She spent way too long checking and rechecking to make sure she didn't make a mistake. Two people fought with blades—Fergus and Callum. Connell faced off against two men. He defeated one of them, but the other gave him more trouble.

And then she found Duncan's tracks. They vanished right here next to the fire.... but he never left that spot. Connell, Fergus, and Callum never left their positions, either. They just.... vanished.

She frowned. This was all wrong. It couldn't be. How could someone just snatch these men without leaving any sign?

She didn't see any tracks of the strangers coming into the camp, either. They just appeared. They must have used magic. That was the only explanation and now all four of them were gone. Was Duncan dead? Did the Laird finally kill him?

He couldn't have. Duncan's call kept ringing in her head. *Zoe! Help me!* He wasn't dead. He needed her help.... but how? She didn't have any magic and she was all alone.

No. She wasn't alone. Her friends from the Last Division might be scattered all over the country, but they were still here.

Her mind went straight to Icemeet. Jaimee, Lily, and Betty were all there, but she had no idea how to get to Icemeet.

Then she remembered Echo. Zoe knew where Echo was and she wasn't far away. She squatted down to force herself to think, but she made up her mind in a split second.

She found the tracks of herself and Duncan when they left the cave. She followed them back to the cave, and from there, she followed Duncan's tracks to the fort.

The sun rose while she was searching around and she paused in the trees where the sentries couldn't see her. She scanned the fort while she made up her mind what to do next. How the hell was she supposed to get in there without getting shot by archers or impaled by armed Highlanders?

She skirted sideways to position herself in front of the big gate. The voices of women and children mingled with those of men behind the high wall. Then some child laughed. Maybe these rebels weren't so dangerous after all.

She considered walking out there and throwing herself on the sentries' mercy when she spotted movement in the bushes to her right. She crouched in the undergrowth and held her breath as a group of armed men came out of the forest.

They walked single file with several of them carrying dead game animals on their backs and shoulders. They headed straight for the fort and the man at the front yelled out, "Open the gate!"

A flurry of activity sounded behind the wall and the gate scraped back. The men filed inside taking their game with them.

Zoe's heart skipped a beat. She had to get these people's attention. She didn't want to risk her life, but these were the only people who could help Duncan.

What did he say to her on the mountain? He trusted Elliot Ritchie. Duncan decided to come here instead of going home to Icemeet to get help from his brothers. He trusted Elliot with his life.

Zoe made her decision and started to stand up. As soon as she did, the rebels would be able to see her and she wasn't looking forward to their reaction.

Then she saw the very last person in the line of hunters. It was Echo Boxwood, but Echo didn't look anything like how Zoe remembered. Was it only two or three days ago that they parted in Washington, DC? It seemed like years ago and Zoe hardly recognized Echo anymore.

Echo wore her hair braided down her back and dirt and dried blood stained her leather clothes. She carried a dead pig strapped across her back and Echo's eyes scanned the undergrowth with a hint of wildness. Zoe had never seen that look in all the years she lived with Echo at Ironforge.

The sight of her friend hardened Zoe's resolve and she stood up. She started walking on an intercept course to meet Echo. Echo stiffened and her hand flew to the dirks at her belt before she realized who it was.

Echo veered out of line and charged Zoe. She grabbed Zoe in a hug and gasped out, "Oh, my God! Are you okay?"

Zoe tore out of Echo's arms and blurted out everything. "You have to help me! Duncan's in danger! He got captured by the Laird and the Laird sent wizards and I think they killed all the Buchanans that were trying to find Duncan and then they all just vanished and Duncan called out to me for help and woke me up and I couldn't find him or the Buchanans or anything and I don't even know if he's alive or dead!"

Echo stared up at Zoe's distraught face with huge eyes and nodded fast. "Okay! Okay! We'll find him! Come on! Let's go tell Elliot."

She grabbed Zoe's hand and led her toward the open gate. Several armed men stood around watching the two women. Zoe's heart jackhammered out of her chest and she struggled to breathe, now that she'd finally found someone to help her.

The sentries and hunters who had been with Echo looked at Zoe strangely when she walked into the fort, but none of them questioned. Echo released the ropes strapping the pig to her body and the carcass thumped in the dirt right inside the gate.

She turned to a grizzled old guy standing nearby. "Will you please take care of this for me, Athol? This is a scout bringing news about the offensive against the Laird. I need to take her to see Elliot right away."

The old man measured Zoe up and down and then nodded like he knew more about the situation than he ever wanted to know. "Aye. I'll take care of it."

"Thank you." Echo took Zoe's hand again. "Come on."

She led the way to an enormous roundhouse and Echo talked nonstop on her way down the corridor. "Duncan was just here two days ago. He told us you were here. He said he was going to get you and bring you back and then he disappeared."

"Yeah. He was just coming to get me when the Buchanan team showed up and tried to capture him. We've been tied up with them until.... until tonight."

Echo frowned at her over her shoulder. "Tied up with them? That doesn't sound good."

"It wasn't."

Echo turned into an office and then into a large, beautiful apartment. It wasn't as nice as the tree room, but it was still very nice.

"Elliot!" she called. "Where are you?"

"Back here!" A male voice drifted from what sounded like the back of the building.

Echo pulled Zoe through three different sitting rooms and a kitchen to the back door. It exited the roundhouse through a hidden doorway leading out into the forest behind the fort.

A man squatted on the ground outside the door. He wore a kilt with his white shirt untucked, but that was it. He wore no shirt or shoes and his hair had come mostly undone. He didn't look like much more than another scruffy rebel living in the woods.

"Zoe's here," Echo told him without any introduction. "She says Duncan is in danger and has most likely gotten captured by the Laird."

The guy shot to his feet and spun around. He looked nothing like what Zoe had been expecting. Duncan said that Elliot Ritchie was the leader of this rebel faction. She knew from sharing Duncan's memories that Grant and Elliot were the Laird's grandsons just like Duncan was.

Elliot didn't look the same now as he did in Duncan's memories. He had been wearing much cleaner clothes then. He looked older now even though it had only been a matter of weeks since Duncan had seen him.

She expected Elliot to be some kind of diplomat or maybe a politician. She didn't expect him to be just a regular guy who had neglected his appearance for a few days. Heck, maybe he had been out hunting with his men until just a few minutes ago.

As soon as he stood up, she saw that he held a dirk in his gnarled, callused hand. Dirt darkened the lines on his knuckles and wrist. He had been whittling a long, thin arrow shaft and he still turned it in his muscular fingers. This was definitely not a diplomat or a politician. He looked more like a soldier or maybe a mountain man.

His eyes widened when he saw her and he started talking to her like he knew her as well as Echo did. "Where did it happen? Do ye have any notion where the Laird's taken him? Are ye certain Duncan is even still alive?"

Zoe scrambled to keep up with all his questions. She hesitated when he finished and she looked into her heart. "He's alive. I'm certain of it."

Neither Elliot nor Echo questioned how she knew. Did they understand that Duncan and Zoe could have bonded so quickly?

"We must find him immediately." Elliot jammed his dirk into his belt and sidestepped around the two women heading back into the apartment. "I'll mount a search party. Ye must tell me where he disappeared, lassie, so our scouts can find the spot."

"You won't find anything," she replied. "I already checked. There's nothing there and there are no tracks leading away from the spot. None of the Buchanans or Duncan left the place on foot. The Laird took them by magic."

"Get a messenger off to Icemeet straight away," he told Echo. "We must alert Colton and Reid to help us. They have wizards who can track Duncan down...."

"Not anymore," Zoe interrupted. "They sent a wizard out with their search team—Connell Buchanan. I met him....and now he's gone, too."

"Damn!" Elliot muttered.

"What about finding the Creighton team?" Echo asked. "Grant and Lily sent Tristan Brodie out with their team. He might be able to find Duncan."

"The Creighton team might have changed loyalties along with all the rest of the Creighton forces. We've no way of kenning, and if Tristan hasnae found Duncan by now, he winnae be able to find Duncan now that he's the Laird's prisoner. Tristan and Connell dinnae stand a chance against the Laird. The only wizard who might be able to do anything is Betty."

Zoe gasped. "Betty....is a wizard? That's impossible!"

Echo rested her hand on Zoe's arm. "A lot has happened here while you were back home. I'll try to get you caught up, but it's gonna take time."

"It will take time we dinnae have," Elliot added. "If Betty can do ought, that's all the more reason we must send a messenger to Icemeet straight away." He pointed at the two women. "Keep her here, lassie. We cannae lose her to the Laird as well."

He walked out and the door swung shut. Zoe had been in the same room with him for a matter of minutes and now he was gone just like that. Everybody she met just kept disappearing.

All the adrenaline and worry of a moment before kept her on edge. She couldn't relax or decide what to do. Wasn't Elliot going to call her back into battle against.... whoever?

Echo brought her back to her senses by touching her arm. "Come on. Let's find somewhere for you to lie down. You look exhausted."

Zoe blinked and then remembered. "I didn't sleep very well last night and then this happened."

"All the more reason. Come on."

Echo led her into a bedroom. It was a nice room—not as nice as the tree room, though. Zoe's heart twisted when she thought about the tree room. Would she ever see Duncan again?

Echo read her thoughts. "He'll be all right. These Buchanans are tough. You just can't kill them."

"Yeah, you can." Zoe looked down at her hands. Exhaustion and despair were catching up with her. "I forgot to tell Elliot, but the Laird's wizards killed one of them a few hours ago. He's still lying at their camp. I should have done more to save him. I should have been there."

"Then you would either be a prisoner of the Laird along with Duncan or you would be dead."

Zoe didn't answer. Her throat hurt. If she was a prisoner of the Laird, at least she would be with Duncan. She wouldn't be here safe and sound while he was in danger.

She couldn't tell Echo that, though. She couldn't throw Echo's hospitality and Elliot's help back in their faces, but she couldn't think of anything but going back out and looking for Duncan.

She wished now that she had some magic. Maybe then she could help him or at least find him.

Echo pushed her down on the bed. "Lie down and try to get some sleep before you fall over. You won't be any good to anyone if you collapse. Besides, it will take a while to get all our people together and to alert the Buchanans."

"What about.... This is all so crazy, you know. I still can't believe you're here." She looked around the room. A window gave a view of the fort outside and some houses built inside the wall. "It's amazing that you're here and the other three are at Icemeet. I have trouble believing it when I hear about some of the things you've all been doing while I've been gone."

"I have trouble believing it, too, and I haven't even been in the middle of it. The others have been through a lot more. I know what you mean. It doesn't seem real."

"Do you think....?" Zoe looked down at her hands again. "I just don't know where I fit into all this. You're all so closely knit and married off with these guys. I'm the only one left on the outside looking in."

Echo only smiled at her and patted her on the shoulder. "You fit into it with Duncan. That's obvious, isn't it?"

"How can I? He's supposed to marry Lady Rhona—whoever that is."

Echo shrugged, but she looked away and wouldn't make eye contact with Zoe again. "Anything could happen, I guess."

"Connell said...." Zoe shut her mouth fast. She couldn't tell Echo what Connell said about Duncan and Zoe being mate-bonded for life.

Would Duncan break that bond to marry someone else if it meant bringing peace to the whole country? Would Zoe want him to? What if Connell made a mistake about that part of it?

The whole situation became so confused in her mind that she couldn't think about it clearly. She obsessed over it until it drove her to the brink of insanity.

She didn't want to give up Duncan, not even if it meant ending the war, but she couldn't stop thinking about the President's genealogy. Liam showed it to her in the modern era and it clearly showed Duncan and Lady Rhona as the President's ancestors. They got married. They had children and grandchildren and great-grandchildren. It was all written there as plain as day.

Wasn't that the whole reason for this mission? The dark wizard came back through time to change history. If he succeeded in either killing Lady Rhona or stopping her from marrying Duncan, history would change and that genealogy wouldn't even exist. Everything would be different and the President would never be born.

What if Zoe was the tool the dark wizard used to drive Duncan and Lady Rhona apart? What if the dark wizard planned this whole thing so Duncan would marry Zoe instead? Then the dark wizard's plan would come true, wouldn't it?

Echo touched her arm again. "Go to sleep. Don't lie here thinking about it all. You'll drive yourself crazy. When you wake up, Elliot will be back and we'll know something more."

She slipped out of the room and left Zoe sitting there with her thoughts. She knew Echo was right. Zoe couldn't think clearly about this or anything else when she was this tired. She didn't think she could think clearly at all when it came to Duncan.

He hit her hard in a place she never expected. She cared about him far more than she rationally should have and now he was gone, in danger, and possibly dead.

No, he wasn't dead. He was definitely alive. She would know if he was dead. She would feel it in her innermost guts. They were linked by a force beyond nature, beyond reason, beyond time. Nothing could break that bond.

She stretched out on the bed. She couldn't fall asleep. She would keep spinning in these wild speculations and unanswered questions forever.

Her eyes drifted toward the window and the sun playing on the leaves outside. The combination of colors and dappled light reminded her so much of the riverbank that, before she knew what was happening, she was sound asleep.

Chapter 14

Duncan came to his senses and tried to open his eyes, but all he could see was black. A steady howling drone resounded in his ears. He knew that sound too well not to recognize it.

The wind moaned over bare rocks and ice crystals scoured his scales.... except that he didn't have any scales. He was in his human form and laying on something warm. He wasn't on his mountain.

He sat up and his heart sank when he saw where he was. He was on a mountaintop, but it wasn't *his* mountain. He couldn't get as lucky as that.

The same magical orb surrounded him. It imprisoned him. He didn't have to struggle. He already knew he couldn't get away.

Snow lay in deep drifts outside the orb, and beyond that, deep, black night blocked any view of the landscape. The orb throbbed and pulsed with energy and it blocked the wind so the elements didn't touch Duncan. It kept him warm and gave him just enough light to see an old man sitting on a rock outside the magical barrier.

The old man looked different from the one Duncan had seen in the clearing, but he already knew this was the same man. It was Laird Balfour Creighton as big as life.

He sat on a flat rock and smiled at Duncan with what the Laird probably thought was a kindly, fatherly expression. A long white beard covered his face and long white hair hung over his shoulders. He didn't look as lined or as ghastly as he did in the firelight, but his eyes gave him away.

"Good evening, me laddie," he began. "I'm yer grandfather, Laird Balfour Creighton."

"I know that," Duncan snarled. "Ye killed me cousin—and me brother Ness."

The Laird smiled even more broadly. "I did all that. I've been looking everywhere for ye."

"Well, now ye've found me. Why dinnae ye go on and kill me the way ye planned?" Duncan tried to back away, but the orb left him no options. He had to sit near this man.

This man was a killer. Duncan didn't have to think about all the people the Laird had killed and ruined to know that. Just looking at the Laird gave Duncan a deep sense of menace and ill-will. Whatever this man had been looking to do with Duncan once the Laird found him, it wouldn't be anything good.

"I dinnae want to kill ye, laddie. All right, I *do* want to kill ye, but that's yer own fault, not mine. Everyone wants to put ye on me throne and I cannae have that."

"I never wanted yer blasted throne," Duncan spat. "Ye can keep it for all that. Ye can choke on it for all I care."

The Laird chuckled warmly, but the sound made Duncan's skin crawl. "I ken ye dinnae, laddie. This isnae yer fault. It's none of yer fault that yer mother ran over the Boundless and moved in with Neill Buchanan. It isnae yer fault that she came home and got herself with Ness nor that she hid Grant and Elliot from me all these years. I dinnae blame ye, but that doesnae change the simple fact. All these people want ye on the throne and they'll do whatever it takes to accomplish that. Look at what they've accomplished already. They drove me out of Kald and it's only me own efforts that have got it back for me."

"I had naught to do with that, either," Duncan grumbled. "I wasnae anywhere near Kald during the uprising."

"I ken, laddie. I ken all that. Ye're a grand wee lad just trying to live yer life in peace, but I cannae let ye live. I wish I could, but as ye ken, ye're too powerful. It's only yer own power that's stopped me from killing ye before now. Ye'd always be a threat to me. I have to get rid of ye."

Duncan stiffened and glared at him. "What are ye waiting on, then? Why am I here when ye could have killed me down in the clearing? Why waste yer breathe with all this talk?"

The Laird laughed again. His eyes sparkled with sadistic mirth.

Duncan kept waiting for the Laird to say something, but he didn't. A shifting sensation under Duncan's seat made him look down and he jumped. The orb had shrunk.

It got smaller and smaller and it shimmered with more energy than before. Duncan sprang to his feet and bumped his head on the orb's top edge. He didn't have any trouble fitting inside it at the clearing. Now he couldn't even stand up.

It kept dwindling smaller. Duncan had to crouch to fit inside it and the Laird laughed even harder at Duncan's comical efforts. The Laird didn't try to act kindly now. He cackled with vicious glee as the orb got closer to crushing Duncan inside it.

Duncan shot out both hands, but as soon as he touched the orb, a colossal explosion went off inside it. It slammed him hard from all sides and buckled him to his knee.

The Laird got to his feet and turned to confront Duncan. The Laird didn't have to raise a finger to attack Duncan. The Laird channeled his power through the orb to plaster Duncan with dozens of blasts.

Duncan reeled under the barrage. He couldn't stand up with the orb barely big enough for him to move. Pulse after pulse hit him harder and harder. It would destroy him any second now.

He had to act. He had to fight back. He tried again to summon his magic, but the Laird still squashed it under his own massive power. Duncan couldn't survive this.

Zoe. He had to get back to Zoe. He couldn't let his death destroy her, too. He had to live if only for her sake.

He threw out both arms to either side. He already knew it wouldn't work, but he had nothing left to lose. If this was his dying moment, he would die thinking about Zoe.

He slammed both his palms against the orb's sides and summoned any shred of magic he still had. One deafening boom after another pounded him all over his head and body, but the orb's sides held. He pushed the orb back just enough to stop them from getting any smaller.

An even more brutal concussion slammed down on his head. He wavered under the blow and almost lost his concentration on what he was doing. A second later, he rallied and forced himself to his feet.

The orb adjusted to his height, but it didn't stop pressing in on him. He had to fight with every ounce of his strength just to hold it. The Laird kept hammering him with one strike after another, but the longer this went on, the more confident Duncan became that he could hold on…. just a little longer.

The Laird's grin twisted into an ominous grimace. He bared his teeth and the veneer of a kindly old man evaporated. He changed back into the grim phantasm that Duncan confronted in the clearing. This man was no kindly old grandfather figure. He wanted to kill Duncan.

Duncan no longer cared why the Laird brought him to this mountaintop to kill him instead of finishing him in the clearing. It didn't matter. Duncan had to channel all his power into holding the orb at bay.

Shuddering booms and punishing crashes rained all over his body. Pain drove him wild and threatened to tear him apart, but he had to hold on. He didn't see any way he could get out of this, but at least he was still alive.

The Laird fell back several paces and now more strikes beat the orb from the outside. Every blow made it shrink a little more. Duncan's arms trembled from the effort of holding it at bay, but he already felt his strength ebbing. One of these hits would finish him and then nothing would stop the Laird from crushing the life out of him.

He had to do something—anything. He had to break the Laird's hold on him. He thought fast and came up with anything. He didn't know what to do.

One of his trembling arms buckled at the elbow. The orb collapsed in on him before he straightened his arm to hold it at a safe distance. This couldn't go on.

Panic took over and Duncan floundered for any way to save himself. He had to get out of this orb....and then he had the answer. He gathered himself for his last desperate attempt.

He took a deep breath and shoved the orb's sides. The field wavered just enough for him to take his palms off it and then he straightened both hands. He stiffened his fingers and stabbed through the orb.

It popped and the snowstorm's full might smashed him to the ground. Devastating hammer blows pounded his head and shoulders. He couldn't stand upright. He slammed down on his knees. Stinging ice and snow burned his skin and his mind started to blur from the cold.

The Laird stood before him, unruffled and untouched, but at least the Laird wasn't laughing or smiling anymore. He narrowed his eyes in deadly fury at Duncan. That on its own told Duncan he was winning.... or at least not losing as badly as he might have been.

Duncan summoned as much power as he could muster to strike back only to fall under another crushing strike. Duncan couldn't even tell where these magical assaults were coming from or how the Laird was doing this. The Laird never moved. He just stood there raining hellfire on Duncan's head.

Duncan struggled to stand, but the cold ate away at his insides. It never bothered him in all the years he lived at Icemeet. Now it sapped his strength and made it impossible for him to think. He couldn't rally his magic to defend himself.

His brain flipped back to the one thing he knew he could count on. *Zoe! Help me!* and then an excruciating strike slammed down on him from above. It drilled him to the ground and snow closed over his head.

Chapter 15

Zoe woke up and took a minute to remember that she was in Echo's rebel fortress. Zoe sat up and looked out the window. Families, armed men, and children moved from house to house in the yard outside her window, but none of them noticed her watching them.

She washed her face in the basin and then went out into Elliot's apartment. It was immaculately clean with some food on a plate on the table, but Echo and Elliot were nowhere around. The apartment sounded unnaturally quiet.

Zoe ate some of the food and then wandered out into the roundhouse. It had been teeming with people of all ages when Echo brought Zoe into the rebel headquarters. Now it was all but deserted.

A commotion drew her attention to the yard near the main entrance gate. Zoe halted in the doorway and saw Elliot addressing his people.

Elliot strode over to the sturdy old man that Echo called Athol and Elliot held up a meticulously drawn map. "Athol, ye and yers will assemble here opposite the west wall. Ye winnae likely meet with any dragons that far west, but anything's possible. Ye'll see plenty of soldiers and we'll send our lads in first to raise Clan Brodie to the assault."

"Aye," Athol growled. "Ye can count on us."

Elliot moved on to a young man who couldn't have been more than nineteen. "Bac, ye'll take yer lot to the south and come at Tyrekirk from the flank. Ye'll be closest to the castle there, so ye may encounter some dragons or other. Ye use our new weapons and take down as many as ye can before ye try to get over the wall."

Bac nodded. "Aye. We will."

Elliot crossed the yard to another young man, but this one was much bigger than Bac and his tartan was much newer and cleaner. Elliot started talking to this man in an undertone that Zoe couldn't hear.

She studied the rebels assembled in the yard. Elliot had rallied at least two hundred men. They packed the space between the fence and the houses. They had organized themselves into four companies, each one assembled behind the leaders that Elliot was talking to.

Zoe spotted Echo standing to one side and Zoe inched over to her friend. "What's going on?"

"Elliot wants to mount an assault against Kald right away. We know the Laird is in residence at Tyrekirk. Elliot thinks that the Laird took Duncan to the castle if he took him anywhere."

"I'm not so sure about that," Zoe began.

Echo smiled at her. "How about you help me organize the troops? I can use all the help I can get."

"It looks like you have enough. Where did Elliot get all these guys?"

"They all hate the Laird," Echo replied. "They're even willing to put aside their old hatred of the Buchanans and follow another Creighton if it means removing the Laird from power."

"So what do you want me to do? I don't know anything about waging a war in this time period."

"Don't worry. It's exactly the same as waging war in any other time period except that we use different weapons. Come on. I'll show you."

Echo turned away from the yard, led Zoe back through the roundhouse, and exited into another yard out of sight from any other part of the fort that Zoe had seen so far.

A blacksmith's forge had been set up here, but no one was working it. Instead, at least thirty contraptions sat in lines that filled the yard. These machines looked something like automatic guns mounted on small, wheeled carts, but they were too small to be pulled by horses or even bullocks.

Zoe examined them more closely. "What are these?"

"They're siege engines. Jaimee designed a bunch of them to defend Icemeet. The Laird threatened my life if Elliot didn't attack the Buchanans and destroy Icemeet entirely. He started by destroying their siege machines, but he couldn't bring himself to kill any people. That's the only reason the Creighton dragons were able to smash Icemeet the way they did—because they didn't have their siege machines to defend the fortress. He still feels terrible about it."

"So what are these doing here?"

"We copied them to kill the dragons. That's what Elliot was just telling Bac about. He wants Bac to take these engines south of Tyrekirk and use them to neutralize the dragons."

"Will that actually work?" Zoe asked. "Those dragons are pretty big."

"It's worth a shot and most of the Creighton dragons aren't as big as Elliot and Duncan. It usually takes about ten of them to take down one of these brothers."

"Are you sure this is a good idea—assaulting Tyrekirk when we don't even know if Duncan is there?"

Echo made a face. "Elliot can be very determined when he sets his mind to something."

Zoe snorted. "I'm starting to see that. So what do you want me to help you with?"

"Over here."

Echo went into the forge and picked up a handful of giant arrowheads, each one at least twice the width of Zoe's hand.

"Our blacksmith made these to tip the spears that will fire from the siege machines. I need you to help me mount them on the shafts and then...."

Another flurry of noise interrupted Echo's instructions and a mob of rebel fighters came out of the roundhouse. They streamed into the yard, surrounded the siege machines, and started working on them while the men talked and joked.

Echo pulled Zoe out of the way and steered her over to the forge. Several large wooden staves sat in a neat stack on the blacksmith's worktable. Echo brought them out into the sunshine along with two hammers, a smallish iron anvil about the size of a man's boot, and several other tools.

She set up the anvil on the ground and laid out the staves next to it. Echo held up a handheld drill bit with a large handle. "This is called a...."

Zoe! Help me!

The call came so clear and loud that Zoe froze in place. She couldn't think or see anything around her. Duncan was in trouble again.

She looked around the yard.... except that it wasn't there anymore. She found herself on a snowy mountaintop in the dark, but some otherworldly knowing gave her a perfect view of everything going on up there.

Both the mountaintop and the yard blurred into each other so that she saw both at the same time for a moment. She couldn't tell where she was and where she wasn't and the wind struck her full force. The yard vanished and ice crystals whipped every part of her face and body.

She stared at Duncan standing inside a shimmering blue orb of throbbing magical power. It hummed and thumped trying to implode with him inside it, but he held it in place. His body strained to the breaking point trying to stop it from squashing him.

A wrinkled old man with long white hair stood off to one side leering at Duncan's pathetic efforts, but the old man's triumphant grin faded the longer Duncan held his own.

Deafening booms smashed the orb from outside and flashes kept bursting inside it. Duncan wavered under successive blows and his head kept drooping each time one of them hit him.

Without warning, he shoved outward, straightened his fingers, and stabbed through the orb's outer walls. It burst with a loud pop and an even more brutal thunder of explosions hit him all over. The tempest whipped his hair and body and he collapsed on his knees in the snow.

Zoe shot out both hands even though she couldn't reach him from this distance. "No—Duncan!" she yelled.

The Laird whipped around fast and his countenance went black and furious when he saw her standing there. His expression turned even more murderous if that was even possible.

The Laird unleashed a horrific barrage on her. Blows punched her in the face and pounded her ribs and body. She whipped back and forth from dozens of hits, but the Laird never came near her. She couldn't see anything happening in real life.

This *was* happening in real life. He delivered a nasty punch to her mouth and she tasted blood. The cold built to more than she could stand. Was she about to die out here?

Out of nowhere, another smash struck the Laird from behind and a different magical orb materialized around him. It trapped him in a bubble of safety, but only for a split second.

His rage erupted to volcanic proportions and he spun the other way to confront Duncan. Duncan stood tall and straight glaring at the Laird through slit eyes narrowed in menace.

The Laird rocketed at Duncan in fury, but Duncan wasn't there anymore. He flew at the Laird just as fast. At the last second before they collided in a battle to the death, Duncan veered sideways, streaked around the Laird, plunged down the mountainside, and slammed into Zoe full force.

The next second, they both vanished and reappeared in the yard behind the rebel roundhouse. Zoe pried herself off the ground still trembling in shock, but Duncan didn't move.

He huddled on the ground half-twisted in a ball of agony. He shook much more violently and nearly every part of him had turned blue from the cold. His fingers curled in ice-crusted talons and he couldn't unkink his limbs from their hunched and frozen position.

Zoe rotated onto her knees and bent over him. "Duncan! Can you hear me!"

He gasped for air and made small grunting noises through his nose when he tried to speak. His eyes found hers, but he couldn't say anything. At least he was alive.

Echo hurried over and bent down to look into his eyes. "Don't worry, Duncan. You're safe. You're back at the fort."

He tried again to speak and failed. His eyes kept darting from Zoe to Echo and back to Zoe like he wanted to say something, but he couldn't.

"He's frozen stiff," Zoe exclaimed. "We have to get him inside."

Elliot shouldered his way through the crowd that gathered to stare at Duncan's crumpled frame. "Christ Almighty!" Elliot growled. "Look at the state of him!"

"We need to warm him up, Elliot," Zoe repeated. "He was on the mountain with the Laird...."

"Dinnae bother about the details, lassie." Elliot pushed her out of the way. "I'll take him from here."

He bent down and picked up Duncan in his arms. Zoe and Echo went in front to clear the way and open the doors so Elliot could take Duncan back to their apartment. They put him in the same room where Zoe had spent the night.

Echo raced off to the kitchen. "Get a fire going, Zoe. Warm up the room and get some blankets out of that chest over there."

Zoe got busy, and by the time she got the fire going, Elliot had covered Duncan in blankets. They heated the room to a sweltering inferno and Echo came back with a warming pan loaded with hot coals and a steaming tea kettle full of fragrant simmering tea.

Zoe inched over to Duncan's bedside. He was still shaking and frozen. His lips, nose, cheeks, and eyelids looked even worse in here than they had in the yard.

She laid her hand on his arm. His skin felt icy to the touch. "Don't worry, Duncan. You're safe. You're among friends. We're going to make sure you're all right."

The instant her hand touched him, he collapsed limp and floppy on the bed. He let out a shuddering sigh and his eyes rolled back in their sockets. "Ye came, lassie! Ye came."

"Easy." She pushed his damp hair off his forehead. "Of course I came."

He melted into the mattress and his whole body relaxed, but that only made him look even more wretched and defeated. His eyes drifted closed and he didn't respond to her touch anymore.

Echo pushed a wooden mug of steaming tea into Zoe's hand. "Give him this."

She bent close to his ear and murmured into his brain. "Let me sit you up and give you something hot to drink, Duncan. It will warm you up."

He didn't respond, but he didn't stop her from wedging her arm under his neck and shoulders, heaving him into a semi-sitting position, and holding the teacup to his lips.

He sipped it and sighed much more easily now. She got him to drink as much as possible and then lowered him again.

Elliot stepped in and tucked the blankets up to Duncan's neck. "What happened, lassie? What did ye see?"

"Not here," Echo ordered. "Come into the sitting room and let Duncan rest."

Zoe didn't want to leave, but she was already sweating from the fire and Duncan didn't speak or even look at her anymore.

She let Echo lead her out to the living room and then Zoe had no choice but to explain the fight to Elliot.

"Blast that filthy bastard Laird!" he growled. "I'll find a way to kill the son of a bitch if it's the last thing I ever do."

"How?" Zoe asked. "The most powerful wizards we have are no match for him. No one can defeat him."

"He's only mortal," Echo insisted. "There has to be a way."

Chapter 16

Duncan opened his eyes and groaned out loud when he remembered his miserable effort to fight the Laird. He would be dead now if Zoe hadn't distracted the Laird's attention for a split second.

Happiness and contentment filled Duncan's heart. She must be near him, but he couldn't enjoy that feeling of being back with her. The Laird came perilously close to killing Duncan. The Laird would probably succeed next time.

Duncan remembered everything that happened after he transported himself and Zoe back to Elliot's rebel fort. The thought only gave him another stab of guilt. Now Duncan had put all the rebels in danger of the Laird's wrath, too.

He threw back the blankets and dragged his aching body into a sitting position. The fire had burned out, but he didn't need it anymore. He didn't feel cold.

He was naked and his own Buchanan tartan lay folded on a chair by his bed along with his belt. He hadn't been wearing anything else when he left his mountain hideout, but now someone had laid out a clean shirt, a nice black jacket, clean socks, decent shoes, and several weapons to go along with his usual clothes. Was someone trying to send him a message?

He was a married man now—or he would be once he mated with Zoe. He would have to make a show of being the Buchanan Clan Chief's brother. He wouldn't be able to run around half-dressed like the rest of his luckier Clansmen.

He turned to gaze out the window. This war could only end one of two ways. In the best possible scenario, he and his friends would find a way to defeat the Laird. Then everyone in both Clans would insist that Duncan sit on the Seat of Armstrong in the Laird's place.

Duncan would have to do it to make sure the Creightons and the Buchanans didn't attack each other anymore. Duncan was the only potential replacement who could bring peace.

The only other alternate scenario was that the Laird won and killed Duncan before that happened. Either way, Duncan's days of running around the mountains with his Clansmen were over. He wasn't a wild boy anymore and he would never be again.

He buckled on his kilt, but he didn't put on any of the other clothes. He wasn't ready for that yet and he didn't take the weapons. He probably wouldn't get a chance to use them, either. He would only have to discard them the minute he shifted and they wouldn't work against the Laird anyway.

He gazed out the window for a long time. His body didn't want to move quickly and every move took an age. His brain felt slow and sluggish, too. He still wasn't back to normal after his ordeal with the Laird, but he couldn't lie around brooding about it.

He walked out of the room and headed for the main room. Even putting his feet on the floor made him wince. The Laird took a lot more out of him than the cold did.

He stepped into the main sitting room and spotted Echo, Elliot, and Zoe sitting around the table eating their evening meal. They were talking and Zoe laughed at something Echo said. Would she ever look that happy about seeing Duncan again?

Elliot looked up and saw Duncan first. Then the two women saw him and Echo gasped. "Hey! Look who's alive and on his feet!" She stood up, crossed to him, and hugged him. "I'm glad you're feeling better."

"Thank ye, lassie," he murmured back. "I hate to trouble ye."

"Nonsense," Elliot interjected. "We've all been waiting for weeks to help ye. Dinnae ye ken that by now, lad? Sit down and put some meat on your bones."

Duncan started to laugh and stopped himself when he saw Zoe's expression. She squirmed in her chair and only cast hesitating glances at him before she went back to pushing her food around on her plate. She didn't seem to be eating anything.

Echo guided him to the seat across from Elliot and she served Duncan a plate of his own. He picked up his fork and speared a piece of meat, but when he put it in his mouth, he realized that he didn't want to eat, either.

"I've sent messengers to Icemeet to tell yer brother that ye're here," Elliot was saying. "We'll mount another offensive now that the Laird has struck the first blow."

"Another offensive!" Duncan exclaimed. "Why?"

"It's obvious, isnae it?" Elliot countered. "Our whole position hinged on finding ye alive and in yer right senses. Now we've done that. We've taken Tyrekirk once already. We can do it again, and once we put ye on the throne, that's the end of his Lairdship." He chuckled maniacally.

"I dinnae think so," Duncan muttered.

"Whyever not?" Elliot fired back. "As soon as Colton gets word, we'll have three dragons, several wizards, and all yer Clan fighting with us. We can send word into Kald to the rebel gangs and the Brodies. We're in a better position now than we were before, and with ye on the throne, we've won."

Duncan shook his head down at his plate. Now he really didn't want to eat. "None of that means ought if we cannae defeat the Laird and we dinnae have one person strong enough to do it. I certainly cannae."

"But....ye must!" Elliot countered. "Why would he try so hard to do away with ye if ye didnae have the power to depose him? He'd leave ye to yerself otherwise."

"I doubt that. I cannae fight him as a dragon or the same thing would happen to me that's happened to ye and Grant already. After what I've just seen on the mountain, I ken I cannae defeat him with magic. He's too powerful."

"I cannae believe that. An attack from the Boundless would...."

"No, man," Duncan interrupted. "Put that right out of yer head now. The last insurrection made it as far as it did because ye and yers attacked from the west. If we all attacked across the Boundless from the Buchanan side, we'd be slaughtered in one stroke."

Elliot twisted his shoulders and waved his fork at nothing. "Perhaps."

"I think what Elliot is trying to tell you is that we're at your disposal," Echo chimed in. "We all want to help, so if you think launching another assault will get us anywhere, we're ready when you are. We don't want to sit on our hands and do nothing."

Duncan glanced over at Zoe, but she wouldn't look up from her plate. What was wrong with her? Maybe she just didn't feel comfortable interacting with him around her friend. Maybe she thought she had to walk on eggshells now that she and Duncan weren't alone together anymore.

"I winnae say I like holding back," Elliot added. "It's as Echo says. I cannae stand to sit on me hands and let the Laird to trample the country the way he does. Someone must stop him."

"I cannae say I'm the man to do it," Duncan murmured under his breath. "Ye've all pinned yer hopes on me, but ye're as likely to wind up destroyed thanks to me."

"No!" Echo exclaimed. "No! We would never blame you for that. You're only one man. It isn't your fault the Laird is so much more powerful as a wizard. You're doing everything you can."

Duncan glanced over at Elliot and knew he was right. Elliot didn't think Duncan was doing everything he could to defeat the Laird. Elliot didn't have to say it out loud.

Elliot looked up and met Duncan's gaze. "I'll follow yer lead, laddie. If ye tell me to sit tight, I'll do it with bells on. Just promise me we'll alert Colton and start planning the next attack."

"Ye've already done both of those, am I right?" Duncan asked. "Ye've sent word to Colton and ye've started arming for the next attack. I've seen ye doing it."

Zoe and Echo both looked at Elliot, too. Elliot stiffened for a minute and then he laughed. He shot Duncan a knowing smirk and shrugged. "I might have done, aye."

Duncan relaxed, but he couldn't enjoy the meal entirely. Zoe's reserve unsettled him. What was wrong? Did she change her mind about him? Maybe she didn't want to mate with him, now that she'd seen firsthand that he was incapable of unseating the Laird. He wouldn't blame her for changing her mind.

Connell made it sound like their mate-bond was already in place. Duncan certainly felt that way, but Zoe was a different species. Maybe that meant she couldn't mate-bond with someone so quickly. Maybe she just needed more time.

If she did, that introduced an element of uncertainty that Duncan wasn't prepared for. He didn't want days or weeks to pass before he knew if she would or even could mate-bond with him.

He tried to concentrate on the present and enjoy Echo's and Elliot's company, but he couldn't get these doubts out of his mind. He had to consolidate with Zoe. He couldn't let her slip through his fingers.

Elliot and Echo kept talking through the rest of the meal. They both managed to steer the conversation away from the coming offensive, either real or imagined.

Echo finally stood up and started clearing the table. Zoe jumped up and hurried away to help her. Elliot clapped Duncan on the shoulder and guided him to the apartment's back door where the two men could look out into the dark forest.

"Dinnae mind ought I say about any offensive, laddie," Elliot murmured. "I dinnae ken what's best. If there's a head to be cracked, I dinnae like to leave it uncracked. That's me own way."

Duncan chuckled under his breath. "I ken all that, man. I didnae take any other meaning from it."

"It's Grant ye want for all this strategy and planning. He's the man with the brains."

"Aye," Duncan replied. "Him and Colton. It's as well for us they're in the same place."

"It isnae so well for us that they're in the same place far from us. I wish they were with us now—or that we were with them. I dinnae like going it alone."

"Aye." Duncan sighed. "I never led an army in me life. I always relied on Colton for that. I never thought I'd be ought but his own wild wee brother."

Elliot gripped Duncan's shoulder again. "Ye'll be grand. Ye've all the rest of us behind ye."

Duncan heard himself saying, "Aye," but his heart wasn't in it. He never wanted to lead anyone and he definitely didn't want to become Laird. That was the last thing in the world he wanted to do.

"Is Zoe all right?" he finally blurted out.

Elliot spun around. "Eh? How do ye mean?"

"Is she.... hurt or ought?"

"Hurt—how? She's grand."

Duncan gazed out into the shadows. She definitely wasn't grand. He didn't know what was wrong with her, but something was.

"She was upset when she brought ye back from the mountain. That's all," Elliot went on. "She was shaking and all, but she calmed down right enough. She was only gone a few seconds. That's what Echo says, at least. I didnae see. I only arrived after she'd already brought ye back, see."

Duncan nodded. He knew all that, but the way she was acting at supper made him question.

"If ye ask me—which ye didnae—I'd say she's worried about ye," Elliot volunteered. "I cannae say I ken her more than a hole in the ground. I spent more time with Betty in the forest that first time we found ye. This lassie's a different kettle of fish. She's quiet....and not confident in herself as the others are. Ye've seen Jaimee. This lassie's nothing like her or Betty or even Lily. This one plays her cards close to her chest, like."

"Aye," Duncan murmured. "She does that."

She never played her cards close to her chest when she was with him on the mountain-top, but he could see her doing it now. What made her change her mind? He had to find out.

"Ye cannae ken how it does me heart good to have ye, laddie," Elliot half-whispered. "I dinnae like to load ye with more than ye're already carrying and I'm not speaking of the war. All me life, it was naught but me and Grant. Now ye're here and I can take all the rest kenning ye're with us at last. It's the end of a long road I didnae ken I was on......"

He broke off and the silence hung heavily between them. Elliot's confession wrung Duncan's heart. He felt the same way. Elliot put into words something that Duncan had always felt but couldn't articulate.

He'd always had his brothers. Colton had always taken care of Duncan the way a father would. Duncan hardly noticed his father's absence because Colton and Reid always filled that place—them and all Duncan's cousins, uncles, and other Clansmen.

Finding out that Grant and Elliot were his brothers threw Duncan's whole world into turmoil. Not even meeting Elliot in the woods could bring Duncan back from his madness, but now it was all different.

Elliot had always treated Duncan like his little brother ever since Grant and Elliot found out the truth about their relationship through their mother's line. Elliot had become another brother to Duncan—a different kind of brother.

Duncan could let Elliot make a fuss over him and show his affection in ways Colton and Reid never could. Duncan was too close to Colton and Reid—or maybe Duncan just didn't know if they would because he hadn't seen his brothers since Duncan ran away from Icemeet.

How should he know what kind of relationship he had with his brothers? Duncan had become a completely different person since he last saw Colton and Reid. Duncan had gone completely out of his mind and come back to sanity as this wizard hybrid shifter the world had never seen or known before.

Then he had a terrible thought. What if Colton and Reid expected Duncan to lead them, too? What if Colton tried to make himself subordinate to Duncan? Duncan couldn't stand that.

He didn't want to live in a world where Colton wasn't in charge. The world couldn't function without Colton in charge. He was every man's leader. He was the best of men and born to lead—unlike Duncan.

Duncan was a wild, unprincipled boy. He was the last person qualified to lead anyone, much less a whole offensive assault against Tyrekirk and Laird Balfour. Forget about leading the country. It wasn't going to happen—ever.

Chapter 17

Zoe snapped awake when someone touched her shoulder. "Lassie!" Duncan breathed in her ear. "Wake up."

"Huh!" She shot off the bed staring into the dark. "What's happening? Is someone attacking?"

"No one's attacking, lassie. Get up and put yer shoes on."

"What—why?" She searched and her dark eyes finally found him in the shadows. "What's going on?"

"I want to talk to ye and I cannae do it here. Come and dinnae make any noise. Dinnae wake Echo and Elliot."

She stood up and shoved her feet into her shoes. She struggled to calm her racing heart. Something must have gone wrong. Was the Laird coming back to attack the rebel fort?

She tiptoed out of the bedroom and into the dark living room, but she didn't hear any noise. The fort sounded quiet. Everyone was asleep.

Duncan crossed the living room to the back door where Zoe had first seen Elliot squatting in the dirt. Duncan eased the door open and led her by the hand into the forest outside.

The trees blocked out all light, and as soon as she and Duncan entered the shadows, he slowed to a casual saunter. He held her hand and he kept smiling at her.

"What are we doing out here?" she whispered. "Shouldn't we tell Echo and Elliot that we're leaving?"

"We arenae leaving—not like that. I only wanted to talk to ye, lassie."

"Couldn't you talk to me at the fort?" She frowned into the shadows. "Where are we going, anyway?"

"We're going to the tree room."

She pulled to a halt. "The tree room! That's miles away."

"It's just here, lassie." He turned behind some trees and she blinked in amazement when she saw the grove.

She looked all around her and saw with a jolt that he was right. In the space of a few minutes' stroll, he had covered the distance between the fort and the grove.

He opened the door in the tree and golden firelight flooded out. It cast such a delightful, tempting glow into the darkness that she couldn't resist going inside.

The room looked the same way she remembered. Was it really just a few days ago when she stayed here last time?

The fire crackled as invitingly and the food looked delicious. She hadn't been able to eat at the fort. She had too much on her mind.

He came over to her still smiling. His eyes gleamed with warmth and hidden meaning. She stiffened when he looked at her like that, but she melted when he cradled her cheeks in both his hands.

She saw him moving into to kiss her. He kissed her in the forest after Connell captured her, but this meant something much, much more.

She didn't have a chance to enjoy it then. Now she couldn't escape what it meant.

He lifted her lips to his and his heat exploded through her. It was dragon heat, pure and simple. His whole being pulsed with it. Hidden power coursed in his veins. It had no outlet except to come through his skin and hair. It whispered on his breath and intoxicated her when she smelled his scent.

Even his lips felt hot and they sent a sizzle of electric excitement through her. He excited her. She could finally admit that to herself, now that she didn't have to worry about anyone chasing her or capturing her or trying to kill him.

She also didn't realize how uncomfortable she had been in Echo's apartment. She didn't feel that way when she was there alone. This awkward embarrassment only started after Duncan arrived.

Jaimee, Lily, Betty, and Echo were all married off to great guys. They had all abandoned the oath they took to the Last Division, so why should Zoe feel awkward about getting interested in a guy?

Everyone assumed that she and Duncan would get together. Echo said so.

Zoe never would have dared to kiss Duncan in Echo's apartment. Zoe wouldn't have been able to let down her guard knowing that one of her old friends was sleeping in the next room.

Duncan must have sensed that and brought her here so she could be completely at ease, but she still wasn't. Some shade still clouded her mind. It hung heavily on her shoulders so that she couldn't appreciate that kiss.

She pulled away and the forgotten depths of Duncan's eyes swam before her. They called on her to forget everything and vanish into him the way she did on the mountain. She wanted to. God, she wanted to so badly!

She turned her back on those eyes. She couldn't look at him without aching inside.

She wandered over to the fire and stared down into the flames. What was wrong with her? Why couldn't she give herself to him the way she yearned to? Why couldn't she disintegrate into his influence the way she did when she first laid eyes on him?

Surrendering to him completely and to her love for him would be so easy, but this black despair stopped her from doing what she most desired to do. Her own resistance drove her to distraction, but she couldn't budge it or find a way around it.

He came up behind her and slipped his arms around her waist. He had never touched her like this before or any other way. He had kissed her once before tonight and her whole being dissolved in desire for him. She wanted him with all her heart and soul.

She leaned back into him and his solid bulk held her up. His lips scorched a path up her neck to her ear. Every breath brushing on her skin blasted her out of her mind with impossible sensations.

"What is it, me love?" he whispered. "What grieves ye that ye cannae love me anymore the way ye did on the mountain?"

She gulped down the tightness in her throat. Tears stung her eyes. He knew. He had known all through the meal they shared with Echo and Elliot.

His words stabbed at her heart. "Ye ken I love ye more than me own life. Ye're me own life's mate and I cannae live without ye. I cannae stand to spend another day without ye by me side."

"What happened......?" Her voice cracked with anguish. She couldn't do this, but his arms refused to release her. Everything about him held her captive. She didn't want him to release her. She didn't want to go free without him. "What happened to tradition? You said you couldn't stay here with me until I met Colton."

"I changed me mind. I dinnae want to go another day without making ye me own. Tradition be damned. The thought of losing ye makes me want to die."

She bowed her head and tears streaked down her cheeks. God, she loved him! The thought of losing him made her want to die, too, but she couldn't give herself to him. She couldn't.

"Say ye love me, lassie," he murmured in her ear. "Say ye love me as much as I love ye."

She couldn't say it no matter how much she felt it. She clamped her eyes and lips tight trying to hold back tears. The harder she fought to keep herself under control, the more she shook with sobs.

Duncan unwound his arms and turned her around to face him. He cupped her tear-stained cheeks gazing into her eyes. "Lassie! Me own lassie!"

He tried to kiss her again and she tore out of his grasp. She couldn't be near him—not like this.

She hustled over to the bed, sat down on it, and buried her face in her hands. "I can't! I know what you want me to do and I can't!"

"Why, lass?" He squatted down in front of her, placed his hands on her knees, and peered up into her eyes. The searching depth of his gaze wrenched at her heartstrings even more. "Ye felt the same way about me on the mountain. I'd lay any odds on that. What changed?"

"Nothing, okay?" She heard herself shrieking at him in misery, but she didn't try to hold it back. Echo wasn't here. No one was here to hear her lose it entirely. "Nothing changed. I feel the same way about you as I did on the mountain—maybe more—but I can't."

"Tell me, lass," he murmured. "Tell me what this is all about."

She covered her face and howled in anguish. She couldn't tell him. It hurt too much, but his presence did something to her. The words poured out of her against her will.

"I don't know who I am anymore! I don't know what I am or where I belong. Jaimee and Betty and Echo and Lily all know where they belong. I'm the only one on the outside."

"Ye belong with me, lass," he breathed. "If it's me Clan ye're worried about...."

"You're hardly even a Buchanan anymore yourself!" she countered. "I don't know what's happening with you and me or even who I am anymore. I'm nobody. I'm a zero. Why do you think I called myself that?"

He didn't answer. He just looked up at her with soft, compassionate eyes and that somehow made this so much worse.

"I'm an orphan. I don't have any family. I grew up in foster care. Being a soldier is all I've ever had and the Last Division is the only family I've ever had. Now that's all gone."

"It is ae gone, lass. Jaimee and Betty are part of me Clan now and ye've seen what Echo is. She treats ye like her sister still."

She shook her head as all the conflicting, confused thoughts assembled even before she had a chance to think them.

"If we do this, we'll be mated for life and one of two things will happen. The first is that I'll become a full member of your Clan like Jaimee and Betty are."

"Dinnae ye want that, lassie? Dinnae ye want to be one of me Clan?"

"Of course!" she wailed. "I want that more than anything, but I'm not good enough to be part of your Clan. I don't know how to act around anyone's family. I've never had one....and what if you become Laird? I couldn't be any kind of head of state with everyone watching me and measuring how well I act in public or how ladylike I am."

He remained silent for so long that she really started to wonder if he was changing his mind about her. Of course he couldn't become Laird with a wife who didn't know how to act in public.

When he finally spoke, he murmured so low that she almost didn't hear him. "What's the second possibility, lassie?"

She covered her face and sobbed as though her heart would break. It really felt like it *was* breaking and she wished it would. Maybe then it wouldn't hurt so much to get this out.

"The second possibility....is that we'll finally find Lady Rhona and you'll marry her instead....and I'll be alone with no one."

She couldn't look at him. This despair spilled out through her tears and her whole body ached with the sobs coming out of her.

Losing the Last Division was bad enough. Now she would lose Duncan, too. She felt it in his silence. She cried harder as that silence went on. He didn't reassure her because there was no reassurance for this.

Caring for him—feeling so deeply connected to him—yes, even loving him—it only made it that much harder to realize what they had could never be.

She would give anything to make it work. She couldn't think of any future better than going home with him to Icemeet and staying there with Jaimee and Betty and Colton and Reid. She didn't even know Colton and Reid, but they must be amazing if everyone thought so highly of them.

They would welcome her as Duncan's mate, but that would never happen now because Duncan wouldn't go home to Icemeet. He would go to Tyrekirk to be Laird or he would be dead. There was no other in-between possibility. The Laird made that all too plain.

She couldn't raise her head to look into Duncan's eyes. She couldn't read in his face that he knew as well as she did that it was all true. It couldn't be otherwise.

She didn't understand what was happening when he sat down on the bed next to her and folded his arms around her. She cried even harder when he pulled her down on the bed next to him.

He started by curling around her from behind. His arms felt so blissfully good that she couldn't stand the pain. She would die from this storm of agony inside her.

Then he rolled onto his back and pulled her down on his chest. Her cheek touched the bare skin above his heart and she cried as though she might die. She couldn't be touching him like this if she was only going to lose him later. She didn't want to love him if she was going to miss him and yearn for him for the rest of her life.

Chapter 18

D uncan lay awake and gazed up at the ceiling. An intertwined fabric of twigs and roots formed the tree room's ceiling. They gave him plenty to look at while he let the hours slip away.

Zoe cried herself into an exhausted sleep. He could feel her breathing in his arms and his heart beat against her cheek. The smell of her hair and her sweet breath floated into his nostrils. They lulled him into a more blissful relaxation than he'd ever known in his life.

Connell was right. Zoe was Duncan's destined mate. He knew that now even if she wasn't ready. He didn't have to talk her out of it or try to change her mind. He didn't have to do anything.

She said she wanted to. He didn't need to know anything more and now she lay here with her head on his chest and his arms wrapped around her. He didn't need to take it any further. This was good enough for him.

The picture she painted of herself as unworthy of being his mate broke his heart. She must have suffered unimaginable torment and now loving him made that pain even worse.

He didn't suffer anything like that when he lost his parents. He had his siblings and his Clansmen to take care of him. This time of self-imposed isolation in his mountaintop sanctuary was the first time in his life when he'd been alone.

Even then, he could use his magic to keep track of what all his friends and loved ones were doing. He hadn't been completely isolated and he probably never would be.

She had been alone all her life. The Last Division changed all that and it gave her the home she never had. Now she'd lost that and stood to lose it again—for good this time. She must be suffering the tortures of the damned just thinking about it.

She didn't see any way out of it, either. That was the worst part, and now that he understood her point, he didn't see a way out of it, either.

The Last Division's whole mission was to find Lady Rhona so Duncan could marry her. That was their idea of successfully completing their mission—which meant Zoe would be completely cut off from the people that made her life worth living. How could he even think of doing that to her now that he knew what it meant to her?

If Connell was right the way Duncan suspected he was, then Zoe must feel the same way about him that he felt about her. She was mate-bonded to him for life, which meant that she couldn't break that bond any more than he could.

If he married Lady Rhona, he would leave her destroyed for all time. She would become a hopeless wreck with no life at all anymore. She would mourn his absence for the rest of both their lives. Could he really do that to her....and for what? For a throne? For a crown?

And what about himself? He would mourn for her, too. He would become a waste of a man if he survived at all. He wouldn't be able to rule the country in the Laird's place.

He would spend every day and every night standing on Tyrekirk's high turrets watching the horizon. He would spend every day and night watching and waiting for her to come back to him. He wouldn't be able to function without her by his side and in his arms.

The fire kept crackling through the small hours. His magic kept it at the same level so he didn't have to add wood to it. His magic also adjusted the temperature in the room so it never got too hot or cold.

All those tiny details left him free to think for the first time since she came through the portal. He went over everything Elliot said about launching another offensive against the Laird. Duncan also reviewed everything that happened in his confrontation with his grandfather.

Mostly, though, he thought about what she said. Those words kept repeating in his mind. *We'll finally find Lady Rhona and you'll marry her instead.*

He shut his eyes, turned his head aside, and pressed his lips and nose into her hair. Her smell soothed him enough to relax completely, but he still didn't fall asleep.

He floated out of his body and looked down into the tree room from above. She looked so peacefully in his arms. He couldn't bring himself to disturb her or cause her any distress...but he already had, hadn't he?

He'd already caused her the worst pain she had ever experienced. His connection with her showed him that. He even felt it himself through their bond.

He drifted higher into the cold night sky. The stars looked especially bright to his magical sight.

He soared over the forest, but this magical projection remained removed from everything he saw and felt. The cold wind didn't whistle as loudly in his ears as it did when he flew over the landscape as a dragon.

He surveyed the countryside to the east. The lights of Kald made a carpet of brilliance all the way to the black sea. It looked beautiful with flags flying from Tyrekirk's majestic turrets, but he didn't go in that direction.

He turned north and whizzed over the forest, across the Boundless, and up the mountains toward Icemeet. He spotted light in bedroom windows in the few remaining towers the dragons hadn't destroyed.

A powerfully built man stood at one of those windows. His broad shoulders made an imposing silhouette against the firelight coming from inside. He had his hair down and he wore a loose robe over his muscular frame.

He didn't see Duncan coming closer because Duncan wasn't there. Only this fragment of Duncan's consciousness hovered outside the window. Duncan looked in on the life he'd known and loved since he was a boy.

Now Duncan was the one on the outside looking in. Zoe had been so painfully right about that. Duncan was hardly a Buchanan at all anymore. He wasn't part of this Clan and everyone knew it. He could never be part of it again—not the way he was before he found out that he was also a Creighton and a wizard.

Duncan couldn't stand that. He floated through the window and made himself solid and visible standing next to his brother. "Colton—it's me. It's Duncan."

Colton rushed him and grabbed Duncan against his burly body. "Lad! Where the devil have ye been?"

Duncan's heart ached accepting his brother's affection. Colton pushed him back at arm's length, stroked Duncan's cheek, and feasted his bright black eyes on Duncan's face. "I thought we'd lost ye, lad."

"Ye had," Duncan murmured.

"Ye must come downstairs," Colton insisted. "Reid and the others will be over the moon that ye're back."

"I'm not back, Colton. I cannae come back."

"Why?" Colton exclaimed. "Ye're.... ye're well again. Reid said ye were off yer head and all. We didnae ken what to think....and then when ye came out during the battle...."

Duncan waved that away. "Ye must listen to me, man. Elliot Ritchie wants to get up another offensive to put me on the throne now that I'm found."

"Of course, laddie! We all want that. We'll start arming right away and get over the...."

"No, Colton," Duncan insisted. "Ye cannae cross the water—not yet."

"Why not? Dinnae ye ken how we've all dreamed and longed for this moment? We sent out teams to find ye...."

"I ken all about that, but ye cannae mount any offensive—not yet."

"Why, lad?" Colton murmured. "Give me one reason."

"Because I cannae defeat the Laird. No one can. There isnae any wizard alive strong enough to defeat him. Ye'd all be slaughtered if ye went over the water now. Promise me ye winnae go over nor raise a blade against the Creightons until I find a way. Promise, Colton. I cannae leave until ye give me yer word."

Colton scowled at him and then pursed his lips. "All right, lad. I give ye me word. If that's the way ye want it, we'll follow ye."

"Och, no!" Duncan turned away and covered his eyes. "Dinnae say that! I cannae stand it."

"Ye're meant to be Laird, laddie," Colton insisted. "If this works, we'll all be taking orders from ye."

Duncan shook his head. He couldn't explain any of this even to himself. He trusted Colton to understand if Duncan could just figure out what to do about all these competing feelings eating him up inside.

He turned around to face his brother, but when Duncan looked into Colton's eyes, he saw so much more than he ever bargained for.

Duncan's sight merged with Colton's. Duncan had only experienced this with Zoe, but now he saw Colton's memories playing out in his brother's mind.

He saw women and children crying from hunger in Icemeet and at Stronghold. He saw Betty healing the injuries of Clansmen injured on the battlefield. She helped women in childbirth and gave comfort to old people dying in crushing conditions.

Duncan's throat constricted until he could hardly breathe. He watched his Clansmen and the archers risking life and limb to sneak out of Stronghold, hunt in mountains infested with Creighton soldiers, and take their kills back to Stronghold to feed people on the brink of catastrophe.

Duncan saw Jaimee in Colton's office as they scrambled for some way to save these people from disaster. He saw the two of them in conference with Reid and Betty while they received reports from scouts who brought news that Laird Balfour was rearming to destroy Icemeet once and for all.

Duncan stared in stunned horror at the lines of care and despair around his brother's eyes. He saw through Colton's sight how exhausted and hopeless Jaimee and Betty had become, but they still kept going against all odds. They had no choice but to keep going.

He saw Reid taking over the training of men who were way too old to fight and boys far too young to go to their deaths against the enemy. Duncan saw young Gavin Buchanan taking over as blacksmith now that Boyd was dead.

Gavin was Duncan's age and now Gavin was doing a man's job just like the whole generation of younger Buchanans. They were all growing up way too fast and now Duncan had to do the same thing.

Then he saw Liam and Edeena working together to help the Buchanans, too. Edeena looked happier and more vibrant than Duncan could ever remember. He also saw them alone together in Edeena's old room. He saw Liam taking Edeena in his arms and kissing her. They had grown to love each other and Edeena would never wait on the rocks anymore.

Duncan gazed so deeply into Colton's eyes that he forgot for a moment where he was and what he came here to do. Duncan saw himself reflected in his brother's eyes and he saw the worry and confusion that Colton experienced at Duncan's sudden appearance.

At that moment, something moved in the reflection and Duncan glanced over his shoulder to see what it was.

For the first time, he saw Jaimee stretched out in Colton's bed. The sheet had fallen off her bare shoulder to reveal the upper part of her back. Her long, satin-black hair spilled over the pillow. She hadn't turned over when Colton and Duncan started talking. She was asleep.

A halo of love and contentment shone around the bed. The bond between Colton and Jaimee cast the whole room in a warm glow of serenity and belonging. None of the hardship and suffering in all of Buchanan country could shake that unbreakable bond.

Duncan's vision blurred with tears at the sight. It gave him such a brutal gut-wrenching stab of pain that he couldn't hold it back. He made a choking sound in his throat before he fought himself under control.

"What is it, lad?" Colton whispered. "What ails ye?"

Duncan shut his eyes against the sting of tears. "It's...." He broke off. He couldn't even say her name.

He cast a magical veil over Colton and showed Colton the image that Duncan had just seen a few moments ago of himself and Zoe lying asleep together in the tree room. The firelight glowed on her hair and skin. Her shoulders and ribs rose and fell in a blissful tide synchronized with Duncan's heartbeat. Rapture and love overflowed Duncan's heart remembering how he felt lying in that bed.

"Laddie!" Colton grabbed him by the shoulders, spun him around, and burst out laughing when their eyes met. "Ye've found yer lassie! Congratulations! I couldnae be happier. Ye're a man now." He clapped Duncan on both shoulders and squeezed. "Me own laddie!"

Duncan couldn't look at his brother. He looked down at the floor and fought to keep his composure. "I cannae, Colton. I cannae...."

"Cannae what, lad? Ye love her, I suppose. When are ye bringing her home? Jaimee will be beside herself." Colton laughed again. He didn't see what Duncan saw.

"I cannae defeat the Laird, man," Duncan croaked. "I couldnae stand to become Laird if it means I must marry someone else. This lassie is me own heart's mate. I would rather walk away from all of this than give her up."

Colton's smile vanished and he frowned. "Aye. I see that now. It wouldnae work."

"Ye understand?" Duncan husked. "Ye dinnae think me a coward?"

"Och, no! None of us chooses who's our mate and who isnae. We dinnae even ken if Lady Rhona exists. Ye mate with yer lassie and do as ye will. We'll back ye one way or the other."

Duncan's chin fell on his chest and he felt tears starting to overcome him. "Colton!"

"Listen to me, laddie," Colton went on. "Everything depends on ye bonding with yer mate. Forget the rest."

"But the war.... all of this...." Duncan waved at nothing, but he knew that Colton understood. Duncan didn't have to explain.

How could Duncan turn his back on Icemeet and all the people suffering in this war? How could Duncan walk away from that when he had the power to ease their suffering and bring peace to the country?

How could he do that if he lost his sanity and his life in the process? He would leave the country in worse shape than before if he didn't marry Zoe.

Colton frowned. He kept his lips clamped shut and didn't say anything. What could he say? He didn't have any answers to this.

How could Duncan ever be with Zoe the way Colton was with Jaimee? Duncan didn't see any way it could ever be and that knowing tore his heart apart.

He had to get out of here. He had to find a way back to her. He didn't know how much longer he would have with her. He couldn't squander one more instant.

He turned back to the window. "I must go. Ye remember what I say, Colton. Dinnae take the Clan out against the Creightons so long as the Laird is in place."

"What am I to do if he attacks us first?"

"Defend the Clan and take our people down to Stronghold. Fall back to the safety of the mountain the way we always have." Duncan saw himself making decisions on behalf of the Clan, but he no longer had the luxury of worrying about that. His time as a boy was long over. "If they besiege Stronghold, ye do what we've always done and go deeper into the mountains. I'll do me best to lead the Laird away to the west. Dinnae set foot across the Boundless until...."

A crushing boom rocked the whole fortress. It shook Icemeet to its roots and a blistering fireball burst in the night sky high above the Boundless.

Jaimee shot out of bed holding the sheet over her body. "What the....? Duncan!"

Colton and Duncan didn't turn around. That flash of fire high in the air cast the planes in one brilliant wash of orange and yellow light. It lit up the sky all the way to the clouds above.

Duncan and Colton stared in slack-jawed shock at a massive black dragon high in the atmosphere between Icemeet and Tyrekirk. More explosions lit up his coal-black scales, and when the blasts winked out, his blackness merged with the night so Duncan could hardly see him at all.

"Grant!" Colton whispered. "What the devil is he doing out there?"

Duncan couldn't move or speak. He stared in horror at an old man standing on the highest parapet of Tyrekirk's north tower. The man wore a tattered robe that touched his bare feet and his lank white hair surrounded his ancient, lined face.

The old man raised his hands in the air and fired blast after blast that pounded Grant to mincemeat. The giant dragon tumbled over and over in the air letting out broken roars of pain each time the Laird hit him.

The Laird's spells jerked Grant back and forth. Each time the Laird broke off his attack, Grant plummeted toward the ground before the Laird caught him and slapped him higher.

Jaimee rushed over to them fully dressed. Duncan didn't even see her get out of bed. She took one look over Colton's shoulder at the situation outside and spun away. "I'm raising the Clan! We'll arm and meet you down on the...."

"No, lass!" Colton whipped around and grabbed her arm to hold her back. "Dinnae raise the Clan. Dinnae do ought."

"Are you insane? He'll kill Grant! We have to mount our defenses...."

"No," Colton repeated. "Stand down."

"To hell with that! I won't stand by and let that son of a bitch get away with this!"

She tore her arm out of his grasp and charged out of the room. Colton sighed. "I'd better go and intercept her."

Duncan couldn't move. The next flash erupted over the Boundless, and in the light bursting across the planes, he saw the Laird clearly once again. The Laird wasn't looking at Grant, though. He was staring straight at Colton's window.

"Damn him!" Colton muttered and charged across the room reaching for his clothes.

At that moment, a catastrophic concussion struck Icemeet again. Duncan saw it coming, but he couldn't move to defend himself. He felt the Laird targeting him and Duncan remained rooted to the spot. He couldn't move a single foot to get out of the line of fire.

A punishing strike smashed in the window and an unstoppable force ripped Duncan out of it. The instant he crossed the shattered window frame, he ceased to be a magical projection. The Laird's hold gripped his body. This was all real. It was happening right now and he couldn't do anything to stop it.

The Laird's power held him in a bone-breaking grip. It did something to him at a gut level and he shifted into a dragon without meaning to. The darkness exploded into broad daylight and he plummeted over the planes taking hit after hit along with Grant.

Duncan twisted onto his back trying to find some way to fight back, but he couldn't break free. His head swiveled toward the ground and he looked down in blank horror at a massive battle taking place on the ground.

What looked like thousands of Creighton soldiers poured across the Boundless. They met a skeleton crew of Buchanans fighting a suicide battle to block the enemy from reaching Icemeet, but it was already too late.

Dozens of Creighton dragons swooped over the fortress pounding what was left of its walls. The fortress crumbled to ruins and trapped the Buchanans on the planes. The dragons finished laying waste to Icemeet, wheeled back toward the Boundless, and pinned the Buchanans between the oncoming army and the dragons' fire.

Duncan gave one more ferocious wrench to break the Laird's grip, but nothing worked. The old man leered at him and a sickening tearing sensation racked Duncan's body with more agony than he could stand.

He screamed out loud and his screams mingled with Grant's dying roars. The two dragons pitched and tossed on the wind, totally helpless to save themselves.

Another somersault showed Duncan the faces of people on the ground. Lily, Reid, Betty, Colton, and Jaimee fought with the Clan in the death trap of dragon fire on one side and Creighton blades on the other. The knot of Buchanans got progressively smaller in the surrounding sea of their enemies.

Chapter 19

Zoe shot upright in a flash. The picture of the deadly battle going on over the planes remained etched in her mind. She could still hear Grant's and Duncan's excruciating shrieks as the Laird's magic tortured them to death.

The two dragons jerked up and down on the puppet strings of hundreds of magical strikes. The Creighton troops cut down Buchanans by the dozen on the ground now that the defenders no longer had any way to fall back to Icemeet.

Zoe was starting to understand this kind of thing now and she saw the battle through Duncan's eyes. Jaimee, Colton, Lily, Reid, and Betty were trapped down there. They would fall to dragon fire any second now.

She sprang out of bed and realized a second later that she wasn't in the tree room anymore. She wasn't in the forest. She was in the bedroom that Echo and Elliot gave her at the fort. So much the better. She wouldn't have to go far to find help.

She blasted out of the room not even trying to keep quiet. She charged down the hall to Echo's and Elliot's bedroom and pounded both fists on the door. "Elliot! Elliot! Wake up. It's a matter of life and death!"

Echo pulled the door open. "What's going on? It's the middle of the night."

"Where's Elliot?" Zoe charged into their bedroom without waiting for an invitation. She didn't give a flying shit anymore if she surprised Elliot stark naked.

He wasn't. He sat in a chair by the window and he still had his kilt on, thank God. He turned around to meet her and she blurted out everything in a rush.

"The Laird captured Duncan again! The Creightons are assaulting Icemeet and the Laird is trying to kill Duncan and Grant. We have to get over to Icemeet right now!"

He shot to his feet in a flash. "I'll fly ye there, lassie. If they're in trouble, I'm the only one who can help them. Get outside the fence. Hurry! There's no room for me to shift in here."

"I'm coming with you." Echo dashed over to dresser and grabbed her weapons. "Come on, Zoe."

She hauled Zoe out of the apartment on their way to the back door. Zoe talked fast on the way. "Both Grant and Duncan were in dragon form and they're over the Boundless. The Laird is at Tyrekirk pounding them with spells. The Buchanans and the Creightons are in battle on the ground and the Creightons have the Buchanans encircled. It looks like a blood bath."

"I'll drop ye off on the Boundless to the west," Elliot replied. "Ye'll have to get up to the battle on yer own while I take out any dragons about. Understand?"

"Yeah." Zoe and Echo burst out into the forest. It was still the middle of the night here, but it had been daylight on the battlefield. Did Zoe make a terrible mistake? What if that was all just a dream?

It wasn't. Her instincts told her that Duncan was in danger—mortal danger.

Elliot stormed out of the fort and back around the fence to the open ground outside the gate. None of the other rebels were around to see.

He shifted in a flash and ruptured in a huge dragon. The dragon crouched low to the ground. Echo didn't have to tell Zoe what to do. She stepped on Elliot's knees and swung up to his shoulders. Echo sprang up a second later and took her place in front of Zoe.

Zoe wrapped her arms around Echo just in time. Elliot shot off the ground much faster than Zoe had flown with Duncan. Elliot climbed straight up streaking for the Boundless.

He held a course due north. The hills bordering the Boundless vanished and the estuary glistened silver in the moonlight. Zoe's heart dropped into her stomach when she saw the planes empty and deserted. There was nothing happening here—no Grant, no Duncan, no Laird, and no other dragons.

Elliot tilted over the last hills and plunged for the Boundless at blistering speed. He shot over the estuary and something popped in Zoe's ears the moment Elliot crossed the river.

The whole landscape exploded in daylight and the noise of battle slammed her ears along with the screams of dragons in the air.

Weapons clashed and the Creighton dragons circled the last Buchanan survivors in a black tide of soldiers. It was a miracle any Buchanans were still alive at all.

Elliot whizzed close to the ground and extended his wings to brake. He lowered himself to land and drop off Zoe and Echo when a catastrophic force yanked him away from the ground.

He gave a gut-turning scream as he somersaulted over and over in the air. Blasts ripped out of Tyrekirk and surrounded him in flashes. His giant body soared high over the battle before he turned over completely and dropped Echo and Zoe in midair.

Zoe screamed and floundered to catch hold of Echo. Echo twisted onto her side trying to reach Zoe, but nothing could save them. Gravity stripped them toward the ground at eye-watering speed.

Zoe screamed again and tried to shut her eyes in the face of death, but they remained glued open so she had to see every heart-rending sight.

Grant and Duncan contorted in agony up in the air. Spell after spell pummeled Elliot as he rose to join them in their sky-bound torture chamber. Dragons pounded the Buchanan fighting force with one jet of fire after another.

Zoe tried one more time to shut her eyes when another blast punched through the noise. It caught her and Echo in mid-fall, but it didn't come from Tyrekirk. It held her and Echo suspended for a minute and then it started to lower them gently toward the Boundless on the Buchanan side.

Zoe searched everywhere for the source. A golden net surrounded the two women and a long thread of sparkling golden light trailed from it all the way to the highest peak above Icemeet.

Zoe strained her eyes to see and had to blink several times before she let herself believe what she was seeing. A man stood on those high rocks casting spells all over the landscape. Was it Connell? No, it was Liam.

More spells rocketed from several spots among the Buchanan fighters on the ground. Betty, Connell, and a few other wizards that Zoe didn't know fired again and again at the dragons in the air trying to help them, but the Laird deflected all their efforts.

Betty and Liam fired at the Laird, but he not only defended himself but bombarded both of them with shots while he kept up his brutal assault on Grant, Elliot, and Duncan in the air. The Laird could fire more powerful magical weapons much faster than all the other wizards put together.

A bolt of lightning forked across the plane, ripped through Elliot's left wing, and kept on going. It slammed into the cliff face beneath Liam's position and the mountain caved in. He started to fall and the spell protecting Zoe and Echo blinked out.

They were only about twenty feet off the ground and they both crashed hard on the riverbank. Zoe sprang to her feet and grabbed Echo. "Come on! We have to get up the mountain!"

"What are we going to do when we get there?" Echo asked.

Zoe had no idea what to say to that, but she never got a chance. The Laird thrust out both arms and a deafening shockwave erupted from his hands. The blast struck the three dragons in one blow and shifted them all back into men.

"Elliot!" Echo shrieked.

"Duncan!" Zoe screamed.

Another piercing screech came from somewhere in the Buchanan force. Zoe and Echo charged up the mountain, but it was too late. The three men plummeted toward the ground, but they were nowhere near the planes anymore.

They nose-dived behind the mountain where no one could see them. "NO!!" Zoe screeched. She heard Echo and Lily screaming, too, but their despair meant nothing to her. She heard men bellowing in the Buchanan ranks, but what did she care for their problems?

She ran as she'd never run in her life. She didn't even know where to begin to look for Duncan, but he needed her help one way or the other. She would spend the rest of her life searching for him. She wouldn't give up until she found him.

Someone caught her and she heard a man yelling in her ear. "You can't help him! We have to get out of here!"

"Get off me!" she shrieked. "Let me go! DUNCAN!!"

She heard Echo screaming for Elliot and Zoe looked around wildly for her friend to help her. She spotted Echo a few yards away fighting off Edeena and a bunch of other archers trying to stop her from rushing headlong into the battle.

Liam grappled Zoe's arms to her sides, and when she didn't stop struggling, he picked her up so her feet left the ground.

"DUNCAN!!" she roared. "DUNCAN!!"

Liam kept yelling in her ear, but she couldn't hear him over her own screams. She had to reach Duncan at all costs.

The archers dragged Echo over to Liam and Zoe. He wrestled one arm free and grabbed Echo's wrist. An ear-splitting bang hit the whole group and they vanished.

They materialized somewhere dark and deep underground. Liam let go of Zoe and she spun around, lashed out, and punched him in the jaw with all her strength. "You bastard! What did you do?! I have to find Duncan! Get out of my way!"

Echo was attacking the archers trying to fight her way out of their grip. She and Zoe burst out of their hold and raced off.... somewhere. Zoe didn't think or care where as long as she left right now to go find Duncan.

She made it five steps before something hit her from behind. It bound her arms and legs together so she couldn't move. She toppled and would have slammed down on her face if something else hadn't caught her and lowered her slowly to the floor.

She kicked and struggled, but when she still found herself bound tightly, she started to come out of her hysterical frenzy. Echo lay at her side bound by the same magical force.

Liam strode over to them and squatted down where they could both see him. "Quiet down, both of you. We'll go find them, but you have to calm down. You can't run out there now or you'll both wind up dead."

"Elliot is alive out there!" Echo roared. "He's alive and he's hurt! He needs me! We have to go now!"

"You would run straight into dragon fire, lassie," Edeena murmured from behind Liam's back. "I ken how ye feel. Believe me, no one kens better than I." She rested her hand on Liam's shoulder. "Ye cannae find them nor help them at all if ye're dead. Just lie still until we can mount a rescue party."

Zoe didn't want to listen. She jerked against the magical bonds holding her, but she couldn't move. She couldn't go get Duncan right now and Edeena's words started to sink in.

Going outside right now would be suicide, but that didn't lessen this sick feeling in her guts. Her life wasn't worth a thing without Duncan.

She sensed in a wordless certainty beyond reason that he was hurt and in mortal danger. He needed help and he needed it now. He wasn't alone. He had Grant and Elliot with him, but they couldn't help him. They were just as injured and wrecked as he was.

She wanted to cry and rage and kill someone all at the same time. Her connection with Duncan demanded that she go right now.

Chapter 20

Z oe twisted around on the cold, stone floor searching for a way out. She contorted the other way and finally saw where she was. She, Echo, Liam, and the archers had all appeared in a deep, shadowy tunnel carved out of solid granite.

A few other Buchanans moved around in here. Stacks of cartons, bundles, and chests of supplies lined the tunnel as far as Zoe could see. Women and old people worked tirelessly to unpack the supplies and carry everything up the tunnel and out of sight. Zoe couldn't see where they were taking it.

Another starburst exploded up the tunnel past Echo's head. The light evaporated to reveal Colton and Reid grappling Lily by the arms as she kicked and tried to bite them to break their hold.

Betty spun around and cast a spell over Lily to make her stop struggling, but Lily kept bellowing and shrieking at them to release her so she could go search for Grant.

Betty lowered Lily down next to Echo and Zoe. None of the three women could relax. Jaimee passed her hand across her eyes. "In case you were wondering, that was an unmitigated disaster."

"How many do we have left?" Colton asked Betty. "How many did ye send through to Stronghold?"

"About a hundred and fifty. That was all I could get out." Another ground-shaking rumble shuddered the rock and everyone looked up to the ceiling. "The dragons are still out there. They won't leave much of Icemeet for us to go back to."

"We have to go get Duncan!" Zoe yelled. "He's the only one who can defeat the Laird."

"Are you just going to leave Grant and Elliot out on the mountain to die?" Echo demanded. "Let us go! We have to go look for them now!"

Colton scowled down at them and then sauntered over to where the three of the women lay. Liam moved out of the way and Colton squatted down in Liam's place.

"We will go search for them. Ye lassies have me solemn word of honor on that, but we'll do it when I say and not a moment before? Is that clear?"

"We have to...." Echo began, but Colton held up his hand to silence her.

"Ye lassies have a choice to make. Ye can all pull yer heads together and help us cope with this disaster. We have more than a thousand people living down that tunnel who need yer help a sight more than Duncan, Grant, and Elliot. Ye can pull yer weight and help us make the best of a bad situation, and when we've secured the Clan against any further threat, we'll send out a search party to bring our lads home. Ye can go with the searchers and be there when we find yer men. We'll send Betty and Connell out to heal their injuries and then we'll bring them back here where they can recover. Do I make meself perfectly clear?"

Zoe gulped. She didn't want to accept this. Her mind whirled for a way to lie to Colton, agree to his conditions, get Liam to release her, and then she'd find a way to escape and go find Duncan.

The other two must have been thinking the same thing because Colton read their minds. "Yer only other option is that we keep ye bound up like this for the rest of eternity and dinnae deceive yerselves for a moment that I winnae do it. I'll have Betty and Connell and Liam keep ye bound and gagged for months if necessary and ye winnae set foot outside until we bring the lads home. If ye cannae see reason and behave yerselves, I winnae hesitate to keep ye tied up until ye do."

He stood up and glared down at the three of them. He didn't have to ask again if he was making himself perfectly clear. No one could argue with this man.

Zoe looked away and Echo and Lily didn't answer, either. Zoe finally choked on the words and muttered, "All right."

"I need to hear ye say the words that ye give yer promise not to try to escape or go after the lads on yer own," he insisted. "Ye look me in the eye and give me yer solemn word of honor that ye'll obey me and do it me own way."

Those words ran through the tunnel with the force of a tolling bell. No one breathed or moved as Colton gave his verdict.

Zoe couldn't stand that silence. She looked up into Colton's face and her eyes swam with tears. "I promise. I give you my word I won't try to go after him until you say so."

"Me, too," Echo croaked and then she burst into tears.

Colton turned to Lily. "Say the words, lassie. Dinnae make me hold ye like this. Ye dinnae deserve this."

She barely whispered, "I promise," and the tension dissolved. Colton rested his hand on Zoe's shoulder. "I cannae stand leaving them out there any more than ye can, but we've the whole Clan to think on."

He waved to Liam and Betty who released the three women. All the energy that kept Zoe struggling and scheming drained out of her and she crumpled on the cold stone floor. She didn't want to face the future without Duncan.

Colton held out his hand to her. "Come along, lassies. We must get under cover before the dragons bring down the whole blasted mountain."

The others moved in and helped the three women up. Echo and Lily looked as lost and despondent as Zoe felt. She couldn't even appreciate that the Last Division was back together again after all the chaos that tore them apart.

What did Zoe care about the Last Division compared with how she felt about Duncan? What was she thinking turning him down in the tree room? She should have listened to him. She should have sealed the mate-bond with him when she had the chance. Then maybe none of this would have happened.

Was it only last night when she fell asleep with him there? Was it only last night that she broke down sobbing at the thought of him marrying another woman?

She knew then that he meant more to her than life itself. She never dreamed it would end like this.

Colton and Reid led the way down the tunnel. The Buchanans moved out of the way to let the party through. Jaimee and Betty accompanied Lily, Echo, and Zoe in a protective huddle. Liam and the archers brought up the rear and Edeena kept casting sympathetic glances at the three women—the three widows.

Grant, Elliot, and Duncan might not be dead, but they were as good as. Now Zoe felt like she was going to die, too. Only her promise to Colton stopped her from fighting these people off and charging off on a rescue mission right now.

She followed them a long way down that tunnel. It was the longest walk of her life and more and more Buchanans stopped what they were doing to stare as the party passed. Did they all see the unmistakable signs of three people who had lost everything in one stroke?

Colton and Reid finally exited the tunnel in a large cavern cut deep into the bedrock. Besides the fact that every wall, floor, and ceiling was made out of the same grey stone, the place had been set up in a similar design to Icemeet. It just didn't have any windows.

Magical balls floated near the ceiling to give light to every room. Colton mentioned that over a thousand people were living down here, but Zoe didn't really grasp what he said until she saw it for herself.

The place teemed with men, women, and children of all ages. They streamed in and out of a massive hall to one side and they all seemed to be working on something extremely important.

Colton and Reid descended the stairs to the central foyer where all the corridors met. From here, Zoe could see hundreds of wounded men lined up on the floor in the main hall. Dozens of people moved among them tending to their wounds, cleaning blood off different parts of their bodies, and doing their best to make the fighters comfortable.

Betty shoved past Zoe and Echo. "I gotta go. I'll see you guys later."

She hustled into the hall and started going from bed to bed. Jaimee vanished somewhere and came back leading a whole bunch of women. They all carried stacks of clean linens and they went into the hall, too.

Edeena and the archers left in a different direction and Liam started talking to Reid. "Go out front and conceal the entrances," Reid told him. "Make sure no one can get in or out without one of ye casting some concealment charm—and that includes hunters. We cannae risk the Creightons following them back here and finding us."

"What about the siege engines?" Liam asked. "We left everything back to Icemeet. Someone is going to have to go back there and get everything before we can use the machines against the dragons."

"Concealment first," Reid decided. "If the Creightons breach that, we'll work on defenses."

"We'll need to bring the siege machines down here before the Creightons breach the concealment charms," Liam pointed out. "We can't be running up there to get everything in the heat of battle with dragons pounding us to kingdom come."

Colton turned around and clapped Liam on the shoulder. "I'll send our people up to bring the siege machines down. Ye handle the magic and leave the heavy lifting to someone else."

Liam laughed and went off to carry out his order. Edeena came over to the three women who remained standing there stunned and devastated. "Come along with me, lassies. I'll show ye where ye can spend the night."

Zoe didn't want to go anywhere. She made Colton a promise to pull her weight and help defend this place. She didn't want to go back on her word, but she got a powerful sense that she wouldn't be any good to anyone in this state.

She blundered after Edeena with Echo and Lily at her heels. None of them spoke and Zoe couldn't look at her friends. She didn't want to see anyone but Duncan right now and that was impossible.

Edeena turned into some room and Zoe came to her senses enough to realize it wasn't a bedroom or a guest room. It was a long, low barracks full of bunks stacked three high. No one was in here now.

"This is the archers' barracks. This is where all the unmated lassies stay before they mate and marry. The unmated lads are right next door." Edeena went over to a stack of three bunks. "These three are empty. Ye can take these for now."

Zoe became aware of Lily and Echo standing next to her. All three of them stared at the bunks without saying a word.

How far they had all fallen from just a few hours and days ago. Echo had been running the rebel fort and living in that apartment with Elliot. Zoe didn't even want to think about the kind of luxury Lily had been getting used to at Tyrekirk.

Now they were here. Echo cleared her throat, threw back her head, scaled to the top bunk, and flopped down. "Thank you, Edeena," she said in a low, flat tone that sounded nothing like her usual vivacious self. "This is perfect."

"Yeah," Lily murmured. "Thank you for your hospitality."

She vaulted into the second bunk, crossed her legs, and started doing something with her dirk.

That left Zoe, but she couldn't thank Edeena. She was unmated—unlike all the rest of her friends. She didn't have the kind of established relationship with Duncan that they had with all their men.

She sank down on the lowest bunk and stared at the floor. She didn't have the energy to say anything, but in her heart, she felt nothing but gratitude for being here.

This bunk room gave her the perfect place to lick her wounds. She would have been in despair if the Buchanans put her in a nice bedroom. That would only throw in her face the horrible reality that Duncan wasn't here. Was the tree room ever real at all? Was it just a fantasy Duncan cooked up with his magic?

The way she felt in the tree room was no fantasy. She didn't feel worthy to join his Clan or any other Clan. At the same time, she didn't want to be part of any mission that ended with him marrying someone else, but she couldn't bring herself to leave. She had nowhere else to go and no one else to go to. Everything she had was here.

Chapter 21

Zoe woke up and immediately felt a sick wave of obsessive need demanding that she get up and go look for Duncan. She swept to her feet and checked her weapons.

Lily hopped down from her bunk and surveyed the archers' barracks. "Let's go find Colton and see what's going on with the defenses."

"I was just going there." Zoe checked the top bunk. "Echo's already up."

"Maybe she's found out something."

The two women left and returned to the central foyer. It was as busy as ever except that Zoe didn't see anyone familiar in there or in the large hall where all the wounded had been yesterday.

Clan Buchanan had removed all their bedding, too, and replaced it with long tables where everyone sat around eating. Zoe scanned the crowd for anyone she knew, but every person in there was a stranger.

Echo showed up a minute later. "Where is everyone?"

"We were just going to ask you the same question," Lily replied. "We were looking for Colton to get the news."

"I was doing the same thing." Echo looked over her shoulder. "I don't know where anyone is."

A second later, one of the archers came downstairs from one of the upper levels. The woman was almost as tall as Jaimee, but she had copper red hair, ivory skin, and a million freckles.

"Och, lassies!" she called. "Colton sent me to find ye. He's waiting for ye lot in his room upstairs."

"Where's that?" Zoe asked.

"I'm to take ye there. Follow me."

She went back to the stairs and led the three women into a different tunnel-like passage. These tunnels snaked all over the place and led off into hundreds of rooms.

People worked in practically every single room. Zoe didn't see a single bedroom—not like any bedrooms she had ever seen. Duncan's memories had shown her what life was like at Icemeet in his youth, but she didn't see anything like that now.

The archer finally threw open a random door. It was one of the very few shut doors in the whole fortress and this one *did* lead into a bedroom.

One simple double bed sat in the corner. The whole rest of the room had been converted into a centralized headquarters full of desks and tables. Papers, books, folders, and maps lay piled on every surface.

The three women walked in on Colton, Reid, Jaimee, Betty, Edeena, and Liam all standing around a large table and consulting maps of the surrounding mountains.

Zoe let out a strangled cry when she saw Connell and Fergus standing there, too. She charged them and threw her arms around Connell. "You're here! Thank God you're alive! I was so worried about you."

He smiled and hugged her back. "Aye, lass. I'm back."

"What happened to you guys?" She pushed him away and grabbed Fergus. "I thought you were all dead. I found Fletcher and I thought the Laird got to the rest of you, too."

"We thought we were dead, too," Fergus replied.

"We dinnae ken how we came back," Connell added. "We left the forest and found ourselves in the remote mountains. We've only just returned."

"And it's just as well ye did for we'll need both of ye to help us find our lads." Colton turned back to the three women. "We're just mounting our search party now so ye lassies are just in time."

"Where are they?" Lily asked. "How far out are they?"

"We don't know where Grant, Elliot, and Duncan are," Jaimee told her. "That's the problem. They could be anywhere."

"We've already used all the magic at our disposal to try to locate them," Liam chimed in. "Either the Laird is still hiding the three men from us or there are some other larger forces at play that we don't know about."

"I find that hard to believe," Zoe countered. "The Laird has been trying to kill Duncan and Elliot for ages. After that last battle, it looks like he's turned against Grant, too. He wouldn't throw them into the mountains and then hide them from us so the three guys would die a slow painful death. If the Laird knew where they were, he would have killed them already....and we know they're still alive."

"What are ye saying, lassie?" Reid asked. "If the Laird isnae hiding the lads from us, why havenae we found them yet?"

"There's only one other explanation, isn't there? Duncan must be hiding them."

Everyone turned around to stare at her. "Duncan!" Liam exclaimed. "How could he hide them from the Laird?"

"He's been hiding himself from the Laird for weeks—and from us," Connell pointed out.

"But why did Duncan fall like that if he still has magic?" Echo asked. "He couldn't protect himself from the Laird. We all saw that. If he had any power at all, he would shift and come home.... wouldn't he?"

"Maybe he only has enough residual magic to hide himself and Grant and Elliot," Betty reasoned. "Maybe he's hurt and that's all he can do right now. Maybe that's the only way he can keep himself and his brothers alive."

A tense silence fell over the table. Zoe felt sick to her stomach. She couldn't think about Duncan being hurt and on the edge of death out in the snowy mountains.

Colton finally turned to the three women. "It's like this, lassies. We havenae any other way to find these lads, so ye'll have to do it for us. Ye'll have to lead our search party into the mountains, find our lads, and bring them back."

"How can we do that if we don't know where they are?" Lily asked.

"Ye must use yer mate-bonds to find them," Reid told her.

"But we aren't mate-bonded with them the way you guys are," Echo countered. "Grant and Elliot aren't Buchanans and Zoe...."

She broke off. She didn't say out loud that Zoe and Duncan weren't mate-bonded, but everyone present knew exactly what she didn't say. Zoe looked away.

"It doesnae account one jot if Grant and Elliot are Buchanans," Colton told them. "Ye're mate-bonded whether ye like it or not and we all ken Zoe and Duncan are mate-bonded as much as the rest of us. If it comes to all that, she can lead the search party to Duncan. I'd bet me last tooth he's got Grant and Elliot with him."

All eyes turned to Zoe. Did she hear that right? Did Colton just say that Zoe and Duncan were mate-bonded as much as the rest of them?

Her eyes sliced over to Connell. Did he say something to Colton.... or did they all just get it intuitively?

Every face surrounding her told her the same thing. They all knew, but that only somehow made her feel worse. Why did she have to mate-bond with a man she could never marry? Everyone in this room still held out some hope of finding this mysterious Lady Rhona. The whole future of the United States depended on finding Lady Rhona and making her Duncan's wife.

Zoe couldn't leave Duncan out on the mountain hurt and in danger no matter who he was supposed to marry. She loved him too much.

This rotten, disgusting feeling in the pit of her stomach told her loud and clear that she loved him. Why deny it anymore? She wouldn't care this much if she didn't love him.

She loved him enough to want him for herself. She loved him enough to want to die without him. She wanted to do absolutely anything for him, even if it meant giving him up.

She gulped down the sting of bile in her throat. "Okay. We'll do it. Who's on this search party with us?"

"Me," Liam announced. "Connell and Betty have to stay here to defend Stronghold. That means I'll be your resident wizard. Once we find the three guys, I'll be able to transport our whole party back here."

"We have magical defenses protecting Stronghold from any incursion, including yours," Betty went on, "Liam will contact Connell and me when it's time to bring you in. We'll adjust our spells so you can come through without bringing any unwanted visitors with you."

"Fergus, Callum, and I are going with ye lassies," Reid added. "We've ten more lads standing ready to leave whenever ye lassies are."

Zoe took one more look around the circle. Jaimee smiled at her with a pained, sympathetic light in her eyes. She understood. She and Betty knew better than anyone what losing one's life mate felt like.

Colton sidestepped around the three women on his way to the door. "Ye lassies get down to our storeroom and suit up to go out on the mountain. We dinnae ken if the Creightons are prowling about, so ye'll need to arm for anything."

Zoe caught his arm. "Colton.... thank you. You don't know what this means to us."

"I think I ken a bit about it, lassie. Ye bring me brother home and it'll be me thanking ye instead of the other way round. I dinnae care what condition he's in so long as he's alive."

"He is," she told him. "I'm certain of it."

"Ye're taking all our hearts with ye, lassie. Ye go on with ye and dinnae stand about thanking me for ought."

He gripped her hand and then walked away. He stepped out into the corridor and started calling orders to someone Zoe couldn't see.

Liam turned to Edeena and put his arms around her. "I'll be back real soon. Don't go anywhere, okay?"

She beamed at him and then they kissed each other in front of everyone. They hugged and gazed into each other's eyes much more deeply than Zoe expected considering the stories she'd heard. Liam and Edeena obviously cared about each other and even loved each other.

Fergus moved forward and distracted Zoe from them. "Ye lassies come with me and I'll take ye down to the storeroom.

Jaimee waylaid the party on their way out of the room. "Bring them back....and bring yourselves back safely. We're all counting on you."

She hugged each woman in turn. Zoe tensed when Jaimee came toward her with her arms out, but Jaimee had changed. She was nothing like the stiff, stern lieutenant she had been at Ironforge. None of the Last Division was the same.

Zoe finally hugged Betty and followed Fergus downstairs. He led them to a massive storehouse packed to the ceiling with weapons, food, clothes, blankets, tools—everything.

Zoe, Lily, and Echo got to work with a vengeance. They were on their way out to find Duncan, Grant, and Elliot. All their energy returned and Zoe's spirits lifted. Duncan was out there and she would stop at nothing to find him.

The three put on thick sheepskin-lined jackets, thick padded pants, and snow boots that laced up to the knee. They put on hooded cloaks and scarves to protect their faces from the elements.

Liam showed up a second later wearing the same protective clothing, but none of the Buchanans bothered with it. Reid and his ten men met the women out in the main cavern. None of them wore anything more than their tartans, but they brought plenty of weapons.

"Where are we going?" Lily asked.

"We'll show ye the way out of the fortress," Fergus replied. "After that, it's ye that'll tell *us* where to go."

Zoe exchanged glances with Lily and Echo. Zoe never expected to be thrust into charge over the Buchanans, but if it meant helping Duncan, she could do this and a lot more besides.

Lily and Echo squared their shoulders and the three friends nodded to each other. They all felt the same pull to get outside and find their men. Zoe just had to trust that this mate-bond between her and Duncan was real.

Fergus led them back to the main chamber and out through a different tunnel. It emerged on a giant ice sheet covering a valley between gargantuan mountains. The wilderness seemed so big and forbidding and vast. Duncan and his brothers seemed so tiny by comparison. How far would Zoe have to go before she found him? Would he still be alive then?

Fergus, Reid, and the others fell back and the three women stepped out on the ice. The sun flashed on massive glaciers flowing like rivers through the mountains. Icy wind bit through Zoe's thick clothes and she pulled her scarf over her face.

She had to squint to keep the whirling ice crystals out of her eyes. She got so snow-blind that she couldn't even see where she was going.

She didn't have to see. She bent her head against the wind, shut her eyes, and concentrated on putting one foot in front of the other. She let her instincts lead her away from Stronghold. She didn't have to think anymore. She just had to let this driving compulsion lead her to Duncan.

Lily and Echo didn't speak, either. They fell into a single-file line all marching in the same direction. They didn't have to discuss where they were going because all three of them already knew.

Liam followed the three women at the end of their line, but the Buchanans took a different strategy. Reid unbuckled his saber and dirk and handed his weapons to Fergus. Then Reid shifted and trotted at Zoe's heels in his tiger form.

A few minutes into the hike, the other eight men did the same thing. They gave their weapons to Fergus to carry. He accepted them with plenty of rude jokes and feigned complaints.

The nine tigers surrounded the women for a little while, but pretty soon, they got tired of keeping up the slow, painstaking pace. The cats darted off into the rocks, played at sliding on the ice, and tousled with each other. They kicked up snow off the ice sheet and sneezed snowflakes off their noses. Their fur kept them much warmer than Zoe's fleeces.

They kept this up for a few hours until Fergus threw all the weapons on the ground. "That's it, laddies. Ye've had yer fun. Now it's me own turn."

He shifted instantly and ran off to have some fun with his Clansmen. Another tiger strutted over to the pile of weapons, shifted back into Callum, and he picked them all up.

He shot Zoe a grin on the side. "Ye cannae expect one man to do all the work, can ye?"

"You won't carry them the whole time, will you?" Echo asked. "We could be out here for days."

"Och, no! We'll take our own turns. That's the way we do it. We dinnae usually carry weapons out here, but with the Creightons around, I suppose we dinnae have much choice." He squinted at the sky. "It will snow soon anyway. We winnae have such good weather for all that. We must make tracks, lassies. Step lively."

Zoe walked faster heading up the valley. The glacier flowed out of a pass up there. It looked a thousand miles away, but she knew now that Duncan was over there. She was heading in the right direction.

Lily and Echo matched her pace. Neither of them ever questioned whether Zoe was going the right way. All three knew exactly where they were going.

Callum was right. Cloud blocked out the sun and a blizzard blew in. The wind howled in a deafening shriek. Zoe pulled her scarf and hood completely over her face so she couldn't see a thing.

She kept pushing forward no matter what. She couldn't stop now when she felt herself getting closer.

Someone grabbed her and a male voice bellowed in her ear over the noise. It was Reid. "Come, lassie! We cannae go on in this!"

"We have to!" she yelled back. "We're almost there!"

"We cannae help Duncan if we're all dead. Now come!"

He dragged her sideways. She had no way of knowing where she was or where he was taking her. She didn't want to divert from her course, but he didn't give her the option.

He hauled her into a black tempest of solid snow and stinging ice….and then the noise died to nothing. He pulled off her scarf, studied her face, and then sighed. "Ye havenae any frostbite, lassie. That's good."

She looked around her. Their whole party was inside an ice cave buried under mountains of snow. A glowing magical orb floated over Liam's head to light the place.

Reid squatted down with his Clansmen. "Ye lassies settled yerselves down and get some rest. We cannae go anywhere in this. We'll go on once it dies down."

Zoe glanced over at Lily and Echo. Echo glared at Reid and Lily pursed her lips. None of them wanted to settle down or rest. Duncan, Grant, and Elliot were still out there in this storm. If it wasn't safe for the search party, it would be even more dangerous for the three lost men.

Liam squatted down next to Reid and Fergus. He was sure acting friendly toward them compared to what Duncan showed Zoe in his memories.

The amazing thing was that they acted friendly toward him, too. The Buchanans joked with him and shared their food with him, especially Reid. None of them seemed to remember or care that Duncan and Reid tried to kill Liam when they first met.

Zoe eyed the men, but there was nothing else to do. She finally sat down across the cave from the men. She didn't want to be near them or share their camaraderie. She wanted to be alone with her misery, but at least Echo and Lily understood it.

The men pretended not to see them and the three women opened up their packs to take out some food. The hours wore away, and in a little while, the sound of the wind moaning outside lulled Zoe into a doze.

Chapter 22

Zoe, Lily, and Echo advanced to the mouth of the snow cave where the Buchanan rescue party had spent the night. The sun was out again and Zoe couldn't even look at the blinding ice sheet.

"How far, lassies?" Reid asked. "How many more days' travel have we got before we find the lads?"

"They're just over the pass," Echo told him. "We should be there by noon, I'd say."

"And ye're certain they're all still alive?"

"Absolutely," Lily replied. "They're in pain and distress, but they're alive."

"All right. Lead the way."

The three women walked out of the cave in a trance. Zoe couldn't feel or see or think anything right now. Some power beyond herself moved her legs one in front of the other. She couldn't imagine doing anything other than climbing up the glacier to the pass.

She didn't even think about what she would find there. Duncan was alive and agonizingly close. She couldn't breathe until she found him.

The three friends crested the pass surrounded by Highland tigers. The whole party paused there and looked down at an even bigger ice sheet stretching as far as the eye could see.

It covered the landscape in a carpet of solid white. Nothing interrupted that smooth, flat, empty expanse.

"Duncan!" Zoe cried and took off running with Lily and Echo right with her.

"Where?!" Liam yelled.

None of the three women waited long enough to explain. Zoe had to reach Duncan before it was too late. Her instincts told her loud and clear that he was hanging by his last thread.

The tigers bounded after them with Liam racing to catch up. The three women slid on the ice to the base of a towering sheer cliff a thousand feet high.

The three men lay sprawled on the ice shivering under a heavy crust covering all three of them. It turned them white so no one could see them from a distance.

Zoe burned her hands touching Duncan. "Hold on, Duncan! We're here! We're taking you back to Stronghold! Just hold on...just a little longer!"

Lily reared back on her knees, drew her saber, and started hacking at the solid ice sealing Grant to the glacier. Echo scrambled in her pack for something or other.

Zoe floundered through her supplies trying to find some way to free Duncan and warm him up. Without warning, an ear-splitting crack shattered the ice sheet under her knees. The glacier exploded and the whole section with the three brothers, the three women, and all the Buchanans caved into a massive sinkhole.

Zoe screamed and dove on top of Duncan, but nothing could arrest their fall. The party plunged along with several tons of solid ice and snow.

They slammed down on a stone floor and all the Buchanans in the Stronghold cavern swarmed around them. "Damn it, Liam!" Lily roared. "At least warn us if you're going to do that!"

"There wasn't time! Get out of the way!"

He pushed Lily and Zoe aside and pounced on the three men. He touched each of them in turn and thawed them out. All three collapsed on the floor shivering and shaking.

"Duncan!" Zoe grabbed his hand. It was still frozen solid and all three men had been battered black and blue. "It's okay!" she choked. "You're home! You're safe!"

She heard Lily and Echo talking to Grant and Elliot, but Zoe had to fight back tears at the sight of Duncan's condition. He looked a thousand times worse than she feared.

He couldn't move his trembling, frostbitten lips to speak. He couldn't uncurl his fingers or relax any of his limbs.

Betty shouldered her way through the crowd, took one look at the three men, and gasped. "Jesus Christ!"

Colton and Jaimee showed up a second later and started giving orders to everyone to get the three men out of the cavern, but Zoe hardly heard them.

She clutched Duncan's hand willing herself to push some of her body heat into him, but nothing worked. Liam kept doing things to Duncan and sending waves of magic sparkling over him, but none of it warmed up the depth of cold inside him.

Betty went to work on Elliot and Connell took care of Grant. Zoe's throat hurt from looking at Duncan's many injuries. Horrible black patches of bruising covered him all over and he coughed up blood when he managed to cough at all.

Liam kept cursing under his breath in between bowing his head, closing his eyes, and using different combinations of spells that Zoe didn't understand.

Colton finally gave the word to pick up Duncan. Zoe kept a firm hold on his hand and didn't let him go, but no one argued. Some of his Clansmen rolled him onto a stretcher and carried him to a bedroom upstairs. They put him on the bed, but he kept shaking as though he would never stop.

Liam did something else and another curtain of sparks rippled up Duncan's body. It did more good to heal his injuries, but when it got to his head, he started screaming in agony. He convulsed and contorted in every direction while his screams echoed through the fortress.

Zoe went nuts and tried to do anything to help him, but she was utterly helpless. Tears sprang to her eyes watching him writhe in torment.

Arms surrounded her and started towing her away from the bed. "Come on!" Jaimee yelled in her ear. "You can't stay here! Come on! You have to get out of here!"

Zoe panicked and tried to fight Jaimee off to return to Duncan's bedside. "Let me go! Duncan! Duncan!!"

He couldn't even hear her over his own screams. Reid and Fergus showed up a second later, and between them and Jaimee, they hauled Zoe out of the room. Reid kicked the door shut and it muffled some of Duncan's screams.

Zoe tried one more time to shove past them to get back to Duncan, and in that moment of quiet, she heard Grant and Elliot screaming in other parts of the fortress.

Jaimee planted herself between Zoe and Duncan's door. Zoe drew in a deep breath to curse Jaimee out.... until she noticed tears in Jaimee's eyes.

"Just leave him alone with Liam," Jaimee husked. "Let Liam do his work. We can't do anything for Duncan that Liam can't do."

Zoe gulped down despair that threatened to destroy her. She couldn't leave Duncan alone, not like this. She couldn't have brought him back here only to leave him to face this alone.

She only had to look at Jaimee, Reid, and Fergus blocking her path to know they weren't going to let her into that room. She didn't know if she could go back in there anyway. Duncan's agonized screams kept floating through the door.

She whirled away fighting down tears. Now what was she supposed to do?

Reid came over to her and touched her arm. "Come along with me, lass. Ye cannae stay here."

She didn't want to be anywhere else, but she didn't know what else to do. She couldn't even through the film of tears blurring her vision.

She started walking away at his side. She had no idea where he was taking her. It didn't seem to matter anymore.

He walked for a long time. When she looked up to see where she was, she found herself in a corridor she didn't recognize. "Where are we?"

"We're at Icemeet, lassie."

"But isn't this.... Isn't it kind of unsafe here?"

He shrugged. "It isnae any less safe here than anywhere else." He opened a doorway and stepped into a stone stairway leading upward.

She followed him and they emerged on a high outcropping overlooking the mountains behind the fortress. She had never been here before, but she recognized it from Duncan's memories.

Reid leaned against the parapet, squinted at the surrounding peaks, and pulled something out of somewhere that Zoe didn't see. He didn't have any pockets or sporran. She didn't see where he had it or how he was carrying it.

He broke it in half and she saw that it was a piece of dried meat. He held out one half to her and started chewing on the other while he surveyed the countryside.

"This is where people come when they've lost their mates—well, not *here* exactly, but up there." He pointed to the high rocks towering over Icemeet. "They spend their days up there watching and waiting for their mates to return—unless the mate is dead in which case the surviving mate usually wastes away for years if they dinnae die first."

Zoe looked down at the meat in her hand and then at him. This was Duncan's brother, but he talked and acted like he wasn't all that worried about Duncan.

"Me father locked himself away in a closet for more than twenty years after he lost his mate. Others throw themselves off the rocks to end their misery."

"Why are you telling me this?" she asked.

"That's all naught to ye, lassie. Ye havenae lost yer mate. He's just downstairs at Stronghold. Liam and Betty will heal Duncan and he'll be as good as new."

"Are you sure about that?"

Reid winced and looked away. "He's alive, at least. He isnae lost thanks to ye."

She turned around and gazed off into the mountains. She couldn't explain why, but this place really did soothe her. Her heart and soul revolted that Duncan was downstairs in pain, but Reid was right.

Zoe was a long way from spending her days on those rocks, alone and forlorn for a mate she could never have—at least, she wasn't there yet. She might be someday, but not today.

Chapter 23

Duncan woke up and winced. Every inch of him hurt, especially on the inside. He had lost. He tried to fight the Laird—again—and barely made it out with his life. He would have lost even that if...

His distress became unbearable when he saw where he was. He lay in one of the couples' bedrooms at Stronghold and Zoe sat in an armchair by his bed.

She studied him with such an intense stare that he couldn't look at her. He had to look away, but that only brought him face to face with the room he was in.

He gulped down misery, but it kept rising against his best efforts to pretend it wasn't there. Colton must have put him in this room. Colton had to approve of everyone's accommodation at Stronghold or Icemeet or wherever Clan Buchanan happened to be staying in this disaster.

Colton would only put Duncan in this room if Colton thought Duncan and Zoe were a mated couple—which they weren't. They would never be one now.

She stretched her arm toward his bedside and her hand slipped into his. Her fingers felt incredibly warm and inviting. They dispelled the cold still lingering in his body, but they couldn't touch the cold eating away at his heart.

"You made it!" she breathed. "We were all scared out of our wits when we lost you on the mountain."

He didn't turn his head to look at her. He couldn't stand to see her angelic face looking down at him with so much compassion and love.

She loved him. He knew that and he loved her beyond endurance, but he couldn't let her do this. "Ye shouldnae be here, lassie. Ye should go back to the archers' barracks. That's where ye belong just as I belong with the lads."

"Why?" she croaked. "Don't you want me anymore? Did you change your mind after I turned you down in the tree room?"

He told himself a thousand times not to turn around. He could command himself not to look at her, but that unstoppable force made him do it anyway. "No, lassie! Of course I didnae change me mind. How could you think that?"

"Why are you sending me away, then?" She struggled to control her lips and her eyes brimmed with tears. "I love you. I love you more than anything. I want to spend the rest of my life with you. Don't you know that?"

Now he had to compress his lips to control himself. "I cannae, lassie. Dinnae ye see that? I cannae bring ye into me Clan—not now."

"Why not?" Her voice got louder, only to crack with tortured emotion. "Do you know what I went through after I lost you? Do you know what it took to find you and bring you back here? You know what this means to me. This Clan is all I have left in the world."

"I cannae, lass." He felt himself spiraling into some kind of insanity. He wanted to die rather than say the words. "I lost, lass. I cannae fight the Laird. It's only a matter of time before he comes for me and kills me. I couldnae do that to ye and now I'm a liability to me own Clan. It's me own fault this has all gone so wrong. What kind of man brings ye into his Clan and cannae even take care of ye? Me Clan is worse off now than if I'd never been found."

She stared at him through her tears and didn't speak. He could only hope and pray that she understood why he could never make her a part of his Clan. His best hope was to live alone for the rest of his life.

"I never should have left the mountain. I'll go back there and everyone will be better off. I never should have gone to visit Colton. Then the Laird never would have attacked and Icemeet wouldnae be in ruins now." He turned away clamping his eyes shut. "I've done all that. I've destroyed Icemeet and killed God kens how many of me own Clan. I've put me whole Clan in danger and nearly killed Grant and Elliot...."

He broke off. He couldn't go on.

She didn't leave and she didn't say anything. She kept holding his hand and tracing her fingers across his knuckles.

He wished she would leave him alone with his grief. Her presence made him even more ashamed of himself, but somehow, her leaving would have been a thousand times worse.

"I cannae think why ye want to be one of this Clan, lassie." He sniffed trying to pull himself together. "We're on the verge of being wiped out. I dinnae want to become Laird even if by some miracle we could find a way to defeat the Laird and take Kald. I dinnae want to marry any Lady Rhona. I want ye and that can never happen now."

She sat silently for a long time. Any second now, she would stand up, walk out of that door, and leave him alone exactly the way he said he wanted her to. Why did he tell her to leave? Why did he tell her to break it off with him when that was the last thing in the world that he wanted?

She stood up and squeezed his hand. He couldn't look at her. He couldn't see her walk out that door, never to return. His life was truly over. He would never find anyone as good as her. He would never love anyone as much as he loved her. He knew that to the very marrow of his bones.

She went to the door and opened it. She went out of it, but she didn't shut it. She heard her talking to someone outside. Was that Colton.... or Reid?

He turned away in the other direction. He didn't want to see anyone, especially not his brothers. He didn't want to face just how badly he messed everything up. They would be stupid to keep him here. They should send him away before he brought another catastrophe down on their heads.

She came back into the room and shut the door with herself inside. He almost asked why she was still here, but he stopped when she walked around the other side of his bed.

She climbed onto it, stretched out on top of the bedspread, and cuddled next to his body. She laid her head on his chest right above his heart.

He stiffened against the flood of emotion tearing him apart. He couldn't stand this. She didn't try to convince him, but she didn't do as he asked by leaving, either.

She put her arms around him and sighed as she sank into the bed next to him. His heart beat in her ear and the same smell drifted into his nose. It brought back all the memories of their last night in the tree room.

She was the one then who didn't think she was good enough to join his Clan. Now it was his turn to feel the depth of that life-destroying shame.

He didn't want to smell her lying so close to him. He didn't want to feel her love drowning him through her arms and body. He didn't want to feel this crushing, aching love for her if he couldn't have her. What did he care about becoming Laird without this?

Her smell and her slow, relaxed breath drew him with that impossible power that he didn't understand. His head turned against his will and his nose and cheek touched her hair.

She nuzzled deeper into his chest and she hugged him tight. He felt her breathing through the blankets. She squirmed her body against him trying to get even closer to him.

He couldn't stand to be even this far away from her. One blanket's thickness was too much. He pressed his face into her hair and a tear dampened his cheek where it touched her. He couldn't send her away. He needed her too badly.

Chapter 24

Someone knocked on the door and Zoe sat up. "I better go see who it is. Everyone is in a dither about you."

Duncan raised one arm and ran his fingertips through her hair. "Ye dinnae have to stay here with me always, lass. I ken ye've more important things to do."

"Oh, you better believe I do. It's only by sheer luck that I was here when you woke up. Plenty of other people have been keeping an eye on you since you came home."

He tried to laugh it off. "Ye didnae watch day and night by my bedside?"

She made a face and didn't take the joke. "I tried, believe me. Your brothers wouldn't let me." She opened the door and three maids came in.

Louisa started talking the minute she crossed the threshold. "Aye, there ye are, lassie. Colton says for ye to come down to his room for the conference as soon as ye've eaten yer breakfast—and Jaimee says ye arenae to go near the place until ye've......Och! Duncan—ye're awake!"

"I think so, lassie," he replied.

Another maid walked in carrying what must have been Zoe's breakfast tray. The maid went to put it on the table and screamed in fright when she saw Duncan's eyes open. She dropped the tray on the carpet and the food went flying everywhere.

She sprang away pressing her hand to her heart. "Och, ye daft nupty!" Louisa chided. "Now look what ye've gone and done!"

"I'll help you." Zoe stepped forward and started picking up the broken dishes.

"No ye dinnae, lassie!" Louisa pushed her away. "Ye dinnae clean up like a common maid."

"I have to go to the conference then," Zoe replied. "Colton would have my head on a platter if I was late."

"Ye cannae!" Louisa countered. "He said ye werenae to come until ye've eaten breakfast."

"Then you can bring it to me in his room, can't you?" Zoe shot Duncan a wicked grin. "I can't wait here for you to bring me another one, can I?"

Louisa frowned and then smacked her lips. "I suppose not. On ye go, lassie. I'll bring it to ye."

Zoe bent over and kissed Duncan on the side of the head. "I'll see you later."

She left and all the light and joy went out of the room. Duncan couldn't even get interested in all the news Louisa was giving him about everyone and everything going on in Stronghold.

"And then Reid said we couldn't use magic to hunt as it might alert the Creightons. Liam said he could conceal his spells and Colton said...." She turned around and raised an eyebrow at Duncan. "Arenae ye listening to a word I've said, laddie?"

"I've heard ye." Duncan threw back the covers. His arms and legs and spine didn't want to cooperate, but he forced himself to put his feet on the floor. "Where's me tartan?"

"Ye cannae get up!" She started flapping around him like a mother bird. "Colton said...."

"If ye dinnae give me a tartan to wear, I'll get out of this bed and walk around Stronghold in naught."

She screamed and threw up her hands when he pushed the covers the rest of the way off, but he'd already spotted his tartan and belt across the room.

She and the other maids ran shrieking from the room when he got up and walked over to it stark naked. Good. That would get rid of them for a while.

He got dressed, but he didn't feel right without a shirt on. He could find some socks and shoes in the men's barracks later, but he couldn't go anywhere without a shirt.

He limped out of the room and spotted another bedroom standing open across the hall. A saber lay on the table. It was Reid's.

Duncan went into Reid's and Betty's bedroom and ransacked Reid's drawers until he found a shirt to steal. Duncan didn't want to take the time to look for a jacket. That could wait.

He tucked the shirt into his belt on his way down the corridor. It didn't take him long to locate the room Colton was using as his office as well as his bedroom.

Duncan pushed the door open and stood in the threshold listening to Colton, Reid, Jaimee, Lily, Echo, Liam, Edeena, and Zoe all discussing the situation.

"We can all forget about Kald," Colton was saying. "I dinnae want to hear that name for the rest of me life."

"We cannae get near the place either way," Reid replied. "We cannae even hunt now with so many Creightons patrolling the mountains and searching for us."

"We have to hunt," Jaimee countered. "Your Clan stashed food down here to last a long time, but it won't last forever. We have to hunt to stretch it as far as we can."

"I still say we should use concealment charms to get us in and out of Stronghold," Liam added. "Our spells have kept this place hidden all this time."

"We cannae take the chance one of the Creightons might happen upon us in the mountains," Edeena explained. "If we fought them, they would ken we were hiding out here. If we didnae see them, they could follow us back here."

"It's better than starving to death," Liam countered, "and there's always the chance we wouldn't have to either fight them *or* lead them back here. There's always the chance we could get away with it and they would never be the wiser."

"I ken what ye're saying, lad," Colton told him. "We arenae so desperate as all that—not yet. If our supplies run low, we'll do it yer way. Perhaps by then the Creightons will have slackened their patrols and we'll stand a better chance."

Liam shrugged. "Whatever you say. You're the boss."

"What about using some of the tunnels out of Icemeet?" Zoe pointed at something on Colton's desk. "Most of the fortress is still intact and there are two more tunnels going northeast to Easthollow. We could use them to get out and hunt in parts of the mountains where the Creightons aren't looking for us."

"We have no way of knowing whether the Creightons are looking for us near Easthollow or not," Jaimee countered.

"Then we could send scouts through to the east to find out," Zoe replied. "We wouldn't have to send hunters into the open to risk getting spotted or found out. We could just ask the Easthollow Buchanans if the Creightons are around. Then we would know our position before we get so desperate that we have to endanger our people to find out."

Colton nodded. "That's good thinking, lassie. We'll do that."

"We should make another trip out to get some more fliuralt," Jaimee added. "We should take advantage of this downtime to start arming for our next battle against the dragons."

"We cannae even hunt for food and ye want to go out and mine fliuralt?" Reid countered. "Ye need a lesson in priorities, I suppose."

"We have plenty of food," she told him. "We don't have enough fliuralt to build more siege machines and spears."

"We wouldn't have to put ourselves in danger to get fliuralt," Betty pointed out. "We could ask Easthollow to help us out."

"How do ye figure that, lassie?" Colton asked.

"Easthollow is already mining fliuralt and the Creightons don't think Easthollow is involved in the war—not yet. The Creightons probably wouldn't notice if the Easthollow Buchanans mined a little more fliuralt. We could bring it in through the tunnels so the Creightons never see us getting it."

"It sounds as though ye lassies have already come to a decision on this," Colton remarked.

Jaimee laughed. "I wouldn't go as far as that."

Colton started to say something else when Zoe spun around. Duncan couldn't tell what tipped her off. Maybe it was just his presence. She gasped when she saw him and hurried over to him. "What are you doing here?"

"Ye're all deciding the fate of the Clan." He limped into the room and approached the table. "Where else would I be?"

"Ye shouldnae be out of bed, lad," Reid told him, but he clapped Duncan on the shoulder anyway. "Ye're meant to be recovering."

"I couldnae recover on me back kenning ye lot were down here talking over the position." Duncan glanced over at Lily and Echo. "How are Grant and Elliot?"

Echo shrugged. "Pretty bad, but they'll make it."

Duncan looked down at the floor. "I'm sorry, lassies."

"Why?" Lily asked. "You saved their lives. The Laird would have killed all three of you if you hadn't concealed them."

Duncan shook his head. "He wouldnae have attacked at all but for me. He only attacked after I came back to Icemeet."

"That's a lie, lad," Colton rumbled. "The Laird didnae ken ye were in me room before he attacked Grant. The Laird had Grant in the air tearing him apart before he saw that ye were at Icemeet."

"And it's thanks to you that I was able to raise the alarm and get Elliot to come help you," Zoe added.

"I didnae bring Elliot to do ought but risk his life for no good reason."

"You call defending your homeland no good reason?" Liam snorted. "It sounds like you're the one in need of a lesson in priorities."

"No one blames you," Jaimee told Duncan. "The Laird would have destroyed Icemeet one way or the other."

"Well, ye should blame me." Duncan heard his voice rising against his will to control it. "All of this is because of me. Icemeet is gone because of me. Alastair and Bryce and Fletcher and all the rest are gone because of me."

"Icemeet isn't gone," Betty insisted. "It's still there and we can rebuild it as soon as the war is over...."

"The war winnae ever be over!" Duncan roared. "Dinnae any of ye understand that? The war winnae ever be over and I winnae ever defeat the Laird any more than ye will. I'm leaving. I'm going back to the mountain and ye can all...." He turned to the door. Zoe tried to hold him back, but he shook her off. "Leave me alone! I dinnae belong here."

He blasted out of the room, but he couldn't go anywhere. Leaving Stronghold would only put the Clan in even more danger. He was trapped here.

He set off walking somewhere, anywhere, and wound up heading up the tunnel toward Icemeet. Maybe Betty's words gave him an inkling of what he would find when he got there. He had to see just how bad it was.

He emerged in the corridor outside his father's old apartment. Duncan looked into it, but it looked nothing like Neill's apartment anymore. It had seen more use in the last few months than it had in the previous twenty years. It would never be used as a mausoleum for a hopeless old man again.

Colton had used it as a hospital for the wounded most recently. Blood stained the carpets. Neill never would have tolerated that in his lifetime. Times were changing and a new man was in charge.

Duncan wandered the familiar halls, but nothing felt the same. The old fortress echoed dark and cold and empty. The whole Clan was down at Stronghold. Zoe was down there with her four friends.

Duncan's memories of Icemeet couldn't bring the place back to life. What did Icemeet mean anyway? It was just an empty crypt without the Clan to give it life.

He climbed up to the parapet overlooking the rocks. He could remember dozens of people wasting their lives up there after losing their mates. Would Duncan become one of them if he left Stronghold now? Had he already mate-bonded with Zoe enough that his life would end once he left her?

He lost track of time haunting what was left of Icemeet, but in the end, the life of the Clan called him back. He headed down to the main hall and walked in on a scene of unimaginable chaos.

The tables and benches had been stacked against one wall. Ten washtubs had been set up on the other side with armed men carrying buckets of steaming hot water to and from the washtubs. More men stirred the contents while women and children carried their bedding down from bedrooms and barracks.

They dumped their laundry into the tubs while the men mixed them around with paddles and churned them to get them clean.

More men and women of all ages worked to raise the saturated laundry out of tubs of dirty water, pound the sheets, blankets, and bedspreads, and then put everything into new tubs of rinse water.

Big Ewan Buchanan and his comrades carried the tubs away to empty them, brought them back, and helped fill them.

Duncan stood back out of the way and watched. Everyone in the whole fortress got involved, either by bringing laundry down from the bedrooms or by helping wring the sheets out and hang them up to dry.

The five women of the Last Division strode back and forth giving orders to everyone. Zoe appeared out of the crowd directing Fergus to take a tub away and then to correct Callum's stirring technique.

Laughter, jokes, and complaints flew back and forth. Jaimee supervised teams of children running through the fortress making sure every family, couple, and single person stripped their beds and sent their bedding down to the hall for cleaning.

Betty and Connell had taken up a position at the far side of the hall. Callum lifted a wad of dripping sheets into an empty tub and carried it over to Betty. She worked some magical spell that raised a sheet into the air. Streams of water poured off it and then it dried itself instantly in a puff of steam.

She and Connell worked non-stop to dry all the laundry as it came off the assembly line. Then the two wizards handed each dry sheet off to more children who folded it and stacked it where it would be ready to take back upstairs.

Duncan watched the operation with a mixture of fascination and aching realization. He couldn't remember anything like this ever happening before in his lifetime. No one had ever organized his Clan as well as these five women.

Everyone listened to their instructions and he spotted Zoe joking around with Fergus and Callum. Her cheeks shone and her eyes twinkled. She was having fun. He couldn't take that away from her and why should he?

She was part of this Clan whether he wanted her to be or not. He didn't have to mate-bond with her to make it happen. If he somehow managed to avoid mate-bonding with her or broke the bond that had already formed, she would still be part of this Clan. It was already done and it couldn't be undone.

He gulped, but the ache in his throat wouldn't go away. He couldn't leave her. She was his mate. Lady Rhona might never be found, and even if she was, he wouldn't be able to bond with her. He had already bonded with Zoe and she had his heart in her back pocket. He had completely lost himself to her and he didn't care anymore.

She glanced over and saw him watching her from the doorway. She smiled and blushed even though he couldn't hear what she was saying to those nearest her.

Fergus followed her gaze, and when he saw Duncan, he said something to her that made her laugh and blush even harder. She pretended to look away and fought to bite back a grin. What was Fergus saying about her.... or about Duncan?

He cast another look around and spotted both Echo and Lily smiling at him. What in the world was he fighting this for? Everyone in the whole Clan already knew about him and Zoe. Every Buchanan alive could see what was going on between them. Why else would Colton give Duncan a couple's bedroom? It was as good as running the news up a flagpole.

Children started carrying the bundles of clean, dry, folded sheets back upstairs and Duncan wandered away. He'd seen enough and he was starting to get tired. Fatigue and pain were catching up with him. He shouldn't have been so quick to get out of bed.

Chapter 25

Duncan went back upstairs heading for his own room when he passed a different bedroom. He didn't notice it before probably because the door had been closed. It was open now and he spotted Elliot inside.

Duncan hesitated on the threshold. Elliot had stripped down to his kilt and scars crisscrossed his chest, shoulders, and back. He still hadn't recovered completely from the Laird's attack.

Connell was in there working on Elliot's leg. Elliot leaned back in an armchair with both hands braced on the chair arms. He grimaced in pain with sweat dripping from his face and hair.

Connell squatted in front of him doing something that Duncan couldn't see. Connell looked down at Elliot's ankle and then up at Elliot's face twisted in pain. "Is that better, laddie?"

Elliot collapsed back in the chair, shut his eyes, and let out a shaky sigh. "Aye. It's much better. Thank ye."

Duncan stepped forward and Connell saw him. Connel's eyes widened and he stood up. "Ye shouldnae be out of bed, laddie. Jaimee will thrash ye if she sees ye....and that's saying naught about Colton."

"Dinnae ye worry yerself about me, lad," Duncan replied. "They already ken I'm out of bed. Besides, I'm learning me own self that I shouldnae be up. I'm going back there now."

Elliot twisted around in the chair and stuck out his hand. "Dinnae ye go yet, lad!" He grabbed Duncan's hand and towed him into the room. "Dinnae leave me alone with these cutthroats."

Connell laughed, squeezed Elliot's shoulder, and walked away. "I can see how ye appreciate me efforts, laddie. Call me when ye cannae stand the pain any longer."

He walked out still chuckling and Elliot sank back in the chair. "I shouldnae have said that. I need him too much and he kens it as well as I do."

Duncan shot a critical glance at Elliot's scars. "I dinnae like the look of that. Connell should have healed ye by now."

Elliot shrugged. "He says the cuts are cursed so they take longer. He says it could be months or even years before they go away completely."

"Och, no!" Duncan exclaimed. "I didnae ken it would be like that. I'm sorry, Elliot. I shouldnae have...."

Elliot's head shot up. "Go on with ye, lad! It isnae ought of yer doing!"

"But I should have stopped it! I should have kept to the forest and...."

"Ye should have kept to the forest and let Grant die? Is that it? Ye saved all our lives. Do ye think I'd forget that in a hurry?"

Duncan pinched his lips shut. He didn't want anyone's appreciation for saving Grant and Elliot on the ice when Duncan was the one who got them there in the first place.

"Dinnae ye dare to blame yerself for this, lad!" Elliot scrutinized Duncan's twisted face and grimaced. "Ye *are* blaming yerself, ye blasted fool! Go on. Get out of here and dinnae ye come back until ye screw yer head on the right way round."

Elliot gave him another hard look, but he didn't look away. Duncan looked back down at Elliot's injuries. Maybe Elliot didn't get out of his chair because he couldn't. Maybe he never would be able to again.

Elliot waited for Duncan to leave, and when he didn't, Elliot spoke again in a much softer tone. "Do something useful with yerself while ye're at it, laddie. Do me a favor."

"What is it?"

"Go check on Grant. No one will let me see him and no one will tell me ought about how he's doing. I need a messenger boy."

Elliot pretended to scowl and then smirked at Duncan.

Duncan turned away. "All right. That's about all I'm good for anymore."

Elliot threw up his hands in exasperation. "Och, for God's sake....!"

Duncan didn't listen to anything more. He didn't want anyone trying to make him feel better. He walked out and stopped Louisa who happened to be passing. "Where's Grant Ritchie staying, lass?"

"Just down there.... next to Colton's room."

She hustled away and Duncan frowned after her. He had been in and out of this corridor at least six times this morning, but he never saw anything to indicate that Grant and Lily were staying in the room right next to Colton's.

In fact, the door had been closed every time Duncan had passed. The room had been so quiet that Duncan didn't think anyone was staying in that room at all.

He paused outside the room and listened. Was Grant dying in there…. or already dead? Lily didn't act like it at the meeting earlier. Now she was downstairs helping out with the laundry and having as much fun as the others. She wouldn't act like that if anything was wrong with Grant.

Duncan couldn't bring himself to open the door or even knock. He checked inside himself. Yes, he still had his magic. The Laird hadn't been able to strip him of it entirely—not permanently.

The Laird quashed it during the battle and Duncan had been too weak to use it for more than concealing himself and his brothers on the ice sheet.

Now it was coming back—slowly. He might not be as powerful as he was before, but he could still perform a few simple spells.

He cast his awareness into the room. His magical sight drifted through the door and he approached the bed. Grant lay stretched out on the pillows with his eyes closed. Several cursed scars similar to Elliot's crisscrossed Grant's face. They disfigured his good looks and made him look haggard and beaten, but at least he was alive.

Connell, Liam, and Betty couldn't heal those scars. The cuts would just have to heal on their own if they were going to heal at all. Betty had done her best and healed the internal damage to Grant's organs. Now he was asleep.

Why hadn't the Laird scarred Duncan like that? The answer came in a flash of insight. Duncan's magic protected him right up until the moment when he struck the ice sheet. The Laird hadn't been able to damage him as much as his brothers.

He gazed down at Grant and a pang gripped Duncan's heart. This was his brother—his oldest brother. Grant was older than Colton and Duncan had never known Grant at all.

Duncan got to know Elliot here and there. Duncan had never spent any time with Grant at all except on the ice sheet and none of them talked then.

Would Duncan ever get a chance to get to know Grant—ever? If this war went on the way it had been, Grant could die and Duncan would never know his own brother. He couldn't stand that.

He wasn't sure where he found the power to do it, but it came to him without even trying. He projected his magic into Grant's body and erased the scars from his face and body. Grant's skin became smooth and perfect again. He looked as handsome as ever, but he didn't wake up. He didn't feel a thing.

Duncan sent a second projection of his own memories down the corridor to Elliot's room. Duncan showed Elliot a mental picture of Grant's sleeping form along with the awareness that Grant was healed and asleep.

Duncan felt Elliot's wave of relief….and then Duncan projected his magic into Elliot, too. Duncan passed his magic through Elliot's body and erased all of Elliot's scars, the damage to his legs, and everything else that Connell hadn't been able to fix.

Elliot collapsed back in his chair with a deep sigh of relief and Duncan withdrew. At least he could still do something in this place. His presence wasn't as much of a millstone around his Clansmen's necks as he thought.

He started to pull back out of Grant's room and return to his body when Louisa came back. She halted right next to him and glared up at him. Her eyes flashed with suspicion. "What are ye doing here, laddie? Dinnae ye go bothering Grant. Betty says he's to sleep as long as he likes and dinnae disturb him."

Duncan snapped back into his body in a heartbeat. "I wasnae disturbing him, lassie. I was just standing here…."

"Ye're up to no good, I suppose. Dinnae make me go and fetch…."

"Louisa!" someone called down the corridor. "Did you get that ointment I asked for?"

Duncan and Louisa spun around to see Zoe and Lily coming up the corridor together. Lily didn't notice anything suspicious about Duncan standing outside her room. She lowered her voice to a murmur. "I better go check on him anyway. Will you be able to handle things downstairs, Zoe?"

"Sure. You go on."

"Ye dinnae need to check on him," Duncan blurted out. "He's grand."

He realized his mistake a second later when all three women rounded on him staring. "What do you mean?" Lily asked. "How do you know?"

"That's what I'd like to ken," Louisa snapped. "How do ye ken he's grand if ye havenae been in his room?"

Duncan flushed. "I havenae been in there. I was simply saying…."

Zoe stepped in and saved him from a miserable demise. "Go get the ointment, Louisa. I'll handle this."

She stood guard over Duncan until Louisa humphed and went off somewhere. Lily kept eyeing Duncan with her head on the side waiting for him to answer her question.

He couldn't look at her. His cheeks burned and he kept his eyes averted.

"Duncan?" she asked again. "Do you know something about Grant?"

He flushed even deeper, and when he opened his mouth to answer, he got another blinding flash of awareness of what was going on inside Grant and Lily's bedroom. He really needed to find a way to stop doing this.

Grant stirred in his sleep. His eyes opened and he stared up at the ceiling. Duncan became aware of Grant's thoughts. This was the first time he'd been awake since Liam and Zoe brought the three men back from the ice. He was wondering where Lily was.

Lily's eyes skewered Duncan while she waited for him to say something in his own defense. Then she whirled away on her heel and burst into the room.

She shut the door a second later and Duncan deliberately blocked himself from seeing or knowing what happened next.

He turned away and found Zoe studying him with a very different expression on her face. "Is there something you want to tell me about what's going on there?"

"Aye. Come with me, lass." He took her hand and took her back to his own room—the couple's room that Colton had given him—to them.

He led her inside and shut the door behind him. She jumped a foot in the air when he threw the lock.

"Is everything okay?" she asked.

"Everything's grand." He crossed to her side and turned her to face him.

She shuffled her feet and looked back and forth. She looked everywhere but at him. "What's going on?"

"We're mated."

She stared at him, all trace of uncertainty gone in a blink. He watched the parade of emotions racing across her features—confusion, wild hope, terror, resistance—he loved them all. He loved her more than anything for having them.

He raised his hands and cradled that exquisite face—the face of the woman he loved. "Ye ken it, lassie. It was done long ago—perhaps even before we met—perhaps even before we were born. Everyone here kens it. Ye and I ken it. There isnae any need to hold each other off any longer. Ye're one of this Clan whether we're mated or not, so we might as well go on and put it all behind us."

"What do you mean by 'put it all behind us'?" she asked.

He couldn't contain all the love in his heart for her. He drew her lips to his and kissed her. That kiss banished all doubt from his heart. She was the one—the only one.

"Put all doubt and question aside, lass," he murmured. "Dinnae ask any more questions. It's done and ye're mine and I'm yers. Ye winnae go back to the archers' barracks anymore. Ye'll stay here with me."

"What about....?"

He read the question before she even said it. He didn't need any magical connection to read her thoughts. He knew her too well to expect anything less. "I winnae marry any woman but ye, lassie. Let the country and the Lairdship and the future and yer home country all go. None of them holds any power over us. We're meant to be together and we will be no matter the outcome. Ye'll stay here with me Clan and kin and be one of us.... starting right now."

He pulled her into another kiss—a deeper one. She started to kiss him back in ways she never had before. She probed his lips feeling.... exploring.... testing....and then her whole being melted into him.

The wave started somewhere outside herself and swept inward toward her mouth. Her lips softened last and then her arms surrounded him. She fell against him and her body dissolved in one warm fluid ripple of delicious peace and ecstasy.

She tilted her head to one side and rested her ear on her own shoulder. Her mouth opened for him and her tongue met his in such a peaceful, blissful dance of union that he nearly exploded from the passion of it all.

Being apart from her even in the smallest degree—living under the cloud of uncertainty of whether they would ever be together—he suffered and struggled under that burden for too long.

Now it lifted off his shoulders with so much bliss and harmony that he didn't know what to do with her first. He wanted to attack her and devour her. At the same time, he wanted to crawl into bed with her the way they did in the tree room. He wanted to curl up with her and just be with her. He didn't need anything more.

She straightened up long before he satisfied himself with tasting her wonderful delights. Her eyes shone with a light he'd never seen. Was it happiness? "Are you sure about this?"

"Aye." He burst into a huge smile and traced his fingertips down her cheeks. "I'm sure. Are ye?"

She nodded and then she burst into the most brilliant smile imaginable. All the emotions he'd just seen warring in her—the confusion, the terror, the resistance—they were all gone.

Even the wild hope was gone. She didn't need to hope anymore because the question that made her hope no longer bothered her. She already knew the answer.

"So...." He surveyed the room. "What would you like to do first?"

She burst out laughing—the first real unbridled laugh of glee and merriment that he'd ever heard from her. God, he had so many miles to go to enjoy every shade and mood of her!

She giggled like a schoolgirl and blushed so delightfully that his heart spasmed. She was beyond beautiful.

Her eyes glinted with wicked mischief. She opened her mouth to answer and he saw a joke forming on the tip of her tongue when, at that moment, a loud knock banged on their bedroom door.

Duncan and Zoe jumped. What was that? Were the Creightons attacking again?

He went over to the door, opened it, and Louisa charged inside. "What did ye do, wee laddie Duncan?" she hissed. "What did ye do to Grant and Elliot? If ye did anything to them, I swear I'll...."

"Louisa!" Echo yelled from farther up the corridor.

Louisa whipped around and stared toward the open threshold. Then she shot Duncan one last menacing glare and raced out of the room.

Duncan resisted the urge to use his magic to find out what was going on out there. He didn't need to know. He could well imagine the reaction when Lily and Echo realized that Grant and Elliot were just fine now.

Elliot would tell everyone that Duncan was the one who did it. Duncan didn't want to deal with that right now.... or ever.

He shut the door, locked it again, and made himself a solemn promise not to open it again until morning—barring a real Creighton invasion, of course.

Zoe gave him one of her strange, searching looks. "Did you do something to Grant and Elliot?"

"Me? Of course not. What would I do to them?"

"Why is Louisa saying that you did?"

"I'm sure I dinnae ken ought about that." He took her hand. "Now where were we?"

She laughed again and he led her over to the bed. She pretended to drag her feet. "Shouldn't I tell Edeena or someone that I'm moving up here instead of staying in the archers' barracks?"

"Not a bit of it, lassie. They all ken ye're staying here."

She looked around her without seeing anything. "So you're saying.... everyone already knows....as in.... *everyone*?"

"Aye. Why do ye think Colton put us in this room?"

"He put *you* in this room. You're his brother and you're the one who's supposed to be leading us all."

Now it was his turn to laugh. "I'm not leading anything or anyone, lassie, and believe me when I tell ye that Colton wouldnae hesitate to put me in the barracks with the rest if I wasnae mated to ye."

"Really?"

"Aye." He couldn't stop laughing. "He wouldnae give me any special treatment for being his brother. Look at Grant and Elliot. They're in their own rooms with their wives."

"Yeah. So?"

"Do ye see Colton treating us any differently? Do ye see anyone treating us any differently—anyone at all?"

She blinked. "I guess not."

"They all ken, lass. Ye ken they do."

She looked away. "Yeah. I know."

He sat down on the bed. "We dinnae have to do ought ye dinnae want to. It's all done."

She finally looked down into his eyes. "*All* of it? There's no.... you know...."

"No what?"

She burst out laughing and blushed again. "No ritual or anything?"

"This is the ritual." He pulled her between his knees and raised his mouth to kiss her. She bent down to return his kiss and her hair grazed his cheeks. Her smell enveloped him and now he could give himself to it with all his heart and soul. He didn't have to hold himself back. That smell made him feel whole in so many ways.

She straightened up and her eyes became bright again. "So.... what do *you* want to do first?"

He climbed onto the bed and scooted back to the pile of pillows. He reclined on it and held out his arms to her. "Come to me, lass."

She beamed at him, kicked off her shoes, and climbed up next to him. She laid her precious body against his side, put her arms around him, and rested her head on his chest.

He let out a matchless sigh of so much relief deeper and more heartfelt than any he could remember. She was here and she was all his. He could let go of everything else now that he knew he had her.

Chapter 26

Duncan floated in the delectable rapture of Zoe's kisses. Her naked body seethed over his in a blanket of satin delight. Every breath coming into his nostrils smelled of her. It reconfigured his being at a subatomic level.

He sailed in a vast sea of sensation that covered every inch of his skin. It permeated his mind and rewrote the structure of who he was.

His body moved in time with hers as they taught each other new ways of finding and discovering each other. His body fit together with hers in magical ways—new magic that had nothing to do with him being a wizard.

His hands explored all the silky corners of her, all the crevices and dark mysteries that made her so deliciously herself. He could keep exploring all his life and never lose interest.

Her eyes delved deep into his being. Was she finding new mysteries in him?

She sat up straddling him and her beauty intoxicated his mind almost as much as her body intoxicated his senses. Her rhythm carried him far away to remote dimensions awash with pleasure and connection beyond words.

He followed her beat getting faster and faster. Mesmerized astonishment and shocked passion transfigured her face into a revelation. He couldn't look away even as he felt himself getting swept into a tidal wave of meaning and cosmic understanding.

Touching her didn't satisfy him anymore. He had to become one with her on the inside. He had to pour his heart and soul into her and erase all the lines holding them apart.

He felt himself losing control and an attack of fear gripped him. He first tried to hold himself back and then the dam burst. He exploded inside her and the spasms racking her magnificent body wrung the last juices from him.

The instant he climaxed, he blinked once and zapped away from his room at Stronghold. He didn't recognize where he was except that he was in a large throne room decorated with tapestries, shields, and coats of arms hanging from the walls.

Tall windows behind the throne gave a view across the Boundless toward the planes in front of Icemeet, but Duncan didn't get a chance to look at any of that.

The Laird stood in front of the throne grimacing at Duncan with a mixture of triumph and bloodthirsty menace. He had his back to the windows and a catastrophic blast erupted from the Laird's chest.

Duncan didn't have time to evade it. It struck him square in the torso and would have flattened him on the spot, but it just bounced off instead. He stumbled a step back and caught his balance.

His reaction startled both him and the Laird so much that neither of them did anything for a second. They stared at each other while Duncan's mind raced. What just happened? Why didn't the Laird's assault do what it was supposed to do?

Duncan had already been weakened during the last battle and during his ordeal on the ice. He shouldn't have been able to defend himself at all. He had never been able to counter the Laird's power before. The Laird had always been able to stop Duncan from doing anything in his own defense.

The Laird seemed to come to the same conclusion at the same instant. He strode forward firing one shockwave after another. He didn't raise his hands now. He didn't have to. Magical explosions punched through the air and smashed Duncan all over, but they didn't harm him. In fact, they didn't have any effect at all.

Duncan stood his ground taking hit after hit. They pounded his chest, his head, his legs—everywhere. He shuddered under the rain of impacts, but they couldn't even knock him over.

He felt the Laird change tack again. The Laird raised both hands and fired ten magical filaments from his fingertips. They whipped through the air and lashed around Duncan trying to rip him off the ground.

Duncan's feet remained rooted to the floor. If the Laird's fibers ever came close to unseating him, he only had to think about it to sink those roots even deeper. He barely had to try at all.

The Laird's expression changed and all trace of triumph and confidence drained from his ghastly countenance. He advanced down the steps to the floor in front of Duncan and unloaded with everything he had.

Duncan didn't really have to look at the Laird to understand what his grandfather was trying to do. The Laird bombarded him with dozens of spells getting stronger and stronger. Duncan's legs wobbled. How much longer could he keep this up before the Laird did something that Duncan wouldn't be able to withstand?

Without warning, without thinking about it first, Duncan slashed the tendrils binding him. He waved his hand to one side and they snapped. He shot out a hand and punched out in the air.

He fired a blast of his own that struck the Laird full force, but the old man barely noticed it. It puffed back the old man's hair in a breath of wind and then the Laird opened up with his most vicious barrage yet.

Thunderous blasts hammered Duncan all over. He definitely felt those. Several punched him in the face and he tasted blood. Blows pounded his body and he stumbled back several steps. Another hit like that would knock him over and he couldn't let that happen.

He blinked again and snapped back to his room at Stronghold. He lay on his back with Zoe next to him. Her bare arm crossed his chest and her hair covered her sleeping face on the pillow next to him.

Her slow, deep breathing never changed. Did she ever realize he had been gone?

He stared up at the ceiling for a long time thinking over what just happened. He didn't transport himself to the Laird's audience hall at Tyrekirk. Duncan would never have chosen now of all times to go there.

He definitely transported himself back here, though. The Laird must have taken him to Tyrekirk to kill him. He wouldn't let Duncan leave if the Laird could do anything to stop him.

What changed? How did the Laird so thoroughly overpower Duncan in all their previous encounters but not now? How did Duncan resist the Laird even in a weakened condition?

The Laird must have known that Duncan was weak. The Laird must have chosen now to carry out this attack for exactly that reason.

A thousand thoughts crowded Duncan's mind. He couldn't sort through them fast enough. If the Laird took Duncan from Stronghold, the Laird must know where the Buchanans were hiding. All of Betty's, Liam's, and Connel's protective spells meant nothing, so why hadn't the Creightons attacked yet?

Duncan already knew the answer to that. None of the Buchanans meant anything to the Laird. He only cared about getting rid of Duncan. Once he did that, none of the others would be able to stop him from killing Grant, Elliot, and any other Buchanans foolhardy enough to stand up to him.

The Laird must have believed, as Duncan did, that Duncan couldn't win. Duncan believed the same thing until just a few minutes ago.

What if he'd been wrong about all of that? What if the Last Division was right about him? What if he could defeat the Laird and end the war?

His heart surged at the thought and then he remembered. Becoming Laird meant marrying Lady Rhona.

What if he could end the war without becoming Laird and without marrying Lady Rhona? What if someone else could become Laird? Grant would make a much better Laird anyway. He'd already been doing it for weeks.

No, that would never work. The Buchanans wouldn't stand another Creighton on the throne. That was the whole point of the war—to put a hybrid of both Clans into power in the Laird's place.

What changed? He kept coming back to that one question. What happened to give him the power to defend himself against the Laird?

He could only think of one thing: Zoe. He mated with her at last—mated for real. They mated in body and blood. The bond had been sealed for all time.

Even Duncan felt the difference. He felt calmer, more secure in himself. He didn't feel as afraid to confront the Laird, but his experience in the audience hall had nothing to do with that. His strength came from her.

Chapter 27

Z oe rolled over, sat up, ran her fingers through her hair, and looked around. She always had to take a few moments every time she woke up to figure out where she was. She'd been moving from room to room so much lately that she never woke up in the same place twice.

She wouldn't have recognized the room at all if Duncan hadn't been lying next to her. He lay on his back and blinked up at her with his deep black eyes. He watched her come to her senses while his warm hand stroked up and down her arm.

"Good morning, lassie," he murmured.

"Good morning." She sighed and flopped down. "I should probably get up and go downstairs. I told Jaimee I'd help her get the scouts ready to go to Easthollow."

Duncan didn't say anything. He watched her with a strange expression on his face. His reaction unsettled her. She didn't know what to do so she scooted toward him and put her arm over his chest. She snuggled into him and kissed his shoulder.

He still didn't say anything. His fingers played absently with her hair, but he didn't try to get closer to her. He acted so differently from yesterday that she started to worry that something was wrong.

She leaned back to study him. "Are you okay?"

"Aye," he replied.

That didn't leave much of an opening for conversation. What should she say back? "Do you have any plans today?"

He shrugged, wriggled out from under her, and sat up on the edge of the bed. He put his feet on the floor, picked up his tartan from the place where he'd dropped it, and started straightening it out like he might be getting ready to put it on.

He still didn't answer. He didn't react at all when she touched his bare back.

She tried again. "Duncan? What are you going to do today?"

"I dinnae ken. I'll have to think about it."

Those words fell into a black pit of nothing and they didn't come out. Why wouldn't he even talk to her? He had his back to her and he didn't even try to look at her.

She couldn't stay in the same room with him like this. She jumped out of bed, pulled on her clothes, and raced outside before she even finished buttoning her jacket.

She headed for the stairs and saw people moving around down in the corridors and caverns. The energy and purpose from yesterday's laundry session came back to her and she stood up a little straighter.

This was her Clan. She knew that now. Whatever was going on with Duncan couldn't change that. She would just move back down to the archers' barracks. They would be happy to have her and none of them ever turned their backs on her.

She went into the dining hall and found her four friends sitting together. She sat down next to Echo and pulled the porridge pot toward her. "What's today's excitement? Are we still sending out the Easthollow scouts?"

Jaimee smirked at her. "Are you sure you don't have better things to do than help us out?"

"What do you mean?" Zoe asked.

"Oh, come on!" Betty chided. "You and Duncan."

Zoe made a face to cover up her wince of pain. "I don't know what you're talking about."

"You guys should have stayed in your room for a week," Lily added. "That's the only honeymoon you're gonna get around here."

Jaimee laughed. "Colton and I didn't even get that. We were right back out in the middle of a battle the next morning."

"You and me both," Betty added. "It was the best honeymoon ever."

The others laughed, but Zoe didn't join in. "Lucky you."

"What's wrong?" Echo asked. "Go back upstairs and enjoy yourself while it lasts."

Zoe bent over her bowl and stirred her spoon through her porridge. She saw out of the corner of her eye that her friends were exchanging confused glances. She didn't want to talk about Duncan. "What do we need to do to prepare the scouts?"

Jaimee gasped. "What is the matter with you? You should be on cloud nine after mating with Duncan. He's a great guy and you're acting like you're on your way to your own funeral."

"Can we talk about something other than Duncan?"

"No, we can't," Betty countered. "He's our brother-in-law and we care as much about him as we do about you. After what Echo went through with him in the forest, she has a right to know what's going on and Lily has been involved in putting Duncan on the throne. Now 'fess up. What's the problem?"

Zoe shrugged and wound up flinching again. She tried to look away and then stared down into her food again. Duncan was the last thing in the world she wanted to think about right now. "I don't know what the problem is. We spent the night together last night and now he's...."

"He's what?" Lily asked after a long silence.

"I don't know. He's just acting weird. He wouldn't talk to me this morning."

Jaimee frowned. "That is weird, especially after the way he was acting yesterday."

"Remember how he was at the conference?" Echo recalled. "He could barely walk and he came down there to stick his nose in Clan business. He wanted to get involved."

"And don't forget what he did for Grant and Elliot," Lily added. "That isn't the behavior of someone who wants to distance himself from his Clan's activities."

"Distancing himself from his Clan isn't the same as distancing himself from me." Zoe had to gulp, and even then, her voice cracked. "I guess he just changed his mind."

"Buchanans don't change their minds," Betty told her. "He's your mate no matter what."

"Yeah," Jaimee replied. "I'm sure there's some logical explanation for the way he's acting."

"He has a lot on his mind," Lily pointed out. "The whole war hinges on him defeating the Laird. That's a lot of pressure for one man to carry."

Echo nodded. "Maybe he's worried that taking on the Laird will put you in too much danger. Maybe he didn't realize how much danger he was putting you in until after he mated with you. Maybe he just needs time to think about how he's going to deal with all that."

"The truth is that none of us knows what he's thinking about," Betty added. "Why don't you talk to him?"

"I already tried. I'm not going to ask him again just so he can ignore me." Zoe threw her spoon into her bowl. She couldn't eat anything now. "Can we not talk about Duncan anymore? Can you just give me something to do to take my mind off it?"

"All right," Jaimee replied. "You can come with us and get the Easthollow scouts ready to go."

"Just remember what we said before," Betty chimed in. "Buchanans don't change their minds. Whatever is bothering him, he isn't questioning whether he belongs to you. If you spent the night together, it's a done deal. He couldn't go back on that even if he wanted to."

"And before you ask, he doesn't want to," Jaimee finished. "He loves you and you love him. The rest is just details."

The others nodded, but none of their assurance could quiet the nagging voices in her head. How did she really know that Duncan loved her? A wizard as powerful as he was might be able to find a way to break the mating bond. How should she know?

She felt the others studying her. She couldn't look any of them in the eye. None of them had to worry about their relationships going south, especially Jaimee and Betty. They already knew where they belonged. They never had to question Colton's or Reid's dedication to their relationships.

Jaimee stood up and waved Zoe to follow her. "Come on. Let's go meet up with the scouts and check their gear. We might need to get some stuff from Icemeet and we need to check the tunnels from Icemeet to Easthollow anyway."

Zoe left her bowl on the table. She should have taken it to the kitchen to be washed, but she didn't want to go any deeper into Stronghold. She wanted to get the hell out of here so she wouldn't see Duncan again.

She and Jaimee went out into the foyer and Zoe skidded to a halt when she spotted Duncan on the landing overhead. He wasn't looking at her, though. He stared off into space and didn't see anyone around him. He acted totally oblivious to the activity going on below him.

Jaimee and Zoe headed for the stairs and her face burned. She would have to walk right past Duncan to go upstairs.

The two women passed Colton, Reid, Liam, and Fergus all talking with their heads together near another passage on the other side of the cavern. Duncan didn't see them, either. What was wrong with him?

Jaimee started up the stairs. That left Zoe with no choice but to follow. She gritted her teeth and resolved to walk right past him without acknowledging him at all. If he wouldn't stoop to talking to her, she wouldn't talk to him, either.

Jesus, did it really come to this? Was she really going to ignore him like a teenager after a one-night stand?

Jaimee reached the landing and said, "Good morning, Duncan." He didn't hear her. He rested his elbows on the railing and gazed down at the floor, but he still didn't seem to notice anything going on down there.

He didn't notice Zoe, either. She walked past him without saying anything and he didn't look up.

"Wow!" Jaimee breathed when the two women started down the corridor. "He's really out of it."

Zoe didn't say anything. Her throat hurt and she didn't trust herself to speak. What a fool she was to buy into this whole mating-for-life thing. She never should have let her guard down with him.

Whatever. She didn't need him. She could still be a part of this Clan without him. She could help people as easily here as she did at Ironforge. In a way, the Last Division was still carrying on their original mission. They were just doing it here instead of in Detroit.

Jaimee turned off into a different storeroom. Clan Buchanan had dozens of these stashed all over the mountain. They had socked away decades worth of food, firewood, weapons, clothes, bedding, and everything else they needed to survive in this cavern for many years.

Four archers and four armed Clansmen waited there for Jaimee and Zoe to show up. They all laughed and lounged around doing very little until the two women showed up.

They made no effort at all to straighten up when Jaimee walked in. "What's all this about supplying us, lassie?" Big Ewan Buchanan asked. "We dinnae need much to go through the tunnel to Easthollow. We've been a hundred times already and it's a straight run."

"You need to take some of those wheeled carts so you can bring back some fliuralt." Jaimee went over to one of the nearby crates and messed with something inside.

"Do we have to?" Duncan's cousin Adaira asked. "We're meant to be scouting, not plowing the fields."

The others all laughed and Jaimee joined in. "Okay. You don't have to take the carts. You can carry the fliuralt back in your arms. I don't care. Just make sure you bring back enough to repair the siege engines, forge about a hundred spears for the crossbows, and cast another hundred sabers and as many dirks. Do you think you can carry all that?"

The scouting party stared at her in horror and Zoe bit back a smirk. Jaimee really had these people wrapped around her little finger. Good old Snowflake. She always knew how to command people.

Adaira sank down on a wooden chest with a groan. "Dear God! Are we scouts or mules?"

"How do we ken Easthollow even has fliuralt to spare?" another man asked.

"They do," one of the archers muttered. "They'll have plenty, I'm sure."

Jaimee scrutinized each scout in turn. "You'll all need food and water, too."

"Whatever for?" Ewan protested. "It's a day's travel through the tunnels and our Clan will feed us when we get there."

Jaimee shrugged again. "I just wouldn't want you to find yourselves unprepared in case you run into the Creightons somewhere along the way."

"The Creightons cannac get to us in the tunnels," the second archer pointed out. "We winnae be going outside the whole trip."

"What will you do if the Creightons have attacked Easthollow, too?" Jaimee asked. "What if Easthollow is at war against the Creightons the same way we are and we've all been too busy to hear about it? What if you're all sitting around the table feasting and stuffing your faces and the Creightons attack and you get swept up in the battle? What if you get separated from your Clansmen with no food or water?"

Ewan passed his hand across his eyes. "Och! Ye drive a hard bargain, lassie!"

Jaimee clapped him on the back and beamed up at him in obvious affection. "Be grateful you're going at all instead of being stuck down here washing the bedsheets."

"She's right." Adaira got to her feet. "I cannae stand hanging about mopping the floors. Let's get our supplies and go."

Jaimee elbowed Zoe and grinned. "Let's go check the carts while they get their gear. Then we can go up to Icemeet and see if Gavin left any scrap fliuralt lying around that we can use."

The two women went out into the corridor and headed for the tunnel leading back to Icemeet. They entered the long, low, dark passage with the wheeled carts lined against one chiseled wall.

"You really know how to work these people, don't you?" Zoe remarked. "You speak their language."

Jaimee laughed. "You get used to the way they think after a while. They're strong people. You have to make them see how doing things a certain way works in their favor. Trying to tell them what to do doesn't work. Trust me."

Zoe started to join in her friend's laughter, but all her happiness died in a blink when she spotted Duncan coming toward her. He strode up the passage and he wasn't staring into space anymore.

His dark eyes bored into her soul as he looked right at her. He gave her a deep, searching look and then walked right past her. He headed up the tunnel toward Icemeet and vanished into the dark.

Her heart plummeted into her shoes and all her energy evaporated. She didn't feel like doing anything.

She looked away and found Jaimee gaping at her with her eyes hanging out of their sockets. Zoe couldn't stand that, especially when the scouts came back, got their carts, and started heading toward Icemeet, too.

"I'll see you later," Zoe muttered to Jaimee. "I gotta get out of here."

She took off back downstairs. She didn't want to be anywhere near Icemeet now that she knew Duncan was going there.

Chapter 28

Duncan looked up when the door to Colton's room opened and Zoe walked in with Betty and Echo. He sat in an armchair by Colton's bed and lowered his eyes back down at the map of Kald spread out on his knees.

The three women collected all the papers from Colton's desk and pulled the tables together to make one large table. They covered it with a tablecloth and Duncan heard Echo and Betty talking while they set the table.

Colton had told Duncan hours ago that the five couples would gather to have supper together here, but Colton had been too busy to talk to Duncan about anything—not that Duncan wanted to.

He was grateful when Colton had to leave. Duncan had been free to spend all day studying this map and thinking everything over.

He had made sure to avoid Zoe. He didn't want to give her false hope until he knew for sure that his theory was right. He didn't want to saddle her with any pressure about increasing his power to fight the Laird.

Duncan didn't want to give himself false hope, either. He needed to test his theory before he told anyone about it. He didn't trust himself not to blurt out the whole crazy idea if he went near her.

Reid startled him out of his thoughts by grabbing Duncan's shoulder. "Keeping yer nose to the grindstone, I see, laddie. What is it this time?" He snatched the map away and scowled at it. "What are ye studying Kald for? None of us is going back there for a good long while."

Duncan let the matter drop and rose to his feet. "I was just looking and thinking. None of us has been inside Tyrekirk before...."

"Ye're daft! Grant and Lily have been living there for months and Grant and Elliot were born and raised there. They can tell ye much more about the place than this map."

Reid folded the map and put it back on the stack of Colton's papers. Duncan didn't argue the point. He definitely didn't want to discuss Tyrekirk with Grant and Elliot. That would tip everyone off that he was planning something.

What was he planning, anyway? He couldn't go to Tyrekirk. He wouldn't be able to set foot in Kald without throwing his life away.

That wasn't strictly true, though, was it? He set foot in Tyrekirk last night and he did a lot more than get out with his life. He got out with his life at his own time and choosing. He escaped from the Laird, but that did nothing to set his mind at ease.

What if mating with Zoe did a lot more than just give him the strength to fight the Laird? What if mating with Zoe drew the Laird's attention to both of them? What if mating with Zoe put her in as much danger as it put Duncan?

He wouldn't be able to live with himself if he put her in danger, or worse, if she got hurt or killed because of him.

"Come on over here, laddie!" Colton called out from the table. "Dinnae think we'll give ye a plate to eat over there."

The others laughed. That was Duncan's cue to join the rest of the group, but he didn't really feel like it. He wanted to take Zoe back to his room and spend the night with her again. He wanted to see if the Laird attacked at the point of climax the way he did last night.

The other four couples sat down together and Zoe pulled out her chair next to Duncan's. The other men pulled out their mate's chairs for them. Duncan realized his mistake too late, but Zoe was already sitting down.

Duncan tried in vain to wrestle his mind back to the present. He shouldn't be so preoccupied. He was here to have dinner with his brothers and their wives, not to plan an assault on Tyrekirk that would probably never happen.

He couldn't even get all that excited when he remembered that every man at this table was his brother—Colton and Reid on one side, Grant and Elliot on the other.

Duncan looked down at his plate and floundered in a jumble of conflicting emotions. He was the lynchpin between both Clans. He was the one thing everyone in this room had in common. He was the nexus point where everything and everyone came together. They were all here because of him. They believed in him. They all thought he was something he wasn't.

What a weak lynchpin he turned out to be. Neither Clan stood a chance if they depended on him to solve their problems.

Dishes and cutlery clinked around the table and the others started talking and laughing. Colton served everyone and they talked while they passed plates and platters back and forth.

Duncan kept his eyes down and went through the mechanics of putting the food in his mouth. He could just imagine the others studying him and waiting for him to say something.

They must be waiting for him to step in and lead them. God, what a nightmare of a joke that would be! How could Duncan take the lead from Colton? Duncan had followed Colton all his life. He should be taking orders from Colton instead of Colton taking orders from him.

Even Reid would be better to lead the Clan than Duncan. Duncan was nothing. He was the wild younger brother that no one expected anything from.

He had to stay present just enough to pass the things people asked him for. Once, he passed something down the table and accidentally brushed Zoe's hand when her fingertips touched his.

She yanked her hand away so hard that she almost dropped the dish. It would have made an enormous mess if Duncan hadn't still been holding onto it.

No one noticed. No one seemed to realize the colossal elephant in the room—or the herd of elephants sitting in the middle of the supper table.

After a torturous eternity, Colton finally pushed back his chair, picked up his glass, and started talking to Grant and Elliot about Tyrekirk. The Ritchie brothers described parts of the castle that Colton and Reid hadn't seen in their brief and fateful visits there.

Duncan didn't want to listen to that, either. Grant and Elliot knew the positions of all the servants' quarters, the routines of all the household retainers, and the names and personalities of all the Laird's most loyal retainers.

None of that gave Duncan any information he needed to defeat the Laird—if he could defeat the Laird at all. Duncan only needed one key piece of intelligence and he could only get it from one person.

The five women got up and started clearing the table. Zoe took a stack of plates to the kitchen while the others ferried platters and cutlery away. Duncan took the opening to leave Colton's room.

Duncan went over to his brother and clapped Colton on the shoulder. "I'm off to bed. I'll see ye lads in the morning."

"Stay, lad," Reid told him. "We need ye to help us plan what to do next."

"Not tonight." Duncan pretended to rumple Reid's hair. "Ye laddies dinnae stay up too late or I'll have to take the horsewhip to ye."

He turned to leave. He got halfway to the door when Elliot pushed back his chair. He strode over to Duncan. "Laddie.... if ye've a moment.... I'd like to speak to ye—just ye and me."

Duncan saw at a glance what Elliot wanted. He wanted to talk about Duncan saving Elliot from the Laird.... or any of the other details of their broken association. Elliot wanted Duncan to be his brother the same way Grant was. He wanted the three of them to be as close as Duncan was with Colton and Reid.

Elliot's expression wrung Duncan's heart. Duncan would give anything to be that close to Grant and Elliot, but now wasn't the time. None of that would happen with the Laird's threat hanging over all their heads.

He did his best to smile warmly enough to soften Elliot's pained countenance. "Aye, we will. Ye come and find me in the morning and we'll talk."

Duncan had to summon all his resolve to give Elliot a hug and then left the room. Getting away from the others gave him a rush of relief. Now he had to finish the business that started last night.

He crossed the landing and waited in one of the other passages. Zoe came back a few moments later and he stepped out into the open where she could see him.

She froze at the sight of him and he suffered another pang when he recognized that she was scared of him. He took one more step nearer and she retreated instinctively to keep a safe distance from him.

He didn't dare to go any closer. He held out his hand. "Come to me, lassie."

"Why should I?" she demanded. "You haven't even looked at me all day."

"I've had a few things on me mind. Ye cannae blame me for being preoccupied with all this."

"All of what?" She jutted her chin at him and braced herself as though she thought he might attack her. "What are you so preoccupied with that you couldn't even look at me?"

He furrowed his brow trying to understand why she was acting so defensive. Then he shrugged. "I've been preoccupied with ye, lassie. Is that what ye'd like me to say—that I havenae been able to think of ought else but ye all day?"

"Really? That's funny because I've been right here all day. I've been right in front of you and you ignored me."

"Ignored ye!" he exclaimed. "I didnae...."

"Did you even see me today? Did you see me even once today?"

He frowned and opened his mouth to argue back when he realized with a lurch that she was right. He couldn't remember seeing her once all day until she came into Colton's room for supper. Had he been so wrapped up in his own thoughts that he didn't even notice her right in front of him?

His shoulders sagged. "I'm sorry for that, lassie, but I really was thinking of ye all day. I was thinking about.... last night....and what it means for all this.... *all* of this."

He waved down at the foyer at all the Clansmen and maids and people crowded into Stronghold.

He crossed the last piece of floor separating him from her and another surge of blessed relief drained all the doubt and worry from his being. He slipped his hand into hers and felt her melt at his touch.

"We're mated now, lassie," he breathed in her ear. "Do ye think I could walk out on that after what we shared last night?"

She didn't answer, but something still held her apart from him. He straightened up enough to look into her eyes. He read his destiny written there and he drew her farther down the hall toward their room.

He tugged her arm to draw her inside, but she pulled to a halt on the threshold. She took one look into the room and tears streaked down her cheeks. She dragged her hand out of his grasp and turned away. "I can't, Duncan. I'm sorry."

"What do ye mean, lassie?" he asked. "We're mated now."

She shook her head. "You don't love me. I don't know if you ever did. I don't know what you were doing last night, but we aren't mated."

He gaped at her in mounting horror. "Of course we are, lassie. How can ye think I dinnae love ye? How can ye begin to think that? It isnae possible—not for me, at least. We're mated for life."

"How come you treated me so coldly today, then? How could you turn your back on me like that? What was I supposed to think?"

His jaw dropped. "I would never turn me back on ye, lassie!"

"You did it today! Jaimee and Betty seem to think doing it once is all it takes for one of your people to mate for life. They say that's how it happened with them, but after today...."

"It *is* all it takes, lass." He heard his voice trembling. How did all his hopes go so horribly, disastrously wrong so quickly?

"How do you explain your behavior today, then?" She raised her tear-streaked face to his. God, she never looked so beautiful! She was crying because she loved him. She wanted him more than anything and she thought she had lost him.

He held out his arms to embrace her, but she shoved him away. Was this what she had been feeling all day—rejected, abandoned, gutted by his coldness?

He felt sick that she would push him away like that. Her eyes became hard and unforgiving. She held him at arm's length and stared into his eyes while she waited for him to explain himself.

He fidgeted trying to decide what to do or say. He couldn't tell her about his theory. That would only make her feel even more used and manipulated.

What woman would want to hear that a man wanted to mate with her to increase his power? Even thinking that sounded too low to say out loud.

She finally shook her head and turned away again. "I thought so. I'll go find Liam and tell him to send me back home."

"No, lass!" He lunged for her and tried to hold her back. "Ye cannae leave me. I cannae live without ye!"

"You lived without me just fine today. I'm sure you'll figure something out. I can't stay here when all the others are so happy."

She burst into loud sobs, tore out of his grasp, and raced away into the fortress. He stared after her totally stunned. He couldn't move or even think. He couldn't have found the one key to defeating the Laird only to lose her.

He kicked himself for even thinking that. What did he care about defeating the Laird? He'd found his life's mate—the other half of his soul—and now she was leaving him. He would never see her again. Losing her would wreck him. It would end him and leave him worse than dead.

This gnawing misery in his heart burned a hole in his guts, but he couldn't even rally the energy to go after her. He would have to explain his theory to her if he did go after her.

Mating with her gave him the power to win this war, but it also put a target on her back and put her life in jeopardy. He would have to tell her all of that if he gave her any explanation at all. No woman wanted to hear that and Duncan sure as blazes didn't want to be the man to tell her.

He turned around, but the sight of their shared bedroom only made him feel worse. That room should have been his crowning glory—the ultimate marker that he was a married man in his Clan now.

He had achieved the same status as Colton and Reid. Duncan was now their equal in running this Clan. He might even have surpassed them. He had become something more than Clan Chief, but he didn't even know what that was. It was nothing he wanted to be.

He pulled the bedroom door shut with himself on the outside in the passage. He didn't want to go in there ever again, but he stopped when he got back to the stairs. Where should he go?

He didn't want to be around other people. He didn't want to be anywhere except where Zoe was. Unstoppable magnetic power dragged him toward her through the walls. He didn't have to think hard to know where she was.

She was down in the archers' barracks with the other single women. She was down there crying her eyes out and all the archers would know what a clod her mate was for driving her to this.

He should have told her the truth. He should have explained about his fight against the Laird in the audience hall. He should have told her this morning before they ever left their room. He never should have left her in the dark about what was on his mind. That was his mistake and now he couldn't change it.

Chapter 29

Duncan wandered back into the tunnels toward Icemeet. At least he would be alone there. No one would bother him and he would be able to think in his agony without Zoe.

He had been looking forward to tonight. He had been holding his breath and counting down the minutes until he could be alone with her again without any social considerations standing between them. Now he could look forward to a long, lonely, torturous night without her.

Just thinking that made him sick. She was right here in Stronghold and he couldn't be with her. What could possibly be worse than that?

He didn't go up to the watchtower. Someone else might be there, though he didn't worry that it would be anyone to whom he might have to explain himself. His brothers would all be back in their own rooms with their wives.

His brothers. Grant and Elliot were his brothers, too, and Duncan couldn't even enjoy that. What kind of disgusting mess had his life turned into? Where did it all go so wrong?

He turned aside in Icemeet's deserted foyer. The citadel sounded too quiet. Duncan's screwups had ruined everything for his own Clan. His mistakes and weaknesses had driven Clan Buchanan out of Icemeet. Now the Clan had to burrow in tunnels just to survive.

How could Duncan free his Clan without Zoe? How could he use her to boost his power? How could he manipulate the woman he loved like that? He might never even get her back.

He climbed up to the gallery overlooking what used to be Icemeet's front courtyard. The courtyard had been reduced to a pile of rubble, but the gallery would be quiet. He could watch the moon and the stars. At least no one would disturb him even if he didn't come up with any answers to his many problems.

He froze and almost walked away when he found Colton and Reid already standing there. He would have fled and crawled into a hole to hide, but they both spotted him before he had a chance to retreat.

"There he is!" Reid clapped Duncan on both shoulders. "The man of the hour! When's the wedding, laddie?"

Duncan looked away. "There isnae any wedding."

"Dinnae play it off and expect us to pretend it hasnae happened," Colton countered. "Congratulations, lad! Ye're a man after me own heart."

"There's naught to congratulate me on so save yer celebrations. There's naught to celebrate here, either." Duncan went over to the railing and looked down at nothing.

"What's up yer kilt?" Reid returned. "Ye're mated now. Ye can start wearing a jacket and socks like the rest of us."

Duncan didn't answer. He sensed his brothers exchanging glances behind his back. This wasn't the response they expected.

The silence that followed ate an even deeper yawning chasm in Duncan's heart. He would give anything to confide in his brothers, but he couldn't. How could he tell them what he couldn't even tell his own fated mate? He couldn't betray Zoe like that, not after everything he'd already put her through.

Colton laid his hand on Duncan's shoulder and Duncan's heart bled. It wasn't the powerful clap and squeeze of brotherly support and affection. The aching tenderness of that touch brought tears to Duncan's eyes. How could he tell his brothers that he'd lost Zoe on the very day when he finally won her?

"Look there!" Reid startled Colton and Duncan by shooting his arm past their heads. He pointed down the mountain and all three brothers stared at something moving fast and sure down the steep crags.

"What the devil is that?" Colton growled.

Duncan's guts clenched. He couldn't see it clearly, but he knew instantly what it was. It definitely wasn't a Highland tiger. It was a person running down the mountain at high speed.

Any Buchanan that wanted to leave would have shifted into their cat form and this person came around the mountain from Stronghold. That left only six humans at Stronghold who could be running away at this time of night. It had to be either Liam or one of the five women from the Last Division.

"Zoe!" Duncan whispered.

He shifted in a split second and bounded down the wall. He sprang lightly to the ground and sprinted across the crag to intercept her, but she already had a commanding lead on him.

He came up behind her in a flash and overtook her. She ran over rough terrain without breaking stride, but he could hear her gasping and sobbing as she ran. She was running away from him.

He pelted past her ankles, skidded in front of her, and shifted. He got far enough ahead of her that she saw him shift while she was still running toward him.

"Zoe, wait!" He held up his hands and tried to grab her, but she dodged and bolted onward without slowing down.

He didn't have time to shift again. He didn't stop to think twice. He magicked himself in front of her. "Zoe, please talk to me! I love ye! I love ye more than me own life. I cannae live without ye. I made a mistake. I didnae want to tell ye because I thought ye'd...."

She burst into wild sobs and veered around him a second time, but this time, he used his magic to move faster than she did. He caught her arm and pulled her to a stop. "The Laird ambushed me last night—when I was in bed with ye!" The words tumbled out of him in an uncontrollable rush. "When we were together—at the moment of our highest pleasure—the Laird kidnapped me and took me to Tyrekirk! I didnae want to tell ye because.... because I thought that mating with ye would put ye in danger!"

She yelped in a mixture of indignation and despair. She struggled to pull away from him, but he refused to let her go.

"I fought the Laird...in his audience hall at Tyrekirk.... while I was lying in yer arms. I didnae ken how to tell ye. I thought......I didnae ken what to think....and I suppose I just kept thinking all day. I didnae ken what to do.... or how to tell ye.... or even if I *should* tell ye. I thought ye'd change yer mind about me if ye kenned."

"You!" she bellowed. "You—thought *I*—would change my mind—about *you*?" She sneered at him and started to turn away.

"I didnae ken the mistake I was making until I saw how it hurt ye. Please, lass. I cannae tell ye how sorry I am. Please.... being with ye.... mating with ye.... It's the only thing giving me the power to defeat him. I cannae lose ye now. I didnae like to tell ye in case ye...."

"In case I what?" she shrieked. "You really thought I would leave.... after everything? Did you really think that?"

"I...." He stumbled over the words. "I feared ye'd take it wrong if ye kenned."

"You thought I'd take it wrong!" she roared. "You thought I'd take *that* wrong but not you giving me the cold shoulder all day? You didn't think I'd take *that* wrong?"

"I love ye, lassie." He took hold of her hands. She resisted, but he didn't let go. He couldn't let go—not ever again. "Forgive me, lassie. I've never been mated to a lassie before. I'm bound to muck it up some way or another."

She glared at him and turned away again. She looked down the mountain toward the Boundless and shook her head. "You're an idiot, Duncan."

"I ken I am, lassie. Ye winnae find a bigger idiot than me on the whole blasted mountain—perhaps not even in the whole country or the whole world. I wouldnae blame ye for leaving, only.... Please. I love ye more than anything. I dinnae ken how to love ye with all this bloody nonsense going on. I dinnae ken how to do ought. It's bigger than me and...."

He looked up the mountain toward Icemeet and gulped down the lump in his throat. He just wanted to go home. He wanted to go back to being everybody's wild younger brother with no responsibilities and no one's hopes resting on his shoulders.

Were Colton and Reid up there listening to his conversation with Zoe? Duncan's magic told him that they weren't. He almost wished they were. Then he wouldn't have to explain anything to them.... but they weren't there. She was the only person here. She was the only person alive who knew.

"I thought it sounded too much like I might be using ye for me own power," he choked. "That's why I didnae tell ye. I didnae like to say it aloud that I wanted ye to make me stronger to fight the Laird."

"We *are* fighting the Laird, Duncan!" she fired back. "We're fighting this war together. Christ Almighty, we can't even be together if we don't defeat him! Don't you get that?"

He looked down at his hands. Her words stung because he was too stupid to think of them before now. He needed her to tell him something he should have figured out a long time ago.

"Aye, lass," he murmured. "I get it now because ye're telling me. I'm a fool. This is why I need ye—to hold me up and make me see what's right in front of me."

"Don't you think I would do anything to help you win the war?" she went on. "Don't you think I would do anything to help you survive against the Laird? Don't you think I love you enough to do anything for you? I love you, Duncan. We're in this together. What threatens you threatens me and it has nothing to do with what happened last night. It's been like that from the beginning. It's been that way since before I came through the portal."

He nodded down at the ground. He knew. He'd always known. He should never have forgotten.

"I dinnae ken ought about any of this, lass. All these people...Colton and Reid.... they're all looking to me to....to pull out some miracle.... I'm going out of me mind, lass. I dinnae ken what I'm doing or even if I can do ought. I'm not who they think I am and they keep telling me all their hopes are riding on me. Their very lives are riding on me and I cannae do ought to save them...." He faltered over the last words. He didn't dare to show anyone else how the whole catastrophe weighed on him. "Perhaps I *am* going out of me mind thinking about fighting the Laird when I'm meant to be with ye. I cannae tell anymore what's real and what isnae. Ye'll think I'm insane....and perhaps I am."

He couldn't even tell if she sympathized or not. She kept glaring at him as though his problems didn't concern her, but that couldn't be right. She was his mate. Who could he confide in if not her?

"You can't ever do anything like this again," she snapped. "Do you understand that? You can never keep anything like this to yourself again. No matter what happens, you have to tell me. You can't pull away and expect me to just stand it like nothing's happening. Do you honestly think Colton would pull away from Jaimee if something like this happened to him?"

"No, lass. Ye're right." He looked up into her eyes. They were starting to soften at last. "If I'm to tell ye all and depend on ye and all, ye must do the same with me. We're mated now. We agreed to put all doubt and question aside to take one another as mates. Ye cannae go running off each time it all goes wrong and it *will* go wrong, lassie. I dinnae ken ought else, but I can promise ye that much. It will go wrong again and we must stand together against it all."

Now it was her turn to look down at the ground and her features spasmed in misery. "You're right. I'm sorry. I just.... I needed you and you weren't there. Hearing that being with me makes you more powerful doesn't make me feel used, but you turning your back on me like that sure did."

"I'm sorry, lassie. I dinnae ken how to do all this. I'm at me wit's end trying to figure it out before anyone else dies.... or if you or I die. If I make one mistake, it's all done and I've done naught but made mistakes all over."

"Okay," she breathed and took a step toward him. She slipped her hand into his, all trace of anger and resentment gone. "We'll figure it out. We have to."

"Help me, lassie," he croaked. "I cannae do this without yer help."

"Okay. I'm here. We'll do it together. So.... what exactly do you want me to do? I don't have any magic. Do you need me to go with you to fight the Laird? Is that it?"

"I dinnae ken, lass. That's what I'm telling ye. I dinnae ken ought on what to do. I'm scrambling to figure it out."

"Okay." She took a deep breath and puffed out her cheeks. Duncan's heart soared now that he was holding her hand and talking to her about this. He really was a fool not to tell her everything right away. "Let's go through it one step at a time. He got you last night when we were together...."

"Aye. I wondered if us being together triggered him somehow.... either us bonding alerted him to where we were or else me magic increasing caused him to attack. I wanted to take ye back to our room and see if it happened a second time. I didnae mean to insult ye by implying it, lassie...."

"You didn't. Being with you could never be an insult. I know you didn't mean it that way."

"Thank ye, lass." Duncan's throat hurt. He wanted to completely fall apart, now that she finally forgave him.

"So......." A flash of light blazed in her eyes all of a sudden. "Are we going back to our room to test it out, then? Is that the plan?"

"Aye.... if ye'll have me, lass."

She smiled, tried to bite it back, and failed. She pulled him closer by his hand. "Don't do it again, okay? I don't think I can stand it."

"Neither can I. I cannae live without ye." He wanted to kiss her, but he didn't dare.

She must have read his mind. She towed him the rest of the way toward her and turned her soft bright eyes up to meet his gaze. "I don't think I can live without you, either."

"Aye. That's the mate-bond talking."

"Is it like this for the others?"

"Aye. It makes ye feel sick to be separated from yer mate. It makes ye feel as though ye might die."

She glanced down at his mouth. "I felt that way when you were on the ice. I've felt that way every time I've been separated from you."

"Aye. I've felt it as well."

She met his gaze and opened her mouth to say something else....and stopped herself. She rose on her tiptoes and kissed him.

She started out softly until that kiss built to a fevered whirlwind. Her arms slipped around his neck and he finally dared to embrace her. Sweet, sweet relief overpowered his senses as he melted into her mouth. He crushed her against him in an agony of emotion. He couldn't lose her. He couldn't survive on his own without her.

All his energy came flooding back and his spirits soared. She was right. They would figure it out together. They had to. He let himself sink into her—into the vast depths of his feelings for her. It was his only sanctuary from all this madness.

At that moment, a blast of tempest wind struck him from the side and knocked him off his feet. A blinding light flashed in the night and lit up the whole countryside.... except that he and Zoe weren't on the mountain slopes below Icemeet anymore.

A remote, storm-swept moor stretched away into the dark on all sides. Duncan didn't recognize this place at all, but he didn't have time to study it. The Laird materialized out of nowhere. The wind lashed his hair and robes and snow whirled in Duncan's eyes.

Duncan straightened his arm to push Zoe behind him.... but she wasn't there anymore, either. She had completely vanished.

His adrenaline surged. Where was she? Did the Laird do something to her at the moment when they reconciled and reconfirmed their love for each other? No other explanation made sense.

The light radiated outward from the Laird in such an intense glow that Duncan lost sight of everything else besides the old man. The Laird bombarded him with spells, blows, and invisible weapons that Duncan couldn't see.

Duncan's magic erupted as never before. Zoe loved him. They were mate-bonded for life and their bond told him that she was still alive. He just had to find a way to get to her.

The Laird hit him much harder this time than he did in the audience hall at Tyrekirk. The Laird must have anticipated Duncan's additional power and the old man showed no mercy.

Icy, blistering gales struck Duncan all over and tossed him in every direction. They stung his cheeks and eyes, stabbed through his clothes, and he stumbled in the snow.

Deadly cold took hold and quashed his magic so he couldn't fight back. He staggered a step closer to the Laird and the old man struck him down with unbelievable force.

All the Laird's ferocity and ruthless cruelty came through his magical blasts. No trace of kindness or compassion seeped in. He hammered Duncan with everything he had and Duncan buckled under the assault.

Duncan's mind and heart switched back to Zoe. He loved her. He had to survive for her sake. He had to find a way to get back to her somehow.

He sensed the Laird trying everything possible to kill him. He unloaded all his power on Duncan in an all-out murderous effort to destroy Duncan once and for all. Only Duncan's own magic stopped the Laird from snuffing out Duncan's life entirely.

Duncan couldn't raise a finger or cast a single spell to counter the Laird's attack. Duncan could only kneel before the old man and take it.

Without warning, a punishing blow hit Duncan across the head and he toppled. He struggled to stay conscious, but the darkness swallowed him and he collapsed in the snow.

Chapter 30

Zoe raised her hand in front of her face, but she couldn't protect herself from the driving snow and wind. This was so much worse than the mountaintop where she first met Duncan.

A blaze of light gave her a full view of the battle going on between Duncan and the Laird—or rather, it gave her a full view of the Laird decimating Duncan before her eyes.

"Duncan!" she shrieked, but he couldn't hear her over the howling wind.

The light radiated from somewhere near the Laird. The light itself seemed to bombard Duncan with a million microscopic shards. They got mixed up in the snow.... or maybe the snow was part of the Laird's weaponry.

The storm seemed to come from the Laird, too, but the snow beneath Zoe's feet was all too real. It numbed her toes and a thousand tiny ice crystals got into her eyes and peppered her cheeks. The cold didn't bother her on the mountaintop where she met Duncan, but now she couldn't escape it.

Duncan staggered a few steps toward the Laird. Why didn't he use his magic to fight back? Some part of her sensed that he *was* using it, but the Laird still overpowered him.

She charged forward trying to reach him. She would have thrown herself between him and the Laird to protect Duncan, but he and the Laird kept moving farther and farther away. They always stayed the same distance from her no matter how far she ran.

She fought her way through the storm anyway. She had to help Duncan. He said she made his magic stronger. Was that why the Laird stopped her from reaching him? It had to be.

The Laird glared down at Duncan in venomous fury. The Laird's eyes gleamed with vicious hatred. How could any man hate his own grandson so much?

The Laired unleashed a crushing barrage and Duncan collapsed on his knees. He didn't raise a finger in his own defense, but Zoe's connection with him told her that he was already doing everything possible to save himself.

All at once, the Laird unloaded a catastrophic strike. Duncan folded over on his knees and fell face down in the snow. The light snuffed out and the whole world went dark. The Laird vanished. Only the faintest gleam showed her the still figure lying unconscious a few feet away.

She charged forward, and this time, she made it to his side. She grabbed him panting in despair. "Duncan! Duncan! You have to get up!"

He couldn't be dead. He couldn't be. She rolled him onto his back. He was still breathing, but just barely.

She cast a frantic look around her. She was on a lonely moor in some unknown country. The mountains of Buchanan country—the Boundless—Kald—they were all gone. She was all alone out here and Duncan needed her help.

She grabbed his wrist and nearly broke her spine hauling him out of the snow. His body weighed a ton, but she dragged him into a sitting position and then hoisted him on her shoulder. She had to get him out of here. She had to find some help or at least some shelter.

The storm didn't let up when the Laird disappeared. Forgotten instincts told her that the Laird wasn't causing this storm—at least he wasn't causing it anymore. He might have started it, but now the weather felt natural.

That didn't make it any less dangerous, though. She turned in a complete circle trying to see anything in the darkness. She had to take Duncan somewhere.... somewhere warm.

A dark, massive shape loomed out of the shadows to her right. She couldn't see what it was, but it was better than nothing. She staggered toward it and her feet crunched in six inches of snow. She couldn't feel her legs anymore and her face was going numb.

Her mind started to blur from the cold. How much longer could she go on like this?

Her knees buckled a few times, but she forced herself to push onward. If she held out long enough, Duncan's magic might revive enough for him to help her. She could only hope and pray.

The storm howled so fiercely that she had to shut her eyes. She staggered on, stumbled, and bumped into a solid rock wall in the dark.

She could barely see it when she was standing right in front of it. She probably wouldn't have known it was there even if she'd had her eyes open.

She hit the ground and dropped Duncan, blundered to her feet, and groped at the wall for any sign of weakness, but it was immovable and solid as the Earth itself.

She tripped over to Duncan and bent over him. She touched his cheek and cringed when she felt how cold he was. He might die out here and then where would she be? Where would the country be?

"Duncan...." She patted him down. "Duncan...you have to wake up. I need you to wake up...."

Nothing. She couldn't summon the strength to pick him up again and she had nowhere else to go. If she didn't find a place to hide soon, she might as well lie down here next to him and go to sleep forever. It really had come down to that. The Laird didn't have to use magic to kill Duncan. He just had to abandon him in this snowstorm and let the weather do its work.

She turned back to the rock muttering prayers and promises to whoever might be listening. She patted down the wall holding her breath. Keeping her eyes open did nothing for her so she shut them again. She had to find some way....

She took one more lurching step and her hand vanished into an empty space. She almost fell into it when she lost her footing again.

Her eyes snapped open and she stared into a crack where the rock split. Did she dare to hope? It was big enough for a person to fit inside and it was all she would get in this nightmare.

She charged back to Duncan, grabbed him by his collar, and heaved. He slid in the snow and she hauled him to the crack. She wedged herself into it and dragged him in behind her before she collapsed on her back shaking with cold.

This rock blocked the wind, but it didn't block the snow nor did it warm her or Duncan. They would both probably freeze anyway, but she had done all she could do. Now she just had to wait.

Chapter 31

Duncan's eyelids fluttered and he looked up at a twisted mat of branches overhead. He might have thought he was back in the tree room except that these branches were much smaller and they still had a few specks of foliage attached to them.

He looked more closely. The ceiling above him had been constructed of intertwined heather and it was much lower than the tree room ceiling. He picked up his head and looked around him.

This was not the tree room. He lay on a bed made of the same intertwined heather and Zoe lay asleep in an identical bed next to him. The walls of what looked like a miniature hut surrounded him. The hut was empty except for the two beds and a fire smoldering in the center of the floor. There wasn't enough space for anything else.

He started to sit up. He didn't recognize this hut, and after his battle against the Laird, Duncan didn't even know where he was. If he and Zoe were here, then Stronghold, Kald, and everyone he cared about would be left unprotected.

He could have touched the opposite wall by stretching out his hand. The walls had been woven so tightly that no light came through them from outside. A shaft of daylight shone through a single small hole in the roof. He wouldn't have known if it was day or night without that.

The smoke from the fire rose through the ceiling hole. Duncan heard the storm raging out there, but no wind or snow made it into the hut. It had been built too solidly.

Zoe didn't stir when he saw up. She must be exhausted. He used his magic to scan her memories and his heart contracted when he saw what she endured getting him to safety.

None of that explained how he wound up in this hut, though. She didn't remember anything beyond the crag where she took him during the storm.

He studied the hut more closely, but it didn't give him any clues. How did he and Zoe get here? So many crazy and unexplained things had been happening lately. Duncan couldn't explain any of them, much less find a way to turn them to his advantage.

He put his feet on the floor, and at that moment, the door opened from the outside. Duncan stiffened when an old man walked in, but this wasn't the Laird.

This man wore rough, hand-tanned buckskin clothing. He wore trousers instead of a kilt and his disheveled beard and hair hadn't been brushed in a long, long time. He was much too tall for the hut and he had to crouch under the low roof.

He smiled when he saw Duncan sitting up. The old man's crystal blue eyes twinkled in a way that the Laird's never had.

The old man squatted down by the fire and dropped an armload of logs next to the coals. He put wood on the fire and then smiled up at Duncan again. "You're awake. You've been asleep for a long time."

He spoke with an American accent that sounded strange to Duncan's ear. He had been listening to the five women of the Last Division talk like that for weeks, but he still had to concentrate to follow what this man was saying.

"Am I in America, then?" Duncan asked. "Am I not in Scotland any longer?"

"You're everywhere, son," the man replied. "This place.... let's just say it's a part of you. It isn't anywhere in time or space. It just is."

Duncan didn't understand what he meant, but that didn't matter. "I must return to me own country. The Laird...."

"Do you know who I am, son?" the man asked. "Do you know why you're here?"

"If ye're a wizard, ye must have brought me here for some reason."

The man burst out laughing. "I'm not a wizard. I'm your great-great-great-grandson. My name is Thompson Resler and I'm the President of the United States. I'm the man the Last Division went to Scotland to save by making sure that you take the throne from your grandfather and marry Lady Rhona Armstrong."

Duncan stared at him with his mouth open. "Ye're.... how can ye be if ye're living *here*?"

"It's like I said. This place exists in your memories—your magical awareness of the past and the future. You created this place so we could meet."

"I dinnae understand any of this." Duncan ran his fingers through his hair. "It's impossible."

"I'm a relic of genetic information that knows no time. I'm speaking to you out of an eternal well of cosmic knowledge that already exists within you. You just need to figure out how to access it."

"How do I do that?" Duncan asked. "I dinnae ken how to do ought and what I can do isnae enough to defeat the Laird. If ye ken that much about me, ye should ken."

"You already have the power to defeat the Laird." Resler waved toward Zoe's bed. She still didn't wake up. "Don't you know that by now?"

"She doesnae have any magic," Duncan pointed out. "She cannae do ought but love me and watch me die in defeat."

"Isn't that enough?"

Duncan's head shot up. He'd been so agonized a moment before at the thought that Zoe couldn't help him. No one could.

Those words seared a blazing path to the center of his being. *Isn't that enough?*

It was enough. It had to be. She was his only advantage. She'd been making him stronger from the beginning. He had to hold onto her at all costs.

"You two together can break the Laird's power," Resler went on. "She doesn't need magic. She just needs you and you need her. You have to do it for the future. If you don't, your line will never exist and the course of history will never be the same."

"How can I break the Laird's power," Duncan asked. "He's already come close to killing me even when I'm mated to her."

"You haven't worked together yet, have you? You've fought him since you mated with her, but you used your power accidentally. You've never done it deliberately."

Duncan turned around to study the man. "Are ye really me own descendent? I cannae believe it."

The old man extended his hand and placed it on Duncan's head. It was a fatherly or grandfatherly thing to do—not something Duncan would expect from his great-great-great-grandson.

The instant Resler touched him, a flood of ideas rushed into Duncan's mind. He knew now how to get back to his own country and his own people.

He had to confront the Laird and win somehow, but the Buchanans couldn't get anywhere near Kald.

"Think outside the box, son. A full assault across the Boundless might not work, but that isn't your only option." Resler waved at Zoe and got to his feet. "Why don't you ask her and see what she says?"

Zoe started to stir in her bed. A tanned deerskin with the hair still on it covered her. Duncan gazed down at her feeling the same undertow of love and aching uncertainty that had plagued him ever since he met her.

How could he protect her when he couldn't even protect himself? How could he shelter her and give her a world where she could live in peace? He would do anything for her if he could only figure out how to accomplish it.

Resler turned away behind Duncan's back, pulled open the door, and stepped out into the raging snowstorm without another word. A puff of snow billowed in, but as soon as he shut the door with himself outside, the noise died and everything went quiet. Warmth enveloped the room and Duncan felt relaxed and comfortable again.

Zoe turned onto her back and sighed. Duncan didn't want her to know about the conversation he just had with some phantom from the future. He stretched out on the bed to pretend that he'd just woken up, too.

She rolled over and draped her arm across his chest. She tucked her head into his shoulder and he kissed her hair. She felt so good and right at his side like this. He didn't even care that they weren't in their room at Stronghold.

Without warning, she jolted upright, propped herself on her elbow, and frowned at the hut. "Where the hell are we?"

"I dinnae ken, lass. We're...." He hesitated to repeat what Resler said about this place being a relic of Duncan's cosmic knowledge of the past and the future.

She furrowed her brow and scowled down at him. "Did you bring us here? Did you transport us here after.... after the snowstorm?"

"I didnae bring us here that I can remember.... but anything's possible, I suppose."

She wouldn't stop frowning at him. "How can you be so casual about this? If we're here, that means Stronghold is undefended. We have to go back."

"Not yet, lass." He ran her fingers through her hair and admired her from below. Even her insistence on going back to his Clan delighted him.

"Why not?" she demanded. "What do we have to do here that's more important than defending the Clan?"

"Not yet. Tell me, lassie. Who's this president ye came back through time to protect? What's his name?"

She scowled even deeper. "What does this have to do with anything?"

"Indulge me. Please. What's his name?"

"His name is Thompson Resler. Why do you ask?"

"What does he look like? I mean, what color are his eyes?"

"Does this help protect Clan Buchanan from the Laird?"

"Please, lassie. It's important. I promise ye. I wouldnae ask if it wasnae."

"Fine. His eyes are blue."

Duncan nodded. "Aye."

"What are you talking about?"

"He was here, lass. He brought us here. This is his place."

Her jaw dropped exactly the way he knew it would. She gaped at him almost as if she feared he really had lost his mind. "He.... what?"

"He was just here talking to me.... though I dinnae think ye would have recognized him. He was old and.... well, let's be kind and say he isnae President of the United States any longer."

"What was he doing here?"

"I told ye. He brought us here so he could speak to me. I cannae be sure what good it will do, but he's done it nonetheless. Ye said ye wanted to ken all and I wasnae to keep ought from ye any longer, so there it is."

She blinked a few times and looked around the hut without seeing anything. He didn't blame her. It all sounded insane.

She finally sat up, crossed her legs, and rubbed her forehead. "Ooookkkaaaayyyyy. That's.... not what I expected, but okay. So what are we supposed to do?"

"It's as I told ye, lassie. Ye and I.... our mate-bond gives me the power to defeat the Laird. Dinnae ask me how, but that's the key."

"So....am I supposed to help you fight him? Is that what Resler said?"

"He didnae say. He told me to think outside the square......or box, as he put it. Think outside the box."

"What is that supposed to mean?"

"I dinnae ken, lass. We're meant to figure it out together, I suppose."

"Well.... let's figure out what the box is. Are we supposed to mount another assault on Kald?"

"I dinnae see how we can do that. We've got Elliot's rebels and not much else."

"We have the Brodies and Clyde McKay's people in the city," Zoe suggested.

"We dinnae ken if Clyde survived the last assault. The Buchanans cannae do ought. We can scarcely leave Stronghold as it is. We'd be fighting a suicide battle against the Creightons if we tried it. We cannae take Kald that way."

"Okay." She covered her eyes and heaved a deep sigh. "That's the box. Now let's think outside it."

"Outside what, I'd like to ken," Duncan asked. "There is nowhere outside it."

"That's not true," she countered. "You have other ways to get the Buchanans off the mountain. You have other fortresses farther north and other Clansmen in other areas."

"Aye, but I dinnae like to put them in danger, either. We must make a stand at Stronghold to protect them as much as our own people."

"We have to do something," she insisted. "The Laird won't stop, you know. He'll keep hunting you until he kills you."

"I ken that, lassie," he murmured. "Ye dinnae need to remind me and he's hunting ye now, too. Mate-bonding with ye has drawn his attention to both of us. It's made him even more determined to destroy us both."

"But don't you see?" she went on. "He's more determined because we're stronger. You saw him when he attacked you in the snow last night. He's desperate."

Duncan snorted. "I doubt that, lassie. We're the ones who are desperate."

"You're wrong. He's using all his power to try to kill you and he still can't do it. He keeps escalating and failing because we're getting closer to defeating him. He knows we're getting closer and he's trying everything to end it before we do."

Duncan couldn't help but beam at her. He stroked her hair and cheeks feeling such a painful stab of love that he couldn't stand it. "Do ye really think so, lassie?"

"I know so. Now listen to me. The last offensive got as far as it did because we attacked from multiple sides. We had the rebels in the forest, the townsfolk inside Kald, the Buchanans at Icemeet, and Grant and Lily inside Tyrekirk."

"We havenae any of those things now, lassie. We couldnae mount an offensive like that again."

"What if we could? We have two of the four—the rebels and the townsfolk. We also still have Buchanans in reserve."

"We wouldnae get near Kald by crossing the Boundless."

"Then we'll attack from a different direction. Just listen. I was talking to Echo the other day. Elliot had the idea to send some of his people to attack Tyrekirk from the south."

Duncan pricked up his ears. "The south?"

"Yeah. Tyrekirk is on a peninsula. The ocean blocks it in on the east side. That leaves three sides—the Buchanans on the north side and the rebels to the west. We've already got the Brodies and the townsfolk on the west side. That leaves the south. The Creightons already expect the Buchanans to come from the north, so we'll have to throw them off by attacking from a different direction. We could send the rebels to the south and bring the Buchanans to the western forest. We can get everyone across the Boundless farther west where the Creightons won't see them. Then the Buchanans came come at Kald from the west, join forces with the townsfolk, and assault Tyrekirk from there."

Duncan frowned. "I dinnae ken about that, lassie. The Laird would see what we're up to."

"Isn't there some way to get the Buchanans off the mountain without the Creightons finding out about it? Can you combine your magic with Betty, Liam, and Connell?"

"I suppose I could." He thought it over for a minute and then threw caution to the wind. "All right, lassie. That's farther out of the box than I imagined, but we havenae ought to lose at this stage."

She burst into a grin. "Great! So...how do we get back home?"

"Not yet, lassie. There's something else we need to do first."

"What's that?"

He slipped his fingers into her hair, pulled her down next to him, and steered her lips to his. "This."

He inhaled the heavenly scent of her breath as he swam in her lips. Her body collapsed on top of him and he careened into such a blissful sea of happiness that he could forget about everything else.

She let her weight fall against him and didn't hold herself back. Doubt and uncertainty dissolved—for good this time.

He opened his eyes to find her studying him while they kissed. He didn't want to leave this hut even though he knew he would. He wanted to delay as long as possible and savor this moment of pure contentment. They were alone together, maybe for the first and last time.

He read the same bottomless understanding in her eyes. The Laird might attack right now—at the moment when their love for each other reached its ultimate fruition. Duncan wouldn't be at all surprised.

Her body tensed with rising passion. She was ready, and this time, she knew the stakes. Joining with him and sharing her body with him might trigger the Laird to attack again. They both had to be ready to fight even as they lowered their defenses to bond with each other.

He only had to search her velvet brown eyes to see that she was ready—for anything. She didn't hold herself back even from that. She was his and the Laird couldn't stop that.

That certainty enveloped Duncan in a beautiful bubble of love and protection. The Laird wouldn't be able to do anything to him as long as she was here with him. Their love protected both of them from any intrusion.

She attacked his mouth even more greedily, now that they both recognized the risk and the power of what they were doing. This moment transcended mate-bonding. It transcended love and destiny.

This was pure sex magic. Duncan and Zoe conjured a power stronger than anything Duncan had ever used before because it went beyond himself. She was all mixed up in that. She was the other half of the incantation and he couldn't do it on his own.

She brought an element of wild unpredictability to the process that he didn't understand. Did her mysterious essence give Duncan's magic that one extra unknown ingredient that made it stronger than the Laird?

He could only try it, and when she climbed on top of him, he welcomed her with open arms. He clasped her down on top of him feeling her body rising to the pinnacle of explosive energy. Her passion carried him with it and took him to a different dimension. He didn't have to understand it. He would be safe as long as he was with her.

Chapter 32

Zoe rolled onto her back and knew before she opened her eyes that she wasn't in the hut anymore. She opened her eyes and looked up at blue sky overhead. She sat up and shook Duncan awake. "Duncan—wake up!"

He twisted over. "Eh?"

"Look! We're back on the mountain."

He propped himself on his elbow and frowned at the surroundings. He and Zoe were on the slopes below Icemeet where they had been when the Laird attacked Duncan—was it two nights ago?

Zoe ran through the sequence of events. "The last real thing that happened.... I ran away from Stronghold and you stopped me here. Do you remember? That's when the Laird attacked you. He must have taken you to the moor and then...."

"He couldnae take me there," Duncan muttered. "The whole thing must have happened just here. He must have used his magic to make it happen. Do ye see lassie? The Laird attacked me here and Resler came to me here."

"Are you saying we just spent last night out here, on these rocks, where anyone from Icemeet might have seen us?" She grimaced and glanced up at Icemeet, but it was deserted now.

"We didnae spend the night here because we werenae here, lassie. We were somewhere else." Duncan got to his feet and grabbed her hand to help her up. "Come along, lassie. Let's get back to Stronghold. We've a heap of work in front of us."

He straightened his tartan. He looked none the worse for his ordeal with the Laird.

They both started walking and she caught him examining her with his head on the side. Neither of them showed any sign of the Laird's last attack or their near-death experience in the snow.

Duncan led the way around the mountain to a hidden path through the forest. He paused under the trees and peered up at the mountain.

"Can you get inside?" Zoe whispered. "Betty and Liam have protection charms guarding the place."

"I'm sending a message to Betty to take them down for us." He bowed his head and closed his eyes. He opened them a moment later. "It's done, lassie. I'll conceal us so the Laird doesnae see us go inside."

"Are you sure that will work? If he does see us, he'll know where Stronghold is."

"He already kens where it is, lassie. He took me straight out of our bed the other night. He doesnae care for ought but killing me now....me and ye. He can handle the rest of the Clan afterwards, but that's neither here nor there. We winnae go through the front door at any rate. We'd havenae any end of trouble if we did."

"What do you mean?"

He shot her a grin. "Every man and his dog would have to congratulate us and want to make a fuss over us. We'll sneak in through the back and then we'll go see Colton."

He took her hand. She didn't ask any more questions about what "sneaking in through the back" meant. These Buchanans were full of tricks and these mountains were crawling with secret passages.

He set off through the trees. One of the mountain peaks looked like where she and the rescue party left Stronghold, but she couldn't be certain.

He climbed up a different stand of rock until they perched on the mountain's shoulder. He squinted across the planes toward the Boundless. Tyrekirk stood tall and untouched in the distance. It looked totally undamaged by the last assault. The rebels' sacrifice might as well never have happened.

"Are you okay?" she asked. "What's on your mind?"

"I'm just making sure he isnae watching us."

"Is he?"

Duncan snorted. "He's hiding it if he is. The daft bastard thinks he can trick me with his magic. Never mind. It's naught if he does or he doesnae."

"Are you sure about that? How are we going to get the Buchanans off the mountain if he can see everything?"

"We'll just have to risk it. Even so, it will lure him in to attacking us and that's what we want."

"It is?"

"Aye. We cannae fight him if he's hiding from us always." He turned toward the rock. "Come, lassie. I'm hungry."

She didn't see how he was going to get inside Stronghold from here. She knew enough about these mountains to recognize that she and Duncan were nowhere near Stronghold.

He surprised her by walking straight into the rock. He floated through it like it wasn't even there. She tried to stop herself from going in there, but he didn't give her a chance. He held onto her hand and pulled her through.

She stepped into the cliff face....and then she was in the tunnel between Icemeet and Stronghold. She gasped in surprise trying to see everything at once.

"Easy, lassie," he murmured. "It's naught but a bit of magic."

She shivered. "I don't think I'll ever get used to that."

"I'll make ye a bargain, lass. If we win this war and rid the world of that foul old dobber, I winnae use magic ever again."

She tried to stay serious long enough to kiss him and then broke down laughing. "Are you sure you could actually go through with that? I bet you couldn't. You would end up using your magic to bring you a snack when you didn't want to get out of bed. You wouldn't be able to resist."

He had to join in the joke and his cheeks flushed with pleasure. "Ye're as wicked a rascal as I am, lassie. All right. Have it yer own way. I'll fetch the snacks for us so long as we're in bed together....and I'll use me magic to communicate with ye when we're in different rooms. That's all. Is it a bargain?"

"Deal." She beamed at him. "I love you."

"I love ye as well, lassie. It's something to dream about, am I right?"

"Yeah," she breathed. "Bring it on."

"That's me own lass." He kissed her, took her hand, and led her down the tunnel toward Stronghold, but that vision kept haunting her mind.

This was the first time she'd been able to visualize what life would be like if she and Duncan actually succeeded in winning this war. They would be happy. They would be able to lounge in bed sharing the snacks that Duncan summoned with his magic.

She giggled thinking about what Louisa and the other maids would say if they saw food and drink soaring down the halls from the kitchens to Duncan's bedroom. Zoe could just imagine the fallout.

He glanced over at her. "What do ye find funny, lass?"

"I'm just thinking about what it's going to be like when we win this war."

His eyes sparkled and he squeezed her hand. *When* we win this war. When, not if.

She could almost believe that thinking about it made it a certainty. She could imagine a life after this—a life of peace and happiness—a life where she and Duncan actually got to live like a normal couple. That would be something to fight for.

Thinking about it and dreaming about it made it real. It would happen. She knew that now. She no longer doubted or questioned her bond with Duncan. They would conquer their enemies. They would find a way, one way or another. They had to if they wanted to get to that bright, peaceful future.

He walked past their bedroom and headed for Colton's room. He pushed the door open without knocking and he and Zoe walked in on another Clan conference in full swing.

Colton, Jaimee, Reid, Betty, Elliot, Echo, Grant, Lily, Liam, and Edeena stood around Colton's desk talking fast.

"We havenae seen Duncan nor Zoe since they both disappeared down the mountain the other night," Reid was saying. "We cannae plan our lives around when or even if they'll come back."

"We're back," Zoe interrupted.

Everyone spun around exclaiming and gasping. Jaimee hugged her. "Where the hell have you been? We were worried sick."

"It's complicated," she replied. "We had a few things to work out."

"Did you two get yourselves figured out?" Echo asked. "Are you fully mated now?"

"Aye." Duncan squeezed Zoe's hand again. "That isnae one of the things we had to work out. It's all done."

"Thank Christ for that!" Reid growled. "We can all sleep at night now."

"Do ye ken ought about the position, then?" Elliot asked. "Can ye tell us ought?"

"Aye. We've a plan, but it winnae be an easy one nor is it likely to succeed."

"What kind of plan have we ever come up with that was likely to succeed?" Lily asked. "Let's hear it."

"We need to evacuate Stronghold," Zoe began. "Elliot, you'll take your rebels to the south side of Kald and assault Tyrekirk from there."

"Finally!" Elliot exclaimed. "I cannae stand all this waiting around."

"Echo, you'll need to get inside Kald and alert the Brodies and Clyde's townspeople to attack at the same time."

"We'll need to know when to attack," Echo replied.

"Ye winnae make a move until the Buchanans reach the western forest," Duncan replied.

"Hold up a second," Betty interjected. "You want to take the Buchanans to the western forest? How in God's name do you plan to do that? These mountains are crawling with Creighton scouts searching for any Buchanan they can catch out in the open."

"Ye and Liam and Connell and I will cast a cloak of invisibility over our people," Duncan went on. "We'll evacuate them at night, use our tunnels to get farther into the mountains, and come out on the Boundless farther west where the Creightons arenae searching for us."

"Ye're taking a muckle great risk, laddie," Colton observed.

"I told ye it wasnae likely to work. I dinnae make any guarantees it will succeed any better than the last offensive."

"What's the point of launching it, then?" Jaimee asked. "We're holding our own here. We can't ask our Clansmen to throw their lives away for no good reason."

"We're launching it to lure the Laird into a battle against us," Zoe replied.

"Us?" Elliot waved between her and Duncan. "Ye mean ye two? The rest of us are just a smoke screen. Is that it?"

"Yeah," she murmured. "I hate to put it that way, but yes, this offensive is a smoke screen to get Duncan into battle against the Laird."

"What good will that do?" Betty asked. "You have no reason to think you'll win."

"That's exactly what we do think," Zoe replied. "We think we can win. So far, the Laird has been the one to choose when and where and under what conditions he attacks Duncan. The Laird has chosen times and places that were all favorable to him. If we choose the time and place and the conditions, maybe we can swing it our way."

"It's a long shot," Echo countered. "Like.... A *really* long shot."

"This whole war is a long shot," Zoe replied. "Besides, we have reason to believe that the Laird is on the ropes."

Colton snorted. "Keep dreaming, lassie. He's anything but that."

"I know it sounds crazy, but Duncan and I have seen things you haven't. The Laird realizes that we're getting close to defeating him. He's trying everything and using all his power to defeat us, but he hasn't been able to do it yet."

"Have you looked around you recently?" Jaimee countered. "We're trapped under this mountain with no way out. He can destroy our whole Clan whenever he wants. He already has defeated us."

"You're wrong. He doesn't care about Clan Buchanan—not yet, anyway. Nothing means anything to him unless he can kill Duncan. Don't you see? He's been trying everything—and I mean *everything*—and he hasn't been able to kill Duncan yet. He tried again the other night after we vanished off the mountainside." Zoe turned to Colton and Reid. "You were there. What did you see?"

"We didnae see ought," Colton replied. "Ye were there and then ye werenae."

"That's because the Laird attacked," she went on. "He attacked Duncan then and he attacked the previous night. He tried both times to kill Duncan. Heck, he's been doing nothing but try to kill Duncan for weeks. The Laird keeps escalating and using stronger and stronger magic, but he still can't kill us."

An audible gasp went around the table and Lily screamed. "Us?! He's trying to kill you now, too?"

"We have to put a stop to this," Jaimee snapped. "This can't go on!"

"That's why we have to finish it—both of us. We talked about it and we came up with this plan because we think it just might work—or it's more likely to work than anything else we can come up with."

Zoe gripped Duncan's hand tighter to give herself courage. The whole group stared at her and she saw herself taking a leadership role with all of them, even the people she considered authorities over her.

The others exchanged glances. Grant broke the silence first. "Ye tell us what ye want us to do and we'll do it. We'll all follow ye. Only tell us how and we're with ye."

"Aye," Elliot replied. "I'll fly down to the forest and send me men around to the south."

"Take your siege machines with you," Zoe added. "Echo, you'll go into the city, but there's no point in you going until the Clan crosses the Boundless."

"Do ye need any Buchanans attacking from this side of the Boundless?" Reid asked.

"I don't think so," Zoe replied. "The Creightons will be watching and waiting for the Buchanans to attack from the north. The Buchanans are too exposed on the planes. We need to get everyone inside Kald as quickly as possible." She turned to Duncan. "We can divide up the wizards, too—Connell to the south, Liam in the west, and Betty can go into town with Echo."

"Aye. That's good thinking, lassie. That will force the Laird to scatter his spells wider and make them less effective."

"Are we really doing this?" Betty asked. "Are we really launching another assault on Kald?"

"We cannae do ought until we defeat the Laird," Duncan replied. "The entire war depends on that alone. I must get inside Kald and engage with him. If the offensive doesnae accomplish that, we winnae survive no matter what else we do."

"As soon as Duncan and I get inside Kald, the Laird will turn his attention to us alone," Zoe replied. "He'll have to use all his magic to deal with us. That will leave the rest of you to invade from your own directions."

"And then what?" Echo asked. "What do we do once we get inside Kald?"

"Converge on Tyrekirk the way ye did last time." Duncan turned to Grant and Elliot. "Ye lads will launch from the western forest and deal to the Creighton dragons the way ye did last time. Ye'll keep the skies clear for our people on the ground."

"Aye," Grant replied. "We can do that much."

All eyes turned to Duncan. Zoe had been doing the talking up until now, but she fell silent when Duncan took over. This was his show.

He turned to Colton, Jaimee, Reid, and Betty. "Ye lot go downstairs and start arming our Clansmen to move out tonight. Leave a skeleton crew to guard Stronghold...." He waved to Betty and Liam. "Ye'll put up concealment and protection charms over the fortress. No one can go in or out until we come home. Make that clear to anyone who stays behind."

Betty nodded. "No problem. Consider it done."

Duncan held out his hand to Elliot. "Ye be off, laddie. Go now before they put up their protections."

"How will we ken when to attack? We winnae have any way to communicate with ye."

"Ye'll ken. I'll tell ye when the time comes. Dinnae ye concern yerself with that—any of ye." He surveyed the faces gazing back at him. "I'll communicate with ye all through the whole assault. I'll be able to tell ye the whole time what to do."

"Okay, Duncan," Echo replied. "We trust you."

"Good lassie. Ye and Betty will split off from our Clan as soon as we get across the Boundless. Ye get into Kald and alert our allies." He checked the others. "Ye all ken what to do. Off ye go."

The conference broke up. Zoe stood off to the side as each person came forward to hug Duncan and confirm that they all believed in him.

She didn't say anything else when they hugged her, too. She didn't have to talk to them to see the relief and resolve written on every face. No one wanted to stand around waiting anymore. They would rather take a gigantic risk like this and lose badly than do nothing in the face of defeat.

They had all been waiting for Duncan to take over and tell them what to do. Now he was and they fell in behind them.

Zoe waited until Jaimee, Betty, and Lily left the room. Then she squeezed Duncan's hand one more time and followed her friends downstairs. They had a lot of work to do before tonight.

Word spread like wildfire through Stronghold, and in a few minutes, all the able-bodied Clansmen started arming up and getting ready to move out.

The energy electrified the fortress and Zoe saw a lot more people laughing and smiling than she had since she arrived in this country. The Clan came to life as never before now that they actually had an objective to work toward.

Zoe left one of the Clan's many weapons storerooms and spotted Duncan talking to Echo and Elliot near the cavern entrance. Zoe went over to them just as Duncan and Elliot were embracing for the last time.

"Ye fly safely, lad," Duncan was saying. "Ye do as I say and go into the western mountains before ye come back to the fort from the west."

"Aye, lad." Elliot clapped him on both shoulders. "Ye winnae keep me out of this offensive by getting me shot down beforehand."

"Don't joke about that," Echo interjected.

He faced her and enclosed both her cheeks in his hands. "Ye winnae get rid of me that easily, either, lassie. I only wish ye were coming with me to rally our lads to fight. They always followed ye better than me."

"I'll be with you as soon as you get into Kald."

They kissed and then Elliot turned to Zoe. He hugged her. "Ye look after me laddie, lass. I still havenae had a chance to make a man of him and I winnae get the chance if ye dinnae bring him home for me."

"Ye winnae get any chance at all if I become Laird," Duncan pointed out. "Ye'll be too busy bowing and scraping and licking me shoes."

Elliot laughed. "Ye think so? We'll see who licks whose shoes when ye become Laird."

He and Duncan hugged one more time and Elliot stepped out onto the ice sheet outside the cave. He waved over his shoulder and then sprang into the air.

He shifted in a split second and the blinding sun caught his gold-black scales. The giant dragon rocketed into the clouds climbing higher toward the west.

Duncan and Echo gazed after him. "Can you protect him, Duncan?" Echo asked. "Can you conceal him from the Laird?"

"Dinnae bother yerself about him, lass," Duncan replied. "The Laird is much too concerned with me at the moment to waste any time on Elliot."

Echo peered up at him and frowned, but Duncan didn't notice. He stared after the black speck of Elliot disappearing over the horizon.

Echo shot a questioning glance at Zoe, but she didn't offer any explanation, either. She nodded behind her and guided Zoe away. They left Duncan standing there still looking out at the ice sheet.

Chapter 33

Z oe leaned in close to Duncan and whispered. "Are you ready for this?"

"Aye, lass. Let's go on and get it over with."

She turned back to her friends. The six women and five remaining men stood at the head of another tunnel buried deep into the mountains. Only Elliot was missing.

Two hundred Buchanan fighters, both men and women, packed the tunnel waiting for the word to go. Betty, Liam, and Connell stood at the front. They were only waiting for Duncan to join them.

He shouldered his way to them, but he couldn't leave without saying a few words to his Clansmen.

He turned around and found all his surviving relatives watching him and hanging on his every word. Colton would have been the one to address the Clan before any battle. Now that task fell on Duncan's shoulders. Even Colton and Reid stared back at him and waited for him to give them his orders.

For some reason he couldn't explain even to himself, this reversal didn't bother him as much as it did in the past. If this battle worked, he would become Laird in his grandfather's place. The whole country would be following his orders.

That was the only outcome he needed to worry about right now. If he didn't win this battle, he wouldn't be coming home or dealing with any of the consequences. He would be dead along with everyone he loved in the world.

He scanned the faces one after another and took a deep breath. He couldn't leave without saying something to them.

"I ken all of ye are fierce fighters and ye winnae stop at anything to win this day. I'm placing me faith in each of ye and ye have me pledge that I'll do whatever it takes to end this war today. We winnae come home tonight without kenning the outcome. There'll be no more hiding in holes and concealing our whereabouts from the Laird. That on its own makes this play worth to risk in me book."

Several people nodded and Duncan couldn't help but see the relief in Jaimee's face. This siege had worn on everyone. It would be over in a few hours, one way or the other.

"I want ye all to ken I wouldnae play games with yer lives and yer faith in me. I wouldnae send ye into any battle that I didnae believe we could win. We're launching this assault because I ken we can win." He slipped his hand into Zoe's. "We both do."

A ripple of defiance went through the assembled Clansmen. Duncan felt them rising to the battle. They were ready.

"There isnae anyone in this country stronger and tougher than our Clan. There's no one on that side of the Boundless that can stand against us." He clapped Grant on the shoulder. "We've two of the most powerful dragons in the country fighting on our side...."

"Three of them," Grant corrected.

Someone in the back of the crowd raised a saber and boomed out, "Aye! Ye bloody the Laird's nose for us, Duncan!"

More people cheered, "Aye! On ye go, laddie!"

In a second, everyone took up the chorus and the tunnel disintegrated in yells and cheers. Duncan could think of a lot of other things he wanted to say to his people, but they didn't let him.

He glanced over to find his family beaming at him and Zoe compressed his hand again. It was time.

He raised his hands for silence. It took a few minutes for everyone to settle down.

"I can see ye're all in a muckle great hurry to go out and get yerselves killed." Laughter answered him. "Betty, Connell, Liam, and I will cover the Clan with concealment charms and invisibility spells, but ye'll need to travel as quietly as possible...."

Someone else yelled out, "That isnae ever going to happen, lad," and the whole company burst out laughing.

Duncan joined and waited for them to quiet down. He spotted Colton opening his mouth to tell everyone to pay attention and follow Duncan's orders, but Duncan waved to his brother to stand down. Duncan had to do this himself.

He stayed where he was and didn't say anything until the noise died down to chuckles and a few snorts.

"Ye lads have yer fun now while ye're under cover," he called out. "Ye make a joke out of this once ye get outside and we're all dead. That's about the size of it."

That did the trick and everyone fell silent except for feet shuffling.

"We dinnae ken when nor how the Laird will break through our charms," he went on. "It's only a matter of time so do yer Clansmen and yer families a muckle great favor and make sure it doesnae happen until last possible moment. It will be a blasted miracle if we get over to the western forest with no one in Tyrekirk the wiser. Ye lads keep yer jokes and yer coughing and farting to yerselves until the battle starts. Then ye can yell yerselves hoarse and do yer worst."

The Clansmen nodded much more agreeably and called back, "Aye, lad."

Duncan turned away at last and nodded to Betty. "Go on, then."

She, Liam, and Connell went over to the cave mouth and Duncan went with them. Zoe hung back with the other couples. Duncan didn't like separating from her, but they had already agreed to do it this way.

The four wizards gathered at the exit and Betty extended her hand into the center. Connell and Liam placed their hands on top of hers and Duncan added his last of all.

A surge of power rushed up his arm the instant he touched them. Their power joined with his and jetted from their joined fingers. It spurted through the cave mouth and formed a curved shield over the dark, snowy countryside outside.

The stars glittered in the velvet black sky above, but the moon had set. The sun would rise in a few hours. The Clan had to get across the Boundless and into the western forests under cover of darkness.

Colton waved everyone forward. The Last Division, Liam, Edeena, and Duncan's brothers advanced and the Clansmen followed everyone outside. Duncan kept contact with the other three wizards and the field flexed and adjusted as the Buchanan fighting force emerged outside the tunnel.

The Clansmen stayed much quieter than Duncan dared to hope. No one spoke. No sound disturbed the quiet except for hundreds of feet crunching on the snow crust.

Duncan and the other wizards turned south. This tunnel led them miles away from Stronghold and the Clan stepped out into a clearing surrounded by forest.

They started hiking downhill and followed a frozen stream down, down, down into steep gullies. They walked in silence for hours until they reached level ground at the very bottom.

Duncan paused there and peered through the last fringe of trees. The Boundless snaked past their hiding place and the moon lit up its silvery surface. A solid mass of dark, dense forest cast the landscape beyond in shadow. Duncan wouldn't be able to see what was going on over there if he didn't use magic.

He didn't dare to break contact with the other wizards and he dreaded using any magic at all in case the Laird detected him. He didn't even want to check to see if Elliot's rebels were in position south of Kald.

"How soon do you want me and Echo to break away for Kald?" Betty whispered.

"As soon as we get across," Duncan whispered back.

"When is that?" Liam asked. "If we get separated, we might break the spell."

Duncan glanced over his shoulder. Zoe stood with the others waiting for him to make his move. The whole combined rebel army hung on his word. He had to make a decision one way or the other.

He opened his mouth to say something when, without warning, a massive starburst exploded in the air above his head. It detonated in a fiery blast that lit up the whole landscape as far as the eye could see.

Every detail of the countryside lay exposed, and in that moment, a pulse of magic shattered the concealment charm. It evaporated to nothing with all the Buchanans standing out in the open for all the world to see.

All the Buchanans looked up and Duncan's heart plummeted into his stomach at what he saw. A massive gold and orange phoenix spreading its wings in the air directly over his position. It covered the night sky from one horizon to the other and overshadowed the stars.

A distant groundswell of noise drifted to Duncan's ears. His senses had become so hypersensitive to any sound that he heard it instantly. All his Clansmen heard it at the same moment. It sounded like the tide coming in from the east, but it wasn't that.

He didn't have to keep contact with the other wizards. There was no point, now that their concealment was gone. His magic erupted to life and his magical sight blasted outward in all directions. He saw in a split second exactly what was going on all over Kald.

"Quick!" he roared. "Everybody over the water! Get to Kald! Launch the assault—now!"

He sent out a silent call to Elliot and all his captains waiting to the south. Duncan held Elliot's awareness just long enough to make sure Elliot ordered his rebels to attack. The rebel siege machines unloaded on Tyrekirk.

Duncan shoved Betty forward. He didn't even try to keep his voice down. "Go, lassie! Go, Echo! To the city wall! Go!"

The two women sprinted for the estuary and plunged in up to their calves.

Duncan couldn't wait around to see any more. He waved to his Clansmen. "Forward! To the city! Hurry before they...."

He didn't get the words out. The phoenix apparition overhead exploded and a million licks of fire rained from the heavens. They plastered all the Buchanans standing there in plain sight.

At the same instant, a massive wave of Creighton soldiers swarmed up the estuary from the east. They left their camps on the planes, surged up the Boundless, and overran the Buchanans who stared at them in shock.

"Go!" Duncan thundered. "Get across the water, through the forest, and into Kald! Dinnae stop for ought! Go! Go!"

He pushed people forward, but far too many tried to stand and fight. They slowed the whole force down. A third of the Clansmen followed Duncan's orders. They waded across the estuary and vanished into the forest. Duncan would never know if they made it to their destination.

The Creightons caught the rest on the banks and overwhelmed them in seconds. The phoenix showered fire everywhere and the magical flames burned the Clansmen where they stood.

The Clansmen tried to scrape the flames off and fell to the oncoming Creightons. Screams and roars mingled with the clash of weapons splitting the night. Colton and Reid tried to dive in and protect their Clansmen.

Duncan shouldered his way into the battle and dragged his brothers away. "Come on! We have to get away!" He pushed Grant toward the estuary. "Get in the air! Get over Tyrekirk and handle the dragons for us. Go!"

Duncan sent one last psychic message to Elliot to do the same thing, but Duncan didn't have time to wait and see if Elliot did it. The assault was already in full swing on Tyrekirk's southern flank.

Duncan checked Echo's and Betty's progress. They were just pulling up to the city wall and engaged in hand-to-hand combat against the sentries who tried to stop them from getting inside. The two women would rouse Clan Brodie in a few minutes, and once that happened, Kald would disintegrate into a raging street battle.

Duncan spun away and herded Lily, Jaimee, and Zoe toward the Boundless. "Get across, lassies! Take charge of our men and get to the city—now! Dinnae stand around and wait for us!"

"What about....?" Zoe protested.

"Go, lass!" Duncan thundered. "All depends on getting into the city."

The three women retreated. Duncan made sure they got into the trees and then he dragged Colton and Reid away from their last surviving Clansmen. Duncan could barely see them under the swarm of Creighton soldiers.

The phoenix overhead let out one last volcanic eruption of flame. Thousands of whizzing fireballs pounded the riverbank up and down the Boundless. They ignited fires all over the place, and in a split second, the whole area went up in an inferno.

The fire consumed Buchanan and Creighton alike and the last survivors had no choice but to fall back to the river and beyond. Duncan raised his hand to quell the flames when he happened to look up.

The phoenix hovered above his head. It blazed as bright as the sun, but he knew from his very first sight of it that it had to come from the Laird.

Chapter 34

Zoe, Lily, and Jaimee raced through the forest and veered hard to the east. Zoe didn't have to see where she was going. She and her friends just had to follow the noise getting louder the farther they ran.

Jaimee skidded to a halt and panted for breath while she scanned the woods for any sign. Zoe looked up at the sky and instantly wished she hadn't. That phoenix blazing in the night sky gave her a bad feeling.

It attacked the Buchanans and sent the Creighton forces to ambush the Highlanders on the banks of the Boundless. That phoenix could only have come from the Laird.

Zoe glanced over her shoulder. Duncan and his brothers were nowhere in sight. What if the Laird ambushed Duncan on the banks of the Boundless, too? What if Duncan never made it to Kald at all?

Jaimee bolted into the shadows and Zoe put all doubt out of her mind. She had her orders. Hell, she was the one who came up with this lunatic plan. She couldn't leave the other rebels to fight the war for her.

The three women burst out of the woods and scanned the area up and down. The city wall that should have blocked anyone from entering Kald had been flattened in both directions. Piles of stone and rubble lay all over the place and it didn't take a genius to see the reason why.

Two giant black dragons soared over Kald bombarding the city streets with hellish fire. Towering pillars of flame boomed out of the city and set off the golden glow on Elliot's scales. Grant shone blacker than black against the sky.

At least twenty smaller Creighton dragons soared around the brothers. The Creightons dodged in to attack and zoomed away before Grant and Elliot could fight back, but the smaller dragons couldn't do a thing to stop the destruction.

Grant rocketed out of town and swooped low over the three women. The monster narrowed his eyes at the ground, plunged over the forest, and came wheeling back for another pass.

He let out a thunderous roar and the wind shrieking over his scales drowned out the noise of a battle for a second.

Elliot raced toward the Boundless and both brothers pumped their wings picking up speed as they converged over Tyrekirk. They trapped the Creighton dragons between them, opened fire, and incinerated their smaller cousins in a deadly cauldron of flame and concussions.

They sprinted past each other and Grant sped up heading for Tyrekirk. He unleashed his fire on the high turrets, but more explosions blasted out of the castle and drove him off before he could do any serious damage.

"Come on!" Lily charged the rubble piles and started scaling them to get into the city. A bunch of Buchanans showed up a second later and Colton and Reid scrambled up next to Jaimee and Lily.

Zoe froze staring at them. "Where's Duncan?"

A crushing boom answered her from behind the woods she'd just come from. Was Duncan over there? Was he even still alive?

"Keep going!" Colton ordered. "Dinnae stop!"

Everyone else ran on and Zoe hardened her resolve. Duncan was depending on her to get into Kald and distract the Laird from Duncan's assault—whatever assault that turned out to be.

She couldn't think about Duncan. She scaled the stone blocks and hit the street in time to see Lily, Jaimee, Colton, and Reid racing ahead of her. Zoe put on speed and caught up with them just as a huge army of kilted Highlanders flooded out of a nearby neighborhood.

Zoe didn't recognize their tartans, but she definitely recognized the two women leading the charge.

Echo raised a saber on high and bellowed to the rebels charging behind her. "Brodie!"

A young man led the Clan and magic crackled all around him. It was Tristan Brodie, the young wizard who helped Grant and Lily escape from Tyrekirk.

His Clansmen took up the call and Zoe and her friends got swept up in the invasion. Betty appeared from another street leading an equally impressive throng of scruffy, mismatched townsfolk. They had armed themselves with everything from shovels and kitchen cleavers to pistols, rifles, and plenty of blades.

Zoe and her comrades dashed through one street after another. The noise kept building to a deafening thunder as they left the slums behind and approached the main part of town.

Spears and blazing balls of burning tar vaulted out of the countryside to the south. They hit dragons in the sky and sailed into town to crash and burn in the streets and against the castle walls.

Zoe and the rebel frontrunners rushed into one of Kald's many intersections. The city looked deserted ahead and she spotted Elliot's forest people scrambling over another wall to invade the Kald from the south. It couldn't be this easy.

Colton elbowed his way to the front, raised his saber, and roared, "To Tyrekirk!"

Another cheer rose from the mob behind him, but when they pressed forward into the next neighborhood, a torrent of Creighton soldiers poured out of the streets that had been empty just a moment before.

The rebels recoiled at the enemy's sudden appearance, but Colton, Reid, and some of the Brodies pushed forward. "Attack!" Reid bellowed. "Forward!"

The rebels responded with another breaking wave of weapons and furious war cries. They closed with the soldiers and the whole city exploded into a battle to end all battles.

Zoe got tied up fighting with the rest. Adrenaline and blood rage obliterated every other thought. She hacked her blades in all directions. She didn't have to think too hard to check that she was stabbing and decimating the right people. The soldiers looked so different from the rebels that no one could mistake anyone for someone on the wrong side.

The Buchanans smashed into their enemies roaring in murderous ferocity. Many dropped their weapons and shifted. Tigers rocketed through the Creighton forces leaving a carpet of devastation behind them.

The rebels worked their way deeper into the city one dead body at a time. Zoe checked her direction against Tyrekirk's high turrets, but no matter how many soldiers she killed and maimed, she didn't seem to be getting any closer.

Another tide of fighters overran her position. They came from the south and these people wore a bizarre mixture of tartan and rough beaten leather. The forest rebels attacked the Creighton forces from the south and started pushing the soldiers back toward Tyrekirk.

Grant and Elliot kept circling overhead and plastering the Creightons with fire to herd them into the rebels' blades. The surviving soldiers tightened into a protective knot as the different rebel factions surrounded them to finish them off.

Wild hope and delight gripped Zoe and she threw herself into the battle with new energy. The rebels were winning!

She cast a quick glance around searching for Duncan. Where was he? Did he ever make it across the Boundless?

Her stomach turned when she looked behind her and another massive swarm of Creighton soldiers materialized behind her. They stampeded out of dozens of streets. She wished she could believe that these were the same soldiers who attacked the Buchanans at the Boundless, but there were just too many of them.

If these soldiers came from the Boundless, then Duncan must have fallen, but none of the rebels had time to worry about that. The soldiers surrounded the rebel force and drove them into a ball. The new arrivals consolidated with the soldiers that Zoe and her friends just pinned down.

More soldiers streamed from every direction and converged from everywhere at once. They cornered the forest rebels and attacked Clan Brodie from behind. Did the Laird use magic to send his forces to destroy the invaders?

Elliot let out a piercing shriek overhead. Echo looked up and screamed, "Elliot—no!"

Voices took up the cry all over the city as a new flock of Creighton dragons assembled from nowhere to bombard Grant and Elliot.

Blasts and explosions pounded Kald all over the place. The projectiles that so recently played in the rebels' favor now bombarded the invaders with punishing fire. Fireballs detonated amongst the townsfolk and dying shrieks ripped out of the crowd.

Zoe looked everywhere for a way to escape, but nothing could get the rebels out of this death trap. Betty, Connell, and Liam fired thousands of spells outward at the attacking Creightons, but the Laird's wizards held the rebels at bay no matter what anyone did. The rebels were trapped here where the Laird could finish them off whenever he wanted to.

Chapter 35

Duncan darted from one corner to the next, from one building to another. He heard the battle going on in the distance and he made sure to avoid any fighting. He had something much more important to deal with.

He checked at the next corner and ducked behind a broken wall to hide from a platoon of Creighton soldiers charging through town. They all headed south toward the battle.

He waited until they passed and then ran forward on a dead course for Tyrekirk. He couldn't help his friends in their battle against the soldiers. He had to focus all his attention on defeating the Laird. Nothing else mattered.

He got halfway across the street when another troop of soldiers overtook him from the west. They came up behind him and would have trampled him in an instant.

He shifted into his tiger form in the blink of an eye, sprang onto a barrel, and vaulted up to the roof before they saw him. He streaked along the gutter, sprang onto a low parapet, and kept going. He leapt from one building to another and adjusted his course to stay one step ahead of the soldiers.

They turned off toward the battle a few blocks later and Duncan dropped onto the cobblestones. He shifted back into a man, but only for a second. He pushed on, but when he paused at the next intersection to check the way ahead, the building right behind him exploded next to his head.

He staggered out of the way as brick, mortar, broken glass, and debris cascaded on top of him. He made it halfway across the square before the whole building toppled. It tilted toward him falling faster than thought.

He didn't have time to run. He magicked himself across the street, but even that wasn't far enough away to escape the destruction. He bolted into another street. He didn't realize he was running south until a dragon swooped around the next corner.

It came out of nowhere glowing golden-green in the first light of dawn. It roared at him and cracked its jaws to bite him in half. He shifted without thinking to fight the thing, but when he spat flames at it, his fire did nothing to stop it.

It kept coming so fast he didn't know what to do. Adrenaline and instinct took over. He unloaded a second time and breathed spells and enchantments instead.

They went right through it...and he realized. This wasn't a real dragon. It was an apparition sent by the Laird just like he did outside the rebel fort.

Duncan snapped back to his senses and his mind cleared enough for him to hear the battle up ahead. It was directly in front of him. He was facing south and his gut told him that Zoe was over there. She was in the middle of the battle and she was in danger.

Duncan's magical sight showed him the whole catastrophe about to unfold. The Creighton forces surrounded the invaders on all sides. Smaller dragons occupied Grant and Elliot in the air while their cousins pelted the rebels on the ground with fire. This would turn into a bloodbath with Zoe falling under the assault. Duncan had to act now.

The Laird must have sent this dragon shade to stop Duncan from reaching the battle. The Laird wanted to stop Duncan from rejoining Zoe. Of course.

Duncan glanced toward Tyrekirk. He couldn't see the castle from here, but he didn't need to. A wrinkled old man stood on the highest turret. The blazing phoenix that attacked the Buchanans at the Boundless now outlined the Laird in a corona of flame. It shone over the whole landscape, but only Duncan could see him. The Laird existed for Duncan alone.

Duncan launched off the ground and took wing. The other dragons screeched and darted out of his path, but he barely noticed them. He bombed toward the Laird flying faster by the second, but spitting fire at the Laird wouldn't work.

Duncan had other tricks up his sleeve. He summoned all his magic and his mind switched back to Zoe. He mated with her. She gave him strength. His mate-bond filled him with the power to defeat the Laird. It had to.

The Laird became more distinct as Duncan got closer and Duncan's heart soared when he saw the Laird glaring at him. The Laird didn't smirk in triumph. He wasn't so sure now that he could really win. He would pull out all the stops, but Duncan was ready this time.

He tilted toward the spire and exhaled a torrent of magic. Duncan's barrage struck the phoenix halo and bounced back. It didn't touch the Laird and it all rebounded to smash Duncan out of the sky.

He shuddered under the impact. Had the Laird been taking it easy on Duncan the other night when he ambushed him on the mountain? Was it possible that the old man still had all this power left in reserve? How could Duncan defeat all that?

Duncan's own magic ricocheted back on him and collided with him in a devastating impact. It smashed him away from Tyrekirk and tumbled him head over heel. His own spells tore him apart and flayed him alive.

He somersaulted over Kald. Was he flying back over the forest—over the western mountains? Was he anywhere near Zoe at all?

The spells didn't just hit him and fade. They kept swirling around him hitting him again and again. They gained momentum to attack him over and over. Could the Laird multiply spells—to make them continue reacting forever?

Duncan's head rotated toward the ground and he looked down at the battle from above before another volley ripped him away. He felt his wings tearing off and his scales peeling back. They left his skin raw and bloody. He couldn't survive this.

Zoe! Help me!

He groped in his shattered awareness and found her. The Laird's magical assault stopped Duncan from reading the rest of the battle, but he could still connect with her. The Laird couldn't take that away from them.

The battle raged on all sides with Creighton soldiers hacking their way through the outnumbered rebels. The enemy cut down hundreds of fighters. The soldiers would reach the center any second now and then Zoe would fall.

The battle dwindled to a speck in Duncan's awareness. Zoe alone occupied his mind and he sensed her looking up at him. Did she see him on the brink of defeat? Did she give up hope when she saw all their plans falling apart at the seams?

The soldiers crushed toward the center one more time and she had no choice but to turn back to the battle. The core of friends blocked her in, but for how long?

Out of nowhere, a jet of sparks erupted out of the ring. It soared over Kald and smashed into Duncan from below. Liam, Betty, and Connell combined their magic and broke the Laird's hold on Duncan, but the blast hit Duncan, too.

He transformed against his will, and without the Laird's magic to hold him aloft, he plummeted to earth in his frail, powerless human form. He cartwheeled over and over in a headlong plunge for the ground. He floundered to come up with some spell, some trick to change back into a dragon, but nothing worked.

Grant and Elliot tore out of their own battles and raced toward him, but they couldn't reach him in time. The streets of Kald rushed at Duncan's face too fast and he smashed full force into the cobblestone streets.

Chapter 36

A silent scream ripped Zoe's mind apart and she looked up to see a small, fragile, human body careening through the air. Grant and Elliot rocketed toward Duncan as he fell, but they were too far away.

He vanished behind a building and an unholy thump resounded through her bones. Did she really feel that through the ground or did she feel it through her mate-bond with Duncan?

She cast one desperate glance around. The combined Buchanan, Brodie, and rebel force blockaded her on all sides with the Creightons hemming the invaders in a sea of weaponry. No one could get out.

None of that mattered. Zoe had to reach Duncan. He needed her and he would be hurt after a fall like that.

"Betty!" she yelled. "Betty—Duncan needs help!"

Zoe looked everywhere. She couldn't see Betty in the confusion. Zoe spotted Liam and Connell nearby, but they were too busy using their magic to fend off the Creightons. The soldiers would overcome the rebel defenders if Zoe distracted any of the wizards now.

The soldiers would overcome the rebel defenders no matter what anyone did. If Zoe was going to die out here, she would do it trying to help Duncan.

She took a fresh grip on her blades and lunged for the outer ring. She hacked and sliced with all her might, but she still couldn't get through.

She drove her way toward a knot of soldiers blocking her from leaving the protective circle. She raised her saber to carve into five soldiers who stood in her way.

They all rounded on her and brought their weapons down to chop her in half when, out of nowhere, two more sabers connected above her head. They connected with the soldiers' weapons in a deafening clang.

Zoe's eyes darted right and left to find Jaimee and Lily at her sides. The two women took their places next to Zoe and the three women started to cut their way through the army.

Jaimee turned off to the left and Lily had to swivel right to defend herself. The two friends opened a channel through the Creighton line and Zoe took it.

She dashed between soldiers occupied with other invaders and she took off running through the streets. She didn't know where to find Duncan, but she didn't need to know. Their bond led her with unwavering accuracy.

Missiles catapulted down on the city and crashed in the streets all around her. Paving stones exploded and smashed into walls on every side. Debris and flying shrapnel peppered her sides and face, but she had to keep on running. She would keep running forever if it meant finding Duncan.

She sprinted from one intersection to another searching everywhere. Where was he? If he was hurt, she would need a wizard to heal him.

She veered around a building and she froze in her tracks when saw his body sprawled on the cobblestones. Was he dead?

She fell on one knee at his side and grabbed him. She turned him over and groaned when she saw his face covered in blood.

She rested her hand on his chest. "Duncan...."

The moment she touched him, a colossal force stripped her off the ground. She had a split second to fling herself at Duncan, grab him, and cover him with her own body, but that unstoppable power ripped them both away.

A torrential wind rocketed her upward, past Tyrekirk, away from Earth, and blasted her far, far into space. The stars whizzed past her head and she clung onto Duncan for dear life.

Pounding wind thundered in her ears and she shut her eyes to huddle against his chest. She didn't know where she was going or even how she was going there. She had to concentrate everything to hold onto him. She couldn't let herself get separated from him—not for anything.

Out of nowhere, his arms folded around her. He pressed her to his heart and a rush of relief and contentment flooded her. He was alive. He was holding her. She didn't care where they ended up as long as they ended up there together.

The momentum slowed. She felt herself and Duncan slowing down, but she didn't dare to open her eyes until they floated to a stop.

She looked up to find him gazing down into her eyes. The blood and muck covering his face and body couldn't quell the light in his eyes. They were all alone—together.

He bent down and kissed her, but his eyes refused to release her. She felt herself drowning in the endless bliss of those eyes.

"Are ye all right, lassie?" he murmured. "I feared ye'd fallen in the battle."

"I'm fine." She touched his cheek and her fingers came away bloody. "Are you?"

"Aye. I'm grand now that ye're here with me."

They both looked around. "Where exactly are we?"

"I dinnae ken. I suppose we're out in space somewhere."

They were out in space, all right. Galaxies spiraled nearby and flashes of brilliant light exploded in their centers. They made no sound in the eternal silence.

"I don't see Earth anywhere," she remarked. "We must be really far out."

"Aye. I can imagine why."

She spun around to stare at him. "Are you saying.... The Laird sent us here to stop us from fighting him?"

"No, lass. He didnae send us here to stop us from fighting him."

"Why, then?"

He didn't answer. He rotated to his right and Zoe's stomach clenched when she saw the familiar phoenix blazing in the darkness. She mistook it for a star, but the moment Duncan faced it, it erupted into a massive, towering explosion of light and magic.

Duncan grabbed Zoe and pushed her behind him. He dodged in front of her to block her from the Laird. The old man hovered at the very center of that starburst where the phoenix's body should have been.

Two gargantuan wings of fire surrounded him and every flame-tip spat a razor blade of power at Duncan. He barely got into position before a torrential blast punched him in the chest.

The impact knocked him into Zoe and she grabbed him. She did her best to steady him, but the Laird's assault only bounced off him.

The Laird unloaded one devastating barrage after another. Flame, lightning, and millions of needle shards spouted from the points of his wings to hammer Duncan all over.

Duncan planted himself in one place and took the whole punishing assault on his skin and face and body.

Zoe didn't understand how any of them managed to stay in one place when they were floating around in space, but this last, ultimate battle made sense somehow. The three of them were in a dimension of magical reality where Duncan and the Laird met to pit their magical power against each other.

Zoe hung onto Duncan for all she was worth. She clamped her arms around his ribs for protection from the Laird, but she sensed through her own body that she was helping Duncan. She needed him and he needed her. He couldn't do this without her.

Another crushing barrage shattered on Duncan's chest and she buried her face in his shoulder. She shut her eyes, and for some reason she couldn't understand, she could see the whole battle playing out in her own mind. Was she using Duncan's magic, too?

The Laird grimaced at Duncan in unvarnished hatred. He didn't grin now. He bared his teeth and snarled in rage. His cheeks shivered with the effort of trying to destroy Duncan and Zoe sensed through her connection with Duncan that the Laird was fighting with every last scrap of his power. He wasn't holding anything in reserve anymore because he had no reserves left.

Duncan held firm, but she felt him getting stronger by the second. Every assault the Laird unleashed on him fed into Duncan's power and made him stronger. He vibrated with more mysterious energy than Zoe had never seen or felt before. His whole body stretched the breaking point.

The Laird's wings shot forward aiming straight for Duncan. Millions of flames punched through Duncan's skin and stabbed to his very core, but he only absorbed them into that relentless energy building to an epic climax.

The Laird tried to escalate, but he was already fighting to the limit of his power. He dumped everything he had into Duncan and Duncan drank it in and made it a part of himself.

Duncan stood still for a long time. Did he ever plan to fight back at all? She started to raise her head when he moved his arm behind him and took her hand.

He drew her out from behind him and pulled her to his side. She looked up into his eyes. Sweat streaked his face and his damp hair hung in his eyes, but he was smiling more happily than she could ever remember. Not even mating with her made him this happy.

That happiness beamed out of him in a blinding starburst as bright as the Laird's. No, it was brighter than the Laird's and getting brighter all the time.

It surrounded Duncan and widened to envelope Zoe, too. The Laird's attack didn't hit Duncan anymore. It deflected off that magical corona protecting him and Zoe from the bombardment.

Duncan slipped his hand against Zoe's cheek and pulled her in to kiss her. He made every move with impossible slowness and deliberate care. He took all the time in the world savoring her lips and gazing into her eyes.

That magical energy took hold of Zoe. She felt and saw everything Duncan saw and felt. She didn't need to look at the Laird to feel him getting more enraged and desperate. Duncan's confidence unnerved the Laird, but he couldn't fight any harder than he already was.

Duncan turned very slowly to face his grandfather. Duncan tightened his hold of Zoe's hand and they confronted the Laird together, united inside their protective halo. Duncan's power filled Zoe to overflowing. It wasn't his power anymore. It belonged to both of them and radiated out of both of them.

In that moment, she knew she could control it just as well as Duncan could. He couldn't use it to defeat the Laird without her help. It took both of them to reach this point and it would take both of them to finish this.

He squeezed her hand, and without warning, the field surrounding both of them exploded. It boomed outward with a deafening impact and the shockwave struck the Laird in all its power.

It blasted him away so fast that Zoe never even got a chance to see his startled face. This had been coming for so long that not even his final defeat came as a surprise anymore. It didn't come as a surprise to Zoe. It felt natural and inevitable.

The breaking wave caught the Laird and swept him headlong into the nearest galaxy. He plummeted to its center where supernovas and explosions swallowed him. He vanished into the bubbling cauldron and then a catastrophic boom ruptured out from the very central axis point.

A blinding outward concussion swept past Duncan and Zoe, but it didn't touch them. Their halo vanished and left them hovering there in the middle of black space.

Chapter 37

Duncan gazed down into the boiling mass of stars and burning gas at the center of the galaxy where the Laird disappeared.

"Wow," Zoe breathed. "I can't believe he's actually gone."

"Aye," Duncan murmured. He couldn't stop staring into that hazy brightness. He had trouble believe it himself.

Zoe attacked him from the side. She flung her arms around him, kissed him all over his face, and burst out laughing. "We did it! We did it! We're free! I can't believe it! It's all over."

Duncan didn't say anything. It wasn't over—not quite. He dreaded going back to Kald. He wasn't too worried about his Clan winning the battle. Everything that happened after that was what concerned him.

The Last Division still hadn't found Lady Rhona. This would never be over until they found her and decided who Duncan was going to marry. Duncan couldn't relax until that he settled that one question.

Zoe didn't seem to notice his agitation. She searched the area around them. "Earth is over there. Don't ask me how I know, but it has to be there."

"Aye. It's there."

She faced him and scowled. "What's wrong? Aren't you happy about this? You're safe. He won't threaten you anymore."

"Aye. I'm happy about it." He couldn't keep away from her. He didn't want to throw a wet blanket over her victory.

He met her gaze, and when he saw how delighted and relieved she was, he couldn't help but hug and smile at her. "Ye've done this, lassie. I couldnae have done ought without ye. Ye stayed with me through it all. I have ye to thank for this."

"Of course I stayed with you. I wouldn't leave you at a time like this."

He kissed her again, but all the same questions still waited for them back on Earth.

She pulled away all too soon. "We should probably go back. Things weren't looking too good when we left."

"Aye. They'll be grand, now that the old man's gone, but we should go back nonetheless."

He took her hand and they soared off toward Earth. He felt it long before he saw it. It started as a pinprick in the distance and got bigger as they drew nearer.

He slowed and floated near the moon while studied the planet. "It truly is a thing of beauty, lassie. I didnae have a chance to admire it before now."

"Maybe when everything quiets down, we'll be able to come back out here and look at it again."

"Aye. We will."

He took a deep breath and descended over Scotland. He landed on Tyrekirk's highest spire and watched the battle going on in the city streets far below.

No time seemed to have passed while he and Zoe were out in space. The Creighton forces still surrounded the rebel army in the same positions. The same dragons attacked Grant and Elliot in the skies over Kald.

"What should we do first?" Zoe asked.

"I ken what to do." Duncan raised his hand and snapped his fingers.

Everything he did felt like it took forever. He watched everything happening in slow motion. His body dragged through space and took a massive effort to do everything, but the rest of the battle unfolded so slowly that it didn't make any difference. He could take all the time in the world and the magic pouring out of him acted instantaneously with no effort at all.

All the Creighton dragons in the air shifted against their will. They changed into twenty men all wearing Creighton and Armstrong tartans. Gravity ripped them out of the sky and they plunged toward the ground.

Grant and Elliot leapt away in surprise and Grant spun around to stare toward Tyrekirk. He saw Duncan and Zoe standing where the Laird had been just a few seconds before.

Screams echoed across the city, but Duncan didn't let his enemies hit the ground. He shot spells at them and caught them in a magical net. He snapped again and transported all his cousins to the castle dungeons. He enchanted those so they couldn't shift anymore. He would deal with them later.

Elliot spotted Duncan, too, and he let out a high shriek of joy and triumph. He angled his wings downward and stooped at high speed for the city streets.

He thundered into town with Grant right on his tail. They closed around the Creighton forces and both dragons unloaded their fire on the enemy without mercy. They bombarded the Creighton army from two sides and incinerated hundreds of soldiers in one breath.

The brothers streaked away on either side and spells exploded out of the rebel army. Betty, Connell, Liam, and Tristan fired in all directions to flatten the surviving soldiers before Grant and Elliot came pelting back for another assault.

"Don't you want to go down there and join in?" Zoe asked. "They look like they're having fun."

"Aye," Duncan murmured under his breath. "Let them have their fun. I dinnae belong down there any longer. Me place is here now."

She compressed his fingers. She understood, but that couldn't soften the blow. Duncan had defeated the Laird. The war was over. It was only a matter of time before the rebels finished off the Creighton defenders.

Almost as if his thoughts made it happen, Colton, Clyde, and Tristan called another charge. They blasted out of their protective ring and the rebel factions scattered the last surviving Creightons.

The rebels punched through the Creighton line fighting in several directions at once. Elliot's forest rebels overran the soldiers to the south. Clan Brodie assaulted the soldiers on the west side and Clan Buchanan broke out of the intersection on a dead run for Tyrekirk.

"Come along, lassie," Duncan told her. "Let's go downstairs and meet them. They'll all be anxious to congratulate us."

He turned away. He didn't have to wonder how to get through the castle. He already knew everything about it.

He headed for the stairs, but when he took his eyes off the battle, he spotted the northern hills in the distance. He couldn't see Icemeet anymore because it wasn't there. It had been reduced to ruins. The landscape didn't look right without the fortress standing tall and proud on the mountainside.

He waved at it and all the stone and rubble floated off the ground. Walls and arches and rooms and towers and keeps reformed. He restored it with hardly a thought.

Now the mountains looked the way they should, the way he remembered them. He would be able to look out of his window and see Icemeet waiting for him even if he never lived to go back there. Now he could face what was waiting for him.

He climbed down the stairs and passed through the Fourth Tower where the Laird's family lived. Duncan didn't see any servants anywhere. They were all hiding from the invasion.

He and Zoe entered the great entrance foyer just as a torrential blast of dragon fire blew the giant doors open from outside. A huge black dragon crouched beyond the threshold and stood guard over hundreds of rebel fighters storming in. They brandished their weapons in all directions and took over the place.

Colton stormed into the foyer pointing his saber at everyone. "Secure the perimeter, lassie," he told Jaimee. He turned to Tristan. "Send out yer Clan to bring in the rest of the soldiers. Clyde, ye set up a patrol covering the western slums. Make sure no one gets any ideas about coming after us again."

He pulled up short and his expression changed when he saw Duncan and Zoe standing there holding hands. Colton dipped his chin once. "I'm sorry, lad. I shouldnae have presumed...."

"Not a bit of it," Duncan murmured. "Ye carry on."

The dragon outside the doors shifted and Grant marched in. He headed straight for Colton and Duncan. "We must bring up all the servants and retainers for review. Maxwell and Tristan can advise us on which ones are loyal to the Laird, and once Betty erects the dome, we must...." He broke off, glanced over at Colton, and lowered his eyes before Duncan with a gulp. "I'm sorry, lad. Ye give me yer orders. I'm at yer disposal."

"No, man," Duncan murmured. "Ye and Colton ken what to do better than I do."

Grant and Colton exchanged another glance. Duncan became painfully aware of all the rest of his friends and relatives gathering behind them. Everyone stared at him waiting for him to say something. They were all waiting for him to take over as Laird.

Grant cleared his throat with difficulty and nodded behind Duncan. "Dinnae ye think ye might take a look in there?"

Duncan looked over his shoulder. The big double doors to the audience hall towered behind him. They were closed.

What would he find in there? Going in there meant he really did plan to become Laird. He hadn't let himself think beyond the next battle. He still had to work hard to remember that the war was over. He didn't have to worry about the Laird coming back.

He stood there trying to decide whether he really wanted to do this when Jaimee strode past him. She walked over to the doors and pushed them open. They creaked and then boomed back into place.

The whole party gazed into the audience hall. The Laird had restored it and repaired the roof. The hall looked the way Duncan had seen it in his visions. The big windows gave a beautiful view across the Boundless. He could see Icemeet from here.

Inevitability drew him into that room. He belonged in there somehow, though he still didn't know how he would do any of this. If he stood at those windows and looked out at the planes and the mountains he knew and loved so much, he would only start imagining himself running through the mountains as a boy. Those days were over. He couldn't hope that he would ever be able to go home to Icemeet again.

He walked past the throne without really seeing it. He approached the windows and looked out. In all his visions, he never imagined seeing the world from this vantage point.

He imagined himself lounging in bed with Zoe without a care in the world. He imagined going home to Icemeet and running through the mountains, but never this. Did that mean he wouldn't become Laird after all?

The Laird had stood at these windows late into the night. He had done all his planning and scheming here and made all his most important decisions here. These windows had been the one place where he did his best thinking.

Zoe appeared at his side and slipped her hand into his. The old Laird didn't have a lady to bring him back to the world that needed him.

He turned around and looked down at the throne. The old Laird only sat in this chair during his audiences of state. He never sat in it at any other time.

"Aren't you going to sit down?" someone asked. It was Lily.

She, Grant, Elliot, Echo, Colton, Jaimee, Reid, and Betty all watched him from the floor below the steps. Liam, Edeena, Connell, Tristan, and all their comrades stood behind them in a crowd.

They looked up at him with wide eyes and he read the truth in all their faces. He was Laird now. Everyone knew it, and most importantly, he knew it. He'd known it all along. He was made for this.

He sat down in the chair still holding onto Zoe's hand. It was done.

Colton stepped out of line, covered the last few feet to the bottom of the stairs, and dropped on one knee before the throne. He bowed his head, drew his saber, and laid it on the floor in front him.

Reid went down on one knee next to him, and the next minute, everyone else did the same thing. Grant, Elliot, their wives, and all their Clans and loyal comrades knelt before the new Laird and presented their weapons in pledge to his service.

One man remained standing. Liam strode forward and planted himself at the bottom of the steps. He didn't kneel. He smiled up at Duncan and Zoe with tears in his eyes.

Liam pulled out his dirk and stabbed the tip into the bare skin of his forearm. He sliced the flesh back and pulled out a small square no bigger than a fingernail.

Liam climbed three steps, deposited the blood-stained object in Duncan's hand, and retreated to the floor. He knelt down on one knee, bowed his head, and laid his dirk on the floor with the others.

Duncan turned the object over in his hand. The blood smudged Duncan's palm, but even when he rubbed it off, he couldn't tell what the object was. "What is this?" he asked.

"It looks like a computer chip." Zoe bent over to look at it and prodded it with her finger.

A ray of bluish light shot out of the thing and Duncan and Zoe both jolted back. The beam twirled in the air and flickered faster and faster to form an image.

It finally solidified into a man with short-clipped hair and a fresh, angular face. He couldn't have been more than forty. He wore a suit with a tie around his neck. Duncan didn't recognize him.... Until the man smiled. His brilliant blue eyes sparkled in a way that Duncan would never be able to forget.

A crackling voice came from the chip. "Hello, Zoe. My name is Thompson Resler. I'm your great-great-great-grandson and I'm the President of the United States.... But I guess you already know that." He bit back a grin like he knew who he was talking to, but he looked away in a different direction. He didn't see anything in front of him and Duncan understood. This must be some kind of message that Resler sent back through time.

"You're probably wondering why I had to send you and your friends back in time to ancient Scotland, but I think once you meet Duncan, you might start to understand. My family tree states that Lady Rhona Armstrong marries Duncan Buchanan. They're my ancestors and I had to make sure Laird Balfour Creighton didn't stop them from marrying so the timeline of history would stay the same. That's why I ordered the Last Division to go to Scotland."

Duncan glanced up at Zoe. She stared at the image with her mouth open. All her friends and Duncan's four brothers had raised their heads to watch, too.

"You see, Zoe," Resler went on, "when Felix Margoles first developed this time travel technology, we also found out the rogue elements around the world were using the same technology to fiddle with the timeline. They tried to change the course of time to bring down the United States. They wanted to change the outcome of world wars and other key events in history. We found out that they had sent a dark wizard back in time to assassinate one of my ancestors. It took us years to figure out who the wizard was and who he was trying to kill."

"That makes no sense," Jaimee interjected. "Laird Balfour has been here for seventy years. He couldn't have traveled back in time."

The image of Resler went on almost as if it heard her. "The man most people know as Balfour Creighton is actually a Russian agent who was working for the KGB. He traveled through time when he was just seventeen. He killed an heir to Clan Creighton and positioned himself to become Laird. He ruled Kald for decades and learned as much magic as he could so he would be in the best position to stop Lady Rhona from marrying Duncan when the time came."

"So Lady Rhona is real?" Betty asked. "Why haven't we been able to find her? Duncan is Laird and we still have no idea who she is."

"That's neither here nor there," Colton pointed out. "Duncan's already mated with Zoe. He cannae marry anyone else."

"When we found out what was going on in Scotland, we did some research on Lady Rhona Armstrong," Resler went on. "We found out where she came from and who her family was. You see, Zoe, you're an orphan. Your parents died when you were a baby and you grew up in foster care. You never knew your original family.... or your real last name. Your name at birth was Zoe Ronna. You were abandoned at a local hospital. No one knew your last name, so the foster home where you grew up gave you the last name of Dutton."

Resler smiled through the airwaves and his expression became even more affectionate than Duncan remembered it from the heather hut.

"You are Lady Rhona Armstrong, Zoe. You were destined to travel to Scotland and marry Duncan. I'm sorry we had to keep you in the dark about this, but it was the only way to convince you to go through with this mission. Maybe when you look at Duncan, you'll understand why I had to do it this way."

Duncan looked up at her at the same moment she looked down at him. The image of Resler vanished and left just the two of them gazing at each other. The rest of the world evaporated and all the old doubts and questions vanished from Duncan's mind. He didn't have to dread the future anymore. He could finally rest.

Chapter 38

Z oe stepped into an absolutely massive bedroom bigger than all of Ironforge. Painted murals covered the ornate ceiling and tapestries hung on every wall. Ceiling-high bay windows gave an almost full circular view of Kald, the northern planes, and the forests to the west.

A dark rim of mountains framed the western horizon. Those must be the mountains where she first met Duncan. They looked so far away from here.

She wandered over to the windows and studied people moving through the streets far below. The Brodies and Clyde's townsfolk were still going through the streets making sure the Laird's troops didn't try to mount another insurgency.

A squad of Brodies came back to Tyrekirk leading a bunch of soldiers under guard. Clyde's people passed between a few businesses several blocks away. Clyde's people consulted a few business owners and then moved on. The rebel fighters didn't harass anyone or interfere in their business.

An air of calm and relief settled over Kald. The city didn't seem the same without that simmering undercurrent of resentment and rebellion that electrified the place just a few hours ago.

The door clicked shut behind Zoe's back and Duncan let out a long, heavy sigh. He flopped back on the bed and threw his arm over his face. "I dinnae ken about ye, lassie, but I dinnae fancy going through an audience like that again in a hurry."

Zoe chuckled and walked over to him. "I hate to break it to you, but I get the feeling you're going to be going through a lot of audiences."

"Not a bit. Grant can handle all the castle business for me."

Zoe sat down next to him, put her arm around him, and laughed. "He only agreed to stay here and help you until you understand enough to do it yourself. You can't make him de facto Laird in your place. We already tried that and it almost ruined everything."

"Dinnae spoil me daydream just yet, lassie." He grinned at her on the side. "What about ye, lass? I cannae wait for ye to start ruling the maids and servants like the lady that ye are."

He laughed at her when she groaned. "Please, no!"

"Count yer blessings that ye have Lily to help ye out. We'd be lost without them."

She joined in the joke. She wasn't ready to start ruling Tyrekirk like some kind of queen. Zoe secretly hoped that Lily would just take over completely so Zoe could hide in her room the whole time.

She didn't envy Duncan at all. He really had to rule the country as Laird. There was no way out of it.

"So...." She began, "how about a snack?"

He burst out laughing again, lunged for her, and tackled her down on the bed. "How about ye be me snack?"

She fought back and then tickled him to make him let her go. They both flopped down on the pillows, rolled onto their backs, and stared up at the ceiling.

"Let's run away to the stars," she suggested.

"Let's run back to the mountain," he added. "No one will find us there."

"Are you telling me they would find us in the stars? No other wizard is powerful enough to go there."

He glanced over at her and his eyes told her exactly what he was thinking. He rotated over to face her and stroked her hair off her cheeks. "I dinnae want to run away. It's too sweet to lie here with ye and ken we dinnae need to go anywhere or do ought. I'd trade all the ruling of the country for that."

He leaned in and kissed her and she let herself collapse into his arms. He was right. The glories of the universe, the rugged beauty of the mountains—none of it was as appealing as this easy contentment.

They didn't have to do anything or defeat anyone or prove anything to anyone. Neither of them had to worry about the Lady Rhona problem anymore.

Everything sounded too quiet and she had to remind herself more than once that she didn't need to stay vigilant and watchful anymore. She could just lie here and enjoy kissing him.

His arms enfolded her and blessed, blessed quiet descended over Tyrekirk. He let out another matchless sigh as he settled deeper into the pillows. He must feel that lingering doubt even more painfully than she did.

How many months would it take him to fully release all the tension that had been eating him up since this started? How long would it take him to start sleeping at night without waiting for the Laird to ambush him again?

He broke off her lips and buried his face in her neck. He wrapped his arms around her and his breath in her ear became long and deep and even. His body relaxed more and more until he didn't move.

Zoe stayed still and gazed at the ceiling. The paintings up there showed dragons, tigers, people, armies, lovers, kings, and townsfolk in different scenes out of fairy tales.

It would take Zoe years to decipher them all, but she had plenty of time to lie in this bed and figure out what they all meant. She would be staying in this room for the rest of her life.

She turned her head aside and kissed Duncan on the forehead, but he didn't respond. He kept breathing in that endless tide of relaxation. He was sound asleep.

Zoe smiled to herself and let herself sink back on the pillows. She wasn't tired enough to sleep, but she didn't dare to get up. She didn't want to disturb him. He had fought harder and gone farther than anyone to win this war. He had earned this rest and she wouldn't be the one to take it away from him.

She must have fallen asleep anyway because she snapped awake when someone tapped on the bedroom door. It wasn't loud enough to wake up Duncan.

The sun had migrated around the sky to the west. It must be afternoon now. She must have been a lot more exhausted than she realized.

She compressed her arm into the pillow and winced when she slid out from under Duncan without waking him up.

She tiptoed over to the door, checked to make sure he was still asleep, and slipped out. She shut the door behind her and looked back and forth between Lily and a rotund older woman.

Lily had changed into a magnificent dress that showed off her cleavage. Her tight corset made her waist look much smaller and her massive skirts completely hid her legs all the way to the floor.

Lily had piled her curly hair on top of her hair in a towering bun with stray curls coiling around her moon face. She looked nothing like the fighter who had just been battling on the street a few hours ago.

"What's going on?" Zoe made a face at Lily's dress. "Please tell me you didn't come here to tell me I have to dress like that now."

Lily grinned at her. "You don't have to until you're ready. Everyone around here is used to seeing me going around in pants and a leather jacket. I'm sure they won't mind if you do." She waved at the other woman. "This is Rosie Brodie."

Zoe's eyes popped. "Brodie!"

"She's Tristan's grandmother and she's the housekeeper of Tyrekirk," Lily went on. "She's been my righthand woman for months and I'm sure she'll be yours, too."

Rosie bobbed a curtsy and held her skirts out to both sides before she straightened up. "At yer service, Lady Rhona."

"If there's anything you need and I'm not around, you just ask Rosie." Lily rested her hand on Zoe's arm. "And I do mean *anything*. She's very loyal. She's been helping Grant and me against the Laird all this time. We would have been dead a dozen times without her."

Zoe glanced back at Rosie. She beamed at Zoe with a broad, open expression and her chubby cheeks glowed with color. She looked like the nicest grandmother that Zoe had ever met.

Rosie handed over a square of plaid folded into a neat bundle. "Here's a new Armstrong tartan for His Lairdship....and here's a new Buchanan tartan." She pushed both tartans into Zoe's hands. "I dinnae ken which he fancies wearing, but I dinnae suppose he wants to give up Buchanan tartan for all that and I wouldnae dream of giving him Creighton colors." She laughed at her own comments.

"Um.... Thank you," Zoe exclaimed. "That's very thoughtful of you. I'm sure he'll appreciate it."

"This...." Rosie handed over another bundle. "Here's a dress for ye, me Lady.... Just in case ye take it into yer head to put it on....and here's a new set of clothes after Lady Lily's fashion." Rosie glanced over at Lily and blushed. "Excuse me, me Lady, but I cannae think of her as anything else even if there's another Lady in Tyrekirk."

"That's all right," Zoe replied. "I think you should keep calling Lily and Grant.... Whatever it is you call them."

Lily blushed, too. "I'm sure the servants will all get used to it soon."

"Maybe not," Zoe replied. "Grant is Duncan's older brother. Maybe Duncan won't mind if the servants call Grant...."

She stopped herself. She had been about to suggest that the servants call Grant "Laird" the same as Duncan, but that would never work. Tyrekirk could only have one Laird and that would always be Duncan. It had to be.

"At any rate, ye can sort yerselves out, and if ye need ought, ye'll let me and Lady Lily ken about it." Rosie dropped another curtsey. "Me Lady."

She hustled off somewhere without looking back. She left Zoe standing there with her arms loaded with clothes. "She seems...nice."

"She is," Lily replied. "You're going to learn real quick which of the servants are on your side and which aren't. We found out, too, but there wasn't much we could do to get rid of the ones that weren't. You should keep your eyes open, and if you see any sign of suspicious behavior, you need to get rid of the person right away."

"You mean.... Tell Duncan or something?"

"No. Just get rid of them."

"How?" Zoe gulped. "Do you mean kill them?"

"You don't have to kill them. You can just fire them."

"Fire them!" Zoe cried. "How am I supposed to do that?"

"You aren't at Icemeet anymore. You're Lady Armstrong of Tyrekirk now. Your word is law second only to Duncan's. If you don't want someone around, you just give them the axe and send them packing." Lily's features hardened. "You need to start thinking like a ruler. Duncan still has enemies who want to overthrow him. They might take a while to show themselves, but never fool yourself that they're there. They'll send people into the castle to spy on you and to weaken you behind the scenes. If you see anything—anything at all—don't hesitate even if it means executing someone. Don't take any chances. You might be playing games with Duncan's life."

Zoe swallowed hard. She didn't think of this in the sudden relief of ending the war. She didn't fully realize until right now what Duncan becoming Laird really meant.

Zoe was his lady now. They would be getting married soon, which meant that she would be responsible for pretty much everything that happened at Tyrekirk.

Zoe never let herself think beyond the moment, but now that Lily mentioned it, Zoe realized just how much responsibility she was assuming. Running the country demanded more of her than just standing at Duncan's elbow and looking nice. She wasn't just a trophy on his arm. She had her own role in making sure no one challenged his reign.

Lily nodded toward the bedroom. "The dresser by the north window has all of Duncan's shirts, socks, and jackets in it. There's also a drawer with a few new belts, sporrans, and other stuff he might want to wear. You can tell him. The dresser against the south wall is your clothes."

"Uh...." Zoe looked down at the pile in her arms. "Okay."

Lily laughed and squeezed her arm. "Don't worry if it takes you a while to get used to it. It took me weeks to settle in."

"Really?"

Lily nodded and laughed again. Her cheeks glowed with so much love and understanding that Zoe's heart tightened. "Take as much time as you need. Everybody understands. Trust me." She nodded toward the door behind Zoe. "Go on. None of us is going anywhere for a while."

She walked away and left Zoe standing there wondering what just happened. Her brain couldn't keep up with all these shocks.

She eased the door open and slipped back into the room. She put the stack of clothes on a chair without making any noise. She made it halfway across the room before Duncan stirred in his sleep.

He sighed, rolled onto his back, and ran his fingers through his hair. "Och, I was knackered!" He looked around, saw Zoe standing there, and collapsed on the pillows. "Lassie! Ye're up."

"The housekeeper just stopped by." She sat down next to him. "She left a new Armstrong tartan for you and a new Buchanan tartan. You can pick whichever one you want to wear."

"Aye? That was right kind of her."

"I thought so, too."

Duncan frowned at her. "Is ought wrong, lass?"

She smiled at him and said, "No, nothing's wrong," and she meant it. Nothing was wrong. Everything was all right exactly the way it should be.

Chapter 39

E deena Buchanan threw her arms around Duncan, sniffed into his jacket, and hugged him. "I cannae stand that I'll never see ye again, laddie!"

"Ye never ken what might happen, lass." He squeezed the back of her neck. "I'll ken ye're happy, at least. I winnae need to worry about ye any longer."

She straightened up and held him at arm's length. She smiled at him with tears streaming down her cheeks. "Ye'll still be here if I ever come back. Tell me ye will, Duncan."

"Aye. We'll always be here. Ye can come back anytime."

She moved over to Colton and sobbed even harder when she hugged him. "Ye keep Icemeet for me, Colton."

"Aye, lassie. Always."

She held onto him for a long time and then she hugged Reid and all the women one after the other.

Liam finished hugging Lily, approached Duncan, and dropped onto one knee. He bowed his head and kissed Duncan's hand. "Thank you, my Lord."

"Thank ye, lad," Duncan murmured. "Thank ye for all ye've done. I winnae ever forget it."

Liam stood up and his countenance radiated so much happiness that Zoe hardly recognized him. "I'm at your service if the need ever arises."

"Aye. Ye'll be the first man I call.... right after Colton, Reid, Grant, and Elliot."

Everyone laughed and Edeena came back over to Liam's side. They both looked incredibly happy even though Edeena was crying harder than ever.

Liam took her hand and led her out into the courtyard in front of Tyrekirk's main entrance. He waved up at the people on the steps and then he set the time portal device on the paving stones at his feet.

Edeena turned back toward the castle so she could see her family until the last moment. She gripped Liam's hand in a white-knuckle hold and tears poured down her cheeks, but she never looked happier.

Zoe's throat constricted watching them. They had come farther than anyone and now they were on their way back to the modern day to live the rest of their lives together. Scotland would never be the same without them.

Liam pushed some of the symbols on the time portal device and it started to spin. Zoe's eyes fixed on the device and suffered a pang of regret. This would be the last time she ever saw it. She would never travel back through time to her own world.

She refused to think about which version of America they were traveling to. Had the events of this war completely altered the timeline? America might have become unrecognizable.

That didn't matter because Zoe and the rest of the Last Division would never go back there. They would never find out. That world lay beyond their reach now and the thought flooded Zoe with relief. She didn't want to find out. She wanted to stay here forever and that's exactly what she would do.

The device spun faster and faster. The vortex opened and Liam and Edeena whirled into a blur before they vanished along with the device.

A collective sigh went through the assembled friends. "Wow," Betty breathed. "It's over. I never really thought it could happen and now it has."

Reid put his arm around her shoulders. "It's for the best."

"I know. It's just so....so final."

Silence fell over the group. It really was the last nail in the coffin of a future that would never be. All five women would stay in Scotland now. Their last way home had just disappeared forever.

"We should go, too." Echo stepped forward and hugged Zoe. "We have to get back to the fort and organize all the...." She laughed. "I guess we can't call them rebels anymore."

She hugged Duncan and Elliot came forward. He put his arms around Duncan and held him for a long time. When he stood back, he had tears in his eyes, too. "I cannae believe I'm walking away from ye again so soon. It isnae fair that Grant is staying and not me."

"We'll have plenty of time for all that," Duncan replied.

Elliot nodded and compressed his lips. "Aye. At least I ken ye're here. I winnae lose ye again."

"Never, lad."

Echo hugged everyone else and Elliot stopped in front of Grant. Their eyes met and then they pulled each other into a long, close embrace. Grant gripped the back of Elliot's neck and neither brother looked in any hurry to let the other go.

They parted without saying a word. They looked deep into each other's eyes for a long time before Elliot turned away.

Elliot hugged Lily and jerked his thumb sideways at Grant. "Ye keep him in line, lassie. If he plays up, ye let me ken."

She laughed. "Don't worry. He never does."

"Aye." Elliot tore himself away, but he wasn't finished yet. He walked over to Reid, hugged him, and then handed him something a folded square of tartan.

"What's this?" Reid asked.

"It's Alastair's tartan. Yer Clan should have it."

"Och, no, lad!" Reid tried to push it back at him. "I gave it to ye. Ye keep it."

"No. Ye take it home where it belongs." He held it out until Reid finally accepted it.

Elliot took Echo's hand and they went down to the courtyard, too. He cast one last look over his shoulder and shifted. He erupted into the huge gold-black dragon and crouched there on the paving stones while Echo climbed onto his back.

He gave a deafening shriek and launched himself into the sky. He swooped over Tyrekirk calling on the wind and his wingbeats made all the flags whip in his wake.

Without warning, Grant shot off the ground following Elliot. He sprang upward and shifted in midair. He transformed into a dragon and rocketed into the atmosphere with a deep resounding bellow.

He turned spirals around Elliot and the two dragons circled Tyrekirk again and again. Neither wanted to leave yet.

All at once, Duncan's hand tore out of Zoe's grasp and he lifted off the steps. He shifted in a blinding flash and rose high, high over the land.

The three dragons screeched and roared to each other. They dive-bombed each other, raced back and forth, and tumbled in the joy of flight until Elliot turned away.

He pumped his wings and zoomed away across Kald. Grant and Duncan raced after him. They traveled all the way to the farthest edge of town before Grant and Duncan pulled back.

Elliot kept hurtling over the landscape calling on the wind as he got smaller in the distance. Grant and Duncan stayed aloft watching him out of sight before they came back to the castle.

They both landed on the steps minus their shirts, shoes, and socks. "You better not let Rosie see you walking around like that," Zoe told Duncan. "She'd have a heart attack."

"We wouldnae have our wee laddie any other way to say goodbye to us." Reid stepped forward and embraced Duncan. "Ye're still a Buchanan at heart, lad. Ye always ken where ye belong."

"Aye." Duncan's voice cracked with emotion. "I dinnae fancy ever being ought else."

Reid hugged Zoe and then Colton came forward. He gripped Duncan's shoulders and shook him. "Ye dinnae ken how proud I am of ye, lad. Ye're me own Laird...as it should be."

"Dinnae say so, Colton," Duncan choked. "Ye'll always be me Chief."

Colton compressed his lips and crushed Duncan in a bone-breaking hug. They both had tears in their eyes when they separated and Colton stroked Duncan cheeks. "Me own laddie."

Colton moved over to Zoe and hugged her. Then he squared his shoulders in front of her. "Ye look after me laddie, lass. I'm leaving him in yer hands. I ken he'll be right with ye."

"I will. I'll take care of him for you."

"Aye." He kissed her on the cheek. "Ye dinnae forget where yer Clan is, lassie. Ye come home to Icemeet soon."

"Thank you. I will."

Jaimee put her arms around Zoe. "We'll see you again real soon."

"You bet. We're only a few miles away."

Jaimee stepped back beaming at her and then Betty hugged Zoe. She laughed when she hugged Duncan. "You had to go and repair Icemeet, didn't you? You didn't leave anything for me to do."

He blushed and beamed at her. "I'm sure ye'll find plenty to do at Icemeet, lass."

Everyone laughed and then came the heart-wrenching time for the Buchanans to leave. Colton, Reid, Jaimee, and Betty descended the steps and waved as they crossed the courtyard.

They would be back at Icemeet in no time at all. Most of their Clansmen had already left long ago. They could leave whenever they wanted, now that no soldiers blocked their route home.

The four friends strode out of the courtyard and vanished behind the castle wall. They left Duncan and Zoe standing on the steps with Lily and Grant, the last pair of their group.

Duncan and Zoe turned their eyes up to Icemeet, but there was nothing to see up there. The fortress occupied its age-old position on the mountain...and that was all. No dragons swooped around up there. No siege machines thundered from the cliffs. No soldiers assaulted the fortress or tried to invade Buchanan land.

Peace blanketed the countryside in every direction. How long would it last?

None of the four friends turned away to go back inside. They stood in silence drinking in that beautiful silence. Zoe didn't hold out any hope that it would last forever, but she could stand here and savor it for as long as it lasted.

Whatever happened, whatever this strange, unknown future held in store for her, she and Duncan would meet it and conquer it. She never doubted or questioned that. She would never doubt or question ever again as long as he was by her side.

The End.

Keep Reading

Prideland Series

When a rescue mission goes disastrously wrong.....

Lieutenant Dina Dyer and her team find themselves held captive on an alien planet—the prisoners of an unstoppable power they never could have imagined possible: a race of sentient cats that keeps people as pets, slaves, and as prey for the hunt. In a world where every friend can become an enemy and nothing is as it seems, Dina must find the courage to escape before time runs out.

Caught in a toxic cocktail of attraction, politics, intrigue, and danger, her journey to freedom navigates the depths of human darkness where destinies collide and survival is the only reward worth fighting for. With the fate of millions hanging in the balance and betrayal surrounding her at every turn, can one woman become the firebrand that brings an entire planet out of shadows and into the light of freedom?

You can find it at your favorite book retailer.

Sign Up Once--Get all Theo Mann's free books including brand new releases

S ign Up Once--Get all Theo Mann's free books including brand new releases

Ian Wallace is tall, muscular, magnetically handsome, heroic, and passionately in love with the lady of his dreams--Lady Ada Ross.

Too bad he's just a character in a romance novel......or is he?

When Dayna Roberts finds a mysterious letter tucked between the pages of her favorite book, she decides to write Ian back to warn him of his enemies sneaking up on him. Little did Dayna know that one act would sweep her into a world of the past--a world of danger, intrigue, and powerful forces she never imagined possible. Disaster strikes when Ian's archnemesis Gavin Macauley intercepts her letter and conquers Grimlock Castle with Dayna inside it--but how could he intercept the letter when she wrote it in the twenty-first century?

If Dayna refuses to marry Gavin in Ada's place, he'll take drastic measures that could leave this whole mysterious world in ruins. Forget about Dayna finding a way to get back to the modern world. She'll be lucky if she survives long enough to escape from the castle. Is there any way out--much less a way to get back to the family and the modern life she knows?

Sign up at www.theomann.com to read it for free

About Theo Mann

I write 70 books per year—and yes, before you ask, all these books are my original creative work. Nothing written under my name is AI-generated or ghostwritten because I write better than AI and any ghostwriter out there.

People don't read fiction for entertainment or to escape from reality. People read fiction to see their humanity reflected in another person's character and story.

This is my promise to you. When you read my books, you'll see your own humanity reflected in the characters and stories. I take this commitment to my readers very seriously. My books are an intimate form of communication between us. I would never disrespect my readers by turning that over to a machine or another writer. This is my bond between me and you as my reader.

I write 20,000 words per day as my daily work output. If anyone with a public platform would like to challenge me to prove this in a controlled environment, feel free to contact me on this website's contact page.

I worked as a professional ghostwriter for fifteen years. Now I'm on a mission to set a Guinness World Record by writing 700 books over the next ten years and 1400 books over the next twenty years, all originally written by me. See my website for the full book list.

I'm also the author of *Proof for the Existence of God* and the *Crimes Against Fiction* blog. You can find all my nonfiction work at www.crimes-against-fiction.com.

If you have a story idea, or if you would like me to explore a series in more depth, or if you'd like me to explore a character by writing a spinoff series about that character or world, leave me a message on my website's contact page. I answer all reader emails, so ask me anything, tell me what you liked and didn't like, and let me know where you'd like your favorite series to go. I would love to hear your ideas and find out what you'd like to read next.

Find out more at www.theomann.com.

Also by Theo Mann (so far)

www.ingramcontent.com/pod-product-compliance
Lightning Source LLC
Chambersburg PA
CBHW070508030726
47503CB00004B/1202